tuesday's child II: redemption

Kathy, Debbie
+ Linda

the Saga Continues!

Carol

i

Carolyn Gibbs

tuesday's child II: redemption

CAROLYN GIBBS

Tuesday's Child Novels
P.O. Box 584
Wilbraham, MA 01095
www.TuesdaysChildNovel.com
TuesdaysChildNovel@comcast.net

ISBN: 978-1-466421-21-9

First Edition 10/10/2011

Printed in the United States of America
This novel is printed on acid-free paper.

This book is a work of fiction. All names, characters, locations and events are either the work of the author's imagination or are used fictitiously. Any resemblance to actual people, either living or dead, locations or events is purely coincidental.

Designed by Carolyn Gibbs

To the Lanes, Rays, and Richards hiding in us all,
and to the fans who really want to know
what happens next...

Acknowledgments

I acknowledge the efforts of Rachel DiMaggio of http://proofreaderone.weebly.com.

I extend my gratitude to her for her editorial guidance in taking Tuesday's Child II: Redemption from a spark to a finished product.

Chapter 1 – On the Dock

The bullet slammed into the dock post, splintering the wood into flying, pencil-sized shards and sending Lane Harris into the lake.

In the two months she'd been out of jail, she had managed to successfully stymie Uncle Ray's plans to resume her swimming lessons with an assortment of excuses—her artificial knee ached, she was too tired, had too much homework to do, or the pool at the high school was too crowded. Something was always too whatever, but the once-homeless teenager seldom performed the same song and dance twice.

Her penchant for creative alibis left her woefully unprepared for the fifteen feet of murky water off the edge of the dock. She scooched off the lip and dropped straight down, knowing her only protection now rested in getting under the pier, and knowing that getting there presented a challenge all by itself.

But while the daily temperatures of May on the Washington Peninsula had climbed into the nice "take your coat off" fifties, the water remained a shocking thirty-five degrees, and it immediately forced all the air from Lane's lungs.

Even two seconds out of cover could be fatal if someone had actually shot at her, but another issue, one equally pressing, rattled around her brain. Ice water sapped warmth from her body, wicking it out through her goose-pimpled flesh. A few minutes immersed in Jensen Pond, whether her unplanned dip was warranted or not, could prove just as fatal as a lead projectile ripping through her body.

Lane's fingertips brushed the support column; slime at and below the waterline made it difficult to get a solid hold. Water sprayed into her eyes as she wind-milled her way to haven, closing the distance enough to hook her arm around the pylon and pull herself into hiding behind it.

The dim light of dusk, combined with the post blocking her view, made it impossible to locate the shooter. She hung motionless in the water, which only served to accentuate the cold. In response to her shivering, ripples spread along the surface of the water, the concentric rings growing bigger the farther away they moved from Lane's body.

She fought to control her breathing…if she ran out of oxygen, she would lose control of her muscles, and then she would drown. But her lungs refused to acclimate, and the exchange of air continued as short, tight puffs that prevented her from catching her breath. Her hands slipped on the scum, and she reached up to get a better hold.

Another shot rang out. The sound reached her as a chunk of wood peeled off the colonnade, carving a groove just inches from her exposed arm. An acrid puff of smoke carried the stench of singed moss and wood. She ducked away from the attack, putting more of the post between herself and the shooter and using just her fingertips to hang on.

Ice water stabbed at tender human flesh, causing her to tingle from her feet to her chin. Her muscles tensed, adding to the discomfort, and her teeth chattered in her head hard enough to make her jaw ache. She had to get out of the water…quickly.

Using the sole of her shoe, Lane scraped some of the muck off the post so she would have a stable platform. She gathered what little strength she had and readied herself for a push off, hopefully with enough force to coast to the support diagonally across from her. The move would put her farther out of the shooter's sight, getting her closer to shore at the same time. And if her older male relatives hadn't arrived to save her by then, she'd wedge herself in between the sand and timbers on the beach side of the dock.

Gulping air, she wondered what she had done to provoke someone into taking potshots at her. The day had started out fair, progressed to poor, and had now taken a sudden turn toward crappy. While she shivered in the water, her mind replayed the last few minutes of the argument that sent her out of the house, the same argument that landed her in this predicament.

"Just do as I say," Richard barked, remembering at the last second to be civil. "Please." Exasperation settled on his brow and in the wrinkles on his face.

"You're not the boss of me," Lane screamed as loudly as she could. Despite the laryngeal reconstruction, it came out as little more than a hushed, gravelly protestation.

The look on Richard's face couldn't have been any more smug. "Uh, yeah I am. Until you're twenty-one. And these three years of probation? That would be your doing."

A brisk wind howled out of the forest, stirring up ripples across the length of Jensen Pond and sweeping away the last whispers of Richard's voice, which had risen in volume as Lane headed out the door; in her mind it trailed off in echo. "I'm not done with you!" Her response had lacked any sound at all; she hadn't even seen his reaction to her single-fingered salute as she slammed the door and hobbled across the porch.

Five whole minutes hadn't yet passed, but it felt like the entire incident had occurred hours ago, days even. Like it didn't even matter anymore. The current situation demanded her attention, and the longer she delayed, the more the frigid water sucked energy from her. She kicked off, plowing through the water and leaving a wake in her passing.

At least the water was still too cold for leeches.

Chapter 2 – In the Cabin

"I'm not done with you!" Richard Keates yelled at his daughter. His brows furrowed deep at Lane's non-verbal response, and his hands rose to his hips. "I am getting so sick of that."

Ray leaned back onto the sofa, kicked his feet onto the coffee table, and crooked one arm behind his head, oozing the unconcerned persona that so often eluded Richard in his dealings with his new-found daughter. Ray knew Richard's first mistake was screaming at the girl, but that poor choice of actions paled when compared to his second: expecting her to come back for more. "I told you." Splotches of flour dappled his face and shirt sleeves, and he nibbled on a freshly baked cookie.

"Yeah, that's helpful. If I had ever given Dad the finger, he would have ripped it clean off my body."

"I told you to pick your battles."

"There shouldn't be a battle. I'm the father."

"She hasn't had a lot of genuine parenting, Rich. And I know you're really new at this, but barking orders and expecting her to jump to like one of your deputies isn't always going to work."

"She needs to start living in this world, and she needs to take orders. And she needs to take them from me."

The verbal slap in the face bounced off Ray's priestly armor, and he declined to react even though Richard's meaning was quite clear—Lane listened to everything Ray said without so much as a raised eyebrow, but she always made Richard justify his requests. Ray owed neither apology nor explanation for that.

5

"Don't hold that against me. Or her, either. You need to approach this like any other challenge…with a plan."

"I think I can handle one eighteen-year-old girl."

Ray glanced over his shoulder, craning his neck to see down to the lakeshore and watching his niece struggle to lower herself onto the edge of the dock. He was in complete control of his emotions, at least now that Lane had returned home, but he wasn't above rubbing Richard's face in his mishandling of the situation. "Doing a fine job there, Sheriff."

Richard stared across the room at his elder brother but finally relented, sinking into the recliner when Ray gestured him closer. He spoke through the fingers dragging along his lips. "I don't even know what to say to the kid."

Ray smiled, giving him that benevolent look their father, Rainier, had displayed much more often than his unhappy side. "Just try opening up your body language."

A rising eyebrow dismissed the notion. "Yeah. Right."

"Notice where you're sitting. I invite you over, you sit alone. If everybody's hanging out, you stand apart, hands in your pockets, all withdrawn. All closed up. You know what that says?" A rhetorical question if Ray had ever asked one—he didn't wait for an answer. "It says, "Don't bother me." You want her to open up to you? You gotta do it first. The face you present to the rest of the world really shouldn't be the face you present to your family, especially your daughter."

Richard fell silent, signaling the end of the conversation. Ray knew his brother would analyze the situation, study the events, and replay the actions and reactions until he had categorized every minute of the argument with Lane, determining the instant he had lost and why.

Ray wouldn't intrude on that process; he certainly couldn't add to it, and it was too much work anyway. He changed the subject. "I think it's time for me to move out. I've already contacted the diocese."

Richard balked. "You can't just run out on us." His tone suggested he had the right to rescind Ray's decision.

"You're a big boy now."

"I'm more worried about her," Richard countered.

"You two young people are gonna have to find a way to work this out, and at the moment, I think my being here has begun to impede that. But I think you'll be okay. Besides, I expect one night of the week to be mine. And Sundays are Mom's. And special occasions, and Mass, so it's not like you'll never see me again. I'll be butting in a couple, three times a week. More if you piss me off."

"I think you're discounting how much she needs you."

Ray flicked on the TV, searching the channels for a ball game. "I know exactly how much she needs me. And I know exactly how much she needs no one. And somewhere in there, you two need to find common ground."

The retort of a nearby weapon discharge assaulted the cabin; the brothers abandoned the search for worthy televiewing before the echo faded. Ray reached the window first and saw nothing but the splash Lane left behind on her entry to the lake. "She's in the water!"

Richard charged the gun cabinet, tossed a Remington and a box of shells to Ray, and then grabbed his favorite Winchester rifle. Loading it on the run, he jammed five rounds into the internal magazine and slid a sixth into the chamber before he'd left the safety of the front porch. The second shot rang out; it forced the men to be more cautious, but it didn't really slow their progress.

Quick assessment of the bullet damage revealed the general direction from which the attack had come. Richard threw himself into a pop-up slide, gouging a trail and kicking up gravel as he assumed a defensive position behind their aluminum rowboat.

Ray took the hint; he ducked behind the far side of the dock, using it to shield his body while he peered around it to find his niece. "Lane!" He trained his rifle forty-five degrees from Richard's line of sight, forming a serious wedge of protection against the shooter's relative position. "I don't see her!"

Neither did Richard. His gun never wavered off the forest, but he cast glances to the dock, analyzing the bullet damage against wood and determining the sequence of events. Since a bullet sent her into the water, the mutilation of the upper post came first. That meant the second shot chased her in, and Richard spotted the furrow on a lower post, just above the water line. "She's under the dock!" He scanned the hillside through the rifle scope and caught a brief glimpse of camouflaged movement near the ridge. "I got him."

Ray swiveled to match Richard's mark just in time to watch the shooter scramble up the hill and over the rise.

"I'll cover you," Richard called out.

Ray set his rifle down and waded into the frigid water. "Lane!"

She slipped out from under the dock ten feet from him, arms flopping against the top decking, fingers dragging along the planks. She lost her grip and slid beneath the surface.

Chapter 3 – Out of the Cold

Ice water dripped a line up the porch and through the cabin as Ray carried Lane straight to the bathroom. He perched his niece on the toilet seat and quickly stripped off her outer clothes, tossing the wet things over his shoulder. The shoes and socks hit the shower wall and tumbled into the tub, the shoes popping noisily around on the way down. But the jacket only made it half way in. One arm hung over the edge, perhaps trying to escape, perhaps just determined to leave a puddle on the floor.

As Lane shivered, Ray stripped her sweater up and off without any trouble at all. The fight didn't begin until he tried to get her tee shirt.

No additional shots rang out, and no rustling in the trees signified anyone else lying in ambush, but Richard didn't take any chances. He backed his way toward the cabin, claiming the Remington that Ray had ditched to carry Lane.

The adrenaline zipped through his body. Every sound became a reason for concern—the fluttering of birds in the trees, the alarmed bark of a chipmunk, the rising volume of Ray's voice, muffled but still loud enough to be heard from outside their shared home.

The first two could mean nothing more than a normal day in the woods, or they could mean the shooter had doubled back around the house. If so, Richard was looking in the wrong place. As for the latter, the exasperation in Ray's voice meant that a certain teenaged probationer was doing something to upset her uncle.

And whatever that was, as rare as it might be, it had to take second fiddle to the more pressing situation…an armed gunman in the woods shooting at people. Nothing about the event suggested an accident to Richard, so he toured the exterior of the house, peering around corners before putting himself in the line of fire, and closed all the storm shutters just in case his gut feeling proved correct.

With the exterior of the house as secure as he could make it, he locked the door behind himself, called the office to alert them of the situation, then headed toward the skirmish growing in the bathroom.

If Richard hadn't known that Lane had just taken a cold dip in the lake, he might have been inclined to think she'd gotten plastered. Her clumsy resistance and slurred speech would earn her a night in the drunk-tank if he ever did catch her intoxicated. Fortunately for her, he knew the symptoms of hypothermia.

He stood in the doorway as Ray struggled to get the tee shirt over Lane's head, but she had wedged her arms into the fabric and hunched forward, keeping her uncle at bay.

"Need some help?" Richard stood both rifles butt-end down in the corner by the door and pulled a stack of thick, terry towels from the linen closet.

"Nothing like a little misplaced modesty," Ray said, temporarily giving up the battle.

Richard hooked his thumb over his shoulder. Ray hesitated, eyeing the girl giving him the devil's own time, but he left the room, taking his Remington and closing the door as he went.

"Come on." Richard drew her up from the toilet and leaned her against the wall to keep her balanced. He snapped open a towel and stretched it across her torso, using her arms to pin it in place. And then he pulled her tee shirt up from her otherwise

10

naked back and over her head, a move Lane couldn't easily counter, especially since doing so would mean using her arms.

He left the shirt balled up under her chin and reclaimed the edges of the towel, holding it in front of her. "Slip your arms out." She obeyed, almost quiet about it, her grumblings barely audible over the sucking noises made by the wet tee clinging to her skin. "Might not be such an issue if you'd listen to me once in a while. Maybe now you're figuring out why I want you to wear a bra."

He knew why she wouldn't wear one—she had nothing to fill it with. Even though she'd been eating well for the last three months, her body hadn't fully recovered from starvation mode. She had gained nearly twelve pounds on the carefully constructed diet Doc Williams had created for her, but none of that found its way to her chest. She looked like a boy, periodically made comments about it, and refused to wear what she so often referred to as a "training bra".

Ray knocked and waited for the "all clear" before stepping in with a clean robe. "Thought this might help."

Richard nodded his agreement. "Pants are next." Lane stumbled around him, heading for the door; he looped a gentle but firm arm around her waist and drew her back. "Everything wet has to come off."

"I can do it," she whispered, the sound of her chattering teeth louder than her words.

"I am your father, you know."

"And I can still do it myself."

He considered it, weighing her needs for modesty and privacy against his wishes. Concern shadowed his eyes, and the lines on his face pulled tight. *She's done it before,* he reminded himself. "Okay. One minute. You get out of those jeans and into this robe in one minute flat, because covered or not, I'm coming back in." He noted the time. "Go."

11

As soon as the door closed behind him, Lane dropped the towel. Unsteady on her feet, she teetered backward, bumping against the toilet and collapsing onto it.

"Forty-five," Richard called through the door.

She hauled herself back to her feet, using the towel bar for support, and pushed down against the waistband of her jeans, shimmying back and forth, enticing the pants off. They declined.

"Thirty."

"Crap," Lane whispered. This particular pair of pants had a mind of its own.

She had told Ray they were too small when she tried them on, but he insisted they fit right, "The way clothes are supposed to fit, not pushing your guts out like sausage and not slipping off your buttski." And then he had bought five pairs of them despite her objections; he'd also absconded with all her old pants—or at least those he could find—deciding summarily that they didn't fit her properly. And now those brand new jeans refused to come off.

"Fifteen."

Lane shrugged into the robe, wrapping it fully around herself and then some. The tell-tale scents of cinnamon and vanilla wafted into the air and tickled her nose, reminding her that Ray had been baking cookies while she and Richard had their somewhat unpleasant snit.

The door popped open...not so much as a knock. Richard frowned at his daughter's lack of progress.

"They're too small." Her teeth chattered wildly.

"Are not," Ray countered from the door, sounding just a tad over sixteen.

"Are too."

Richard closed the door on his suddenly adolescent brother. "Okay, kids. Don't make me send you to your rooms." He locked eyes with Lane. As she held tight to the robe, he reached in and tugged down the resistant jeans. His eyes never left hers, but that didn't keep her skin from turning scarlet.

"Sit."

She didn't exactly obey; Richard steered her backward and her legs simply buckled when she hit the bowl. He clamped his thumb and forefinger around the hem of each pant leg, stripping the jeans out from under the robe without any difficulty at all. They, too, ended up in the tub.

"I think you're just plain weak." He snatched a thermometer from the medicine cabinet and stuffed it under her tongue. "Not a good sign."

Hands cupped around her third hot chocolate and flanked by her father and uncle at the kitchen table, Lane's eyes shifted expectantly from one man to the other.

"Drink up," Ray urged, his finger turning circles at her to emphasize his wishes.

"Already had two," she whined.

Richard scowled. "Sound like a request to you? Your temp got down to ninety-three. Not particularly dangerous, but you still need to get warmed up, preferably from the inside out. Drink." His attitude vacillated between annoyed and concerned. Even now he had to explain himself, even though his request obviously centered on her well-being. But she did drain the cup in one long draw.

Ray swept it off the table and refilled it in fifteen seconds flat.

"You gotta be kidding."

"We look like we're kidding?" Richard shot back.

She clucked her tongue at him. "Come on. Shouldn't I be eating some crap right now? Carbs and stuff? High sugar foods?

Cookies?" Her chin nudged toward the counter and the racks of confections cooling there.

"Oh, so now you're the expert. Okay, then you know that you should be walking around and generating some of your own heat."

"No, I didn't mean that!"

But it was much too late. She had opened a door that Richard had no intention of letting close. He wrapped his arm around her, extracting her from the chair despite her objections.

"Let's tour the house," he said, pulling her close and musing over her obvious discomfort. He was sure she would prefer to do it herself, and he might have allowed it if he could be certain she actually would do it. But logic told him that, for a while at least, he'd have to ensure her compliance as well as keep her from falling over.

Richard strolled along with his daughter, exiting the kitchen and snaking around the first floor, around the dining room table twice, through the living room, and circling the sofa before heading into the study-turned-bedroom. His eyebrows rose high on his forehead, but he didn't give voice to the thoughts floating around his head regarding the crap piled on the desk, the clothes on the floor, or the general disarray.

It irritated him that she couldn't clean up after herself, and that's what had started the fight that sent her out of the house, down to the dock, and into the path of someone's bullets. Now she was shivering in his arms; he let the issue go. For now.

Besides, he thought, cutting her some slack isn't such a bad idea. She wasn't exactly sitting on her ass doing nothing...she'd completed her junior year of high school and, if she stayed on schedule pulling double-duty on her senior year studies, she'd graduate with the rest of her classmates. Throw in the assorted therapies, despite her obvious distaste for all of it, and the work required to drag the injured leg around behind her, and the kid was expelling some serious energy.

And Richard had discovered a great use for the little time left over every day…overseeing Lane as she slowly whittled away at her two-hundred and forty hours of community service. Often that involved Lane playing janitor inside the Sheriff's Department, but he wasn't above stopping the car on the way home to have her pick up trash along the road.

In light of all that, what difference can it possibly make if she cleans the damn room? Richard asked himself. Just because he preferred order and structure didn't necessarily mean he couldn't tolerate the mess on a temporary basis, even if it did look like the aftermath of a hurricane. Couldn't I just close the door?

Richard knew he was pushing her hard, spurring her to accomplish too much too quickly, though odds were that she'd say his tactics more resembled strong-arming than persuasion. He decided it might be time to take a step back and cut something from the activities mix.

Community Service looked to be the likely candidate, though the delay would have her serving the required hours until Hell franchised a Dairy Queen. The attack she endured at Morgan's hands had left both physical and emotional scars; having a little time off might relieve some of the issues that tormented her.

Or he could cut her schooling. With ample credits in the Early College Program, Lane could just graduate now. He and Ray had discussed the issue back in December, and they had jointly decided that she would be better off in a social setting, rather than just performing her community service in relative isolation. Returning to school kept her involved, busy, and productive, while also reintroducing her to the human race.

If she couldn't pull it all off, they would be forced to use her ECP credits to secure her high school graduation. Either way, she'd head off to college in four months; probationary meetings could be rescheduled to coincide with her weekend visits home, and community service could be served just as easily at college as in Mills Valley. And the study would be his again. Nice, clean, and back to normal.

Not that he really wanted her to leave, but those plans had been in place for quite some time, since before he even knew that he had a daughter. He rather liked having her around, except perhaps the constant fighting about relatively stupid crap. But he had another few months before that day arrived. And in that time, maybe they could reach an understanding, that common ground Ray spoke of, or perhaps just an uneasy truce that allowed them both to leave a room with their skin and organs intact.

He turned her back out of the room and escorted her to the kitchen just as Ray returned from his own waltz around the house with his dance partner, the Remington rifle he had received on his fourteenth birthday. He butt-ended it against the lower cabinets and helped himself to a cookie, its dough still soft and the chocolate inside just beginning to solidify. "Hmm. Good." He winked at Lane. "Don't see anybody out there now. Hunter?"

Richard didn't really want to talk about it in front of Lane. Since she seemed to have gotten her land-legs back, he sent her on another round of the house.

Her first official act, however, involved sucking her teeth for effect, making sure Richard knew her displeasure. Then she toured herself right to the confections where she snatched one for each hand before gimping away.

The cabin's open floor plan would keep the girl in sight; to prevent eavesdropping, Richard kept his voice low even though Lane's irritating tooth-sucking noise made him want to scream.

"Even with buck-fever, it would be pretty irresponsible to shoot an animal he had no hope of retrieving."

"Maybe he figured it would get back to shore before it died," Ray offered.

Richard shook his head. "That looked like a head shot. Dead on target but a foot wide. If he'd accounted for the wind on the water he'd have splattered her noggin like a watermelon. He did a much better job with the second bullet."

Ray's eyes squinted into skeptical slits. "If he was trying to kill somebody, he could've picked either of us off at any time."

"Best guess? Our shooter didn't think he'd miss, or he didn't expect to have to contend with both of us armed. But I can only think of one person who'd want Lane dead. And if I know Jenna at all, the rest of us aren't particularly safe."

Stunned, Ray's mouth fell open. His fingers wrapped around the barrel of his rifle, pulling it from the floor and heading for the door without uttering any sort of explanation. He got halfway to the front door before his younger brother's hand tightened around his arm. He shrugged free of Richard's grasp. "Mom's alone."

Richard nodded. "Yep." He pulled his cell phone from his pocket, and wiggled it at Ray. "Already taken care of. And you going out there, without knowing who we're up against, or how many...that just makes you a target." He turned back toward the kitchen and stopped. Lane's tour of the house had ended abruptly at the sofa. Cookie crumbs lingered at the corners of her mouth, suggesting that she had at least managed to finish her snack before falling asleep.

Chapter 4 – County Jail

Jenna couldn't decide which was worse—the pumpkin-orange jumpsuit, the food, or the outdated books in the jail's library.

She had been in the general population for an entire week before her attitude toward the rest of the jail's residents earned her a sound beating. Six women cornered her in the cafeteria, pummeling her with their fists and feet. The guards broke up the melee before it got any worse, but Jenna still spent the next week in the infirmary before being sequestered in the isolation unit for her own protection.

Her six attackers had also been confined in solitary as punishment for their misdeed. They had each been given thirty days, and they had all been released to the yard weeks ago. But while they had shared time in the segregation block, they nattered back and forth across the corridor, their taunts, threats, and mocking laughter echoing into Jenna's cell at all hours of the day and night, promising retribution and a good deal more pain.

Morgan had been terrifying at times, and occasionally brutal with her, but at least he had been the only one inflicting the damage. And as soon as he "won" whatever conflict they had become embroiled in, he stopped. Lane had never learned that.

Lane. Even thinking of her daughter twisted the corner of Jenna's lips into a dismissive sneer. She had tried so hard to destroy the Keates brothers, both of whom had ultimately rejected her, and Lane was now free as a lark and living with them. Wearing whatever she feels like wearing, Jenna thought. "Style has never really been the girl's forte." There could be little doubt that Lane had resumed her normal wardrobe—blue jeans, a ratty old shirt, with her hair all chopped off and raggedy. Looking more boy than girl. A snort of disgust pushed out through Jenna's mouth.

The wicket in the solid door slid open, metal scraping against metal and sending a shiver up Jenna's spine. A hand stuck through the opening, and a pair of eyes peered in at her. "Hey, Beauty Queen." The ex-cellmate of one of her tormentors did double-duty as library-cart pusher and terror-spreader. "They moved my cellie because of you. Got her over in D block."

Jenna put up her toughest front. "That's her doing. They attacked me, and they got caught."

Library-girl chuckled. "Don't matter. You the one gonna pay for it. You won't be so high-and-mighty then. Bopper's got lots of friends inside. Do you?" She slid a book onto the small shelf in the door and pushed the cart away. "It's just a matter of time 'fore somebody get you."

"The warden says I'll be staying in protective custody."

Library-girl's snort came out her nose and was clearly audible inside Jenna's cell, as were her words. "Maybe. Maybe not. But they let you out for an hour a day, Princess. And sooner or later, they'll get lazy about watching you. Or they'll get paid to look the other way. Maybe we'll get you today. I hear your lawyer just signed in, and it's a long walk back to visitation."

The room held nothing of comfort. Grey paint adorned the walls, the haphazard sprays on the ceiling and moldings reminding everyone that convicts had splash-dabbed this room in hasty style. The mismatched furniture—a table and two unpadded chairs—only added to the general feeling of poverty and unpleasantness.

Jenna's butt screamed inconsolably at its abuse; never in her life had anyone insisted that she plant her perfect, yet un-cushioned rump, into a chair that didn't conform to her every curve. Unable to find a comfortable position, she fidgeted.

Her skin had even begun to match the drab environment. While her dry, cracked hands rested on the tabletop, she fiddled with her broken and unvarnished nails, tugging at a frayed end and flicking the offal onto the floor.

Her arms fared no better; the alligator crackling extended up and under the sleeves of her bright orange jumpsuit, which blazed a stark contrast against the rest of the room.

The bruises had long since faded, but the scar over her eye reminded her, and everyone else who saw it, of the beating that sent her into the solitary unit. The defect would require cosmetic surgery, just as soon as her lawyer secured her release from this godforsaken place.

"Jenna." The deep, fairly mellow voice held that untamed power Morgan had possessed. "Are you listening?"

Jenna looked up at him. With a few more years and a few more pounds, Barnett could have passed for his elder, and now dead, brother. "Yes."

"Try to stay with me, dear. If they can convince a jury that you were involved, I expect you'll need far more than a day at the spa to get yourself back in order."

She shot him with her best "I'm in charge here" look, but it didn't have the impact she expected. He smiled, almost pleasantly. "Twenty-five to life depending on whether the prosecutor goes for first or second degree. I think the "aiding and abetting" is irrefutable, but she could have died. If the prosecution argues that you were instrumental in the attack," he paused, his shoulders shrugging up and his hands splaying open on the table, "well, I just hope you can live in orange for the rest of your life. You're also not likely to win the civil suit her lawyer has filed against you. She'll end up with a good deal of your assets."

"Most of my assets are offshore."

"If you're comfortable living in the Caymans for the rest of your life, fine. But if you ever plan to come back to the U.S., any money that comes with you is seizable. But I'm sure you'll find plenty of island boys to help you through those lonely nights."

"You're a pig, Barnett."

"Indeed, but that hardly matters. What you need to decide is whether you want to spend some money for your freedom, or if you'll allow your new neighbors to break your hands before you can sign a check."

Jenna's mouth clamped shut, her eyes pinched into a death stare as she glared at him from across the table.

"It hasn't gone well. The funds we expended haven't produced high quality results."

Jenna remained silent, her eyes darting about the room, locating the guards and other inmates passing by.

"We've been through this, my dear. They cannot record our conversations. Doing so would be utterly illegal, a felony, in fact. Actually, it would be better for you if they did record us, because then I could get you out of here faster than you can slap on your vixen facade."

Hearing the words didn't make it easier on Jenna. She leaned forward, her voice dropping into her most threatening tone. "Just remember you can be replaced, too, Barnett. Just like the last lawyer who couldn't do what I wanted."

Barnett turned sideways and crossed one leg over the other, folding his hands in his lap. His eyebrows rose high on his forehead, daring her to lay her cards out. "Or you could just stay here. It may not be Seychelles, but it is warm and dry. Three square meals per day."

"A million per." Jenna leaned back in her chair.

21

Barnett's smile returned, his blunt teeth startlingly different from Morgan's canine grin. He slid a bank draft across the table to her and waggled a pen in her direction. "Is that including the old woman?"

"You do whatever you want with her. I'm only interested in three. Just remember that I want Lane dead first." She snatched the pen from his hand.

"Whatever. While we're on the subject, let's discuss those offshore accounts."

Jenna's victorious smile revealed her to be the holder of the winning hand. "And have you forget all about me? I think not."

Chapter 5 – Oh, Please

"You've come to protect me?" The whimsical tone in Dottie's voice and the laughter in her eyes made it clear that she didn't need some upstart rookie looking after her.

"Sorry, Dottie. Sheriff's orders. I'm to bring you down to the station. Said I could give you fifteen minutes to pack a bag, then I'm to drag you outta here if I have to."

"And you think you can do that? Cuff me and drag me off?"

"Please step away from the door."

Dottie looked past him into the night. The warm glow of the street lights illuminated the road, and moths bombarded the bulbs in kamikaze spirals. Two cruisers sat at odd angles to the curb, their lights flashing incongruent colors against the otherwise serene landscape. "Oh, please. Two cars? The station is across the damn street."

Danny stepped through the threshold, using his body as a shield, his hand latching onto the door. Dottie unconsciously stepped back, allowing him just enough room to block her body with his own and close the door at the same time.

"I did not invite you in." Her tone took on a sudden hint of annoyance, but Danny slipped past her and into the living room, his eyes dancing around in search of hidden dangers, his hand caressing his sidearm.

"Sorry. Sheriff said not to take any lip from you. I'd really rather not have to manhandle the Sheriff's mother, if it's all the same to you, but he does believe you're in danger."

Richard had never been given to needless worry; that was Ray's domain. Still, Dottie thought, why do I need protecting? Not like I've got a list of enemies. Her eyes followed the deputy through the room for a few seconds before locking onto a picture of her granddaughter, Lane, with…that…woman!

"I think you best spill the beans."

That woman, whom Dottie did her level best to never refer to by name, was the only possible enemy Dottie had ever made, but she was supposed to be in the county lock-up at the moment.

"Sheriff said not to worry. Just precautionary," Danny said.

"And the Sheriff's mother wants to know what this was about."

Danny eyed her, and Dottie had the distinct feeling that the young deputy was sizing her up in case he had to make a real go against her. Perhaps if she smacked him with her handbag a whole bunch of times she could delay him, but she couldn't evade him for long. Dottie decided he was more worried about explaining any bruises he might inflict on her—the Sheriff certainly wouldn't look kindly on anyone who brought his mother into protective custody in need of a doctor.

"Sheriff said, if you insisted, I should remind you to trust him just because he's the Sheriff."

Dottie's lips pinched tight, and a moment later she shuffled over to the closet for a suitcase. "Did the Sheriff happen to say how long?"

Chapter 6 – Can I Have Some Money?

No one knew how long it would take the Sheriff's Department to figure out who shot at Lane, whether or not it was an accident, if they'd stick around and try again, or if they had just blown out of town with the weekend tourists.

Three days after the shooting, Richard still had no clues other than an incredibly common shell casing that five out of six hunters in the area might have used. Neil from the sporting goods shop confirmed he had sold fifteen boxes to twelve different people, a mixture of both locals and transients, in the last three weeks alone.

No one had seen any exceptionally suspicious strangers in town or any vehicles lurking in the shadows or behind corners. None of the bed and breakfasts nor any of the lodges revealed guests still around. Most visitors to town had checked out Sunday, but a half-dozen families lingered until Monday, with a few of the stragglers still at Marigold's partaking of a late breakfast before their long drives home.

Richard's buddy Wes reported that he still had three visitors in the campground, procrastinating over the decision to become part-time residents. On top of that, eight of last year's seasonals had shown up this past weekend to open their campers up a couple weeks before the season's official opening.

Wes didn't mind the work or the extra influx of funds, but he couldn't verify where any of them had been on Friday. Considering they were all retirees in their late sixties or better, Richard seriously doubted any of them were involved in anything more strenuous than a rousing game of bingo.

It had even begun to look like it might have been an isolated incident, most likely some jerk with buck-fever shooting at whatever moved. A poacher would never have been so stupid, so the blame fell by default on a weekend-warrior, some yahoo up from the city to kill something but lacking the intelligence to know he couldn't retrieve it in fifteen feet of frigid water. Fortunately, the moron missed his intended target, but Richard berated himself for his inability to solve the incident more precisely.

"So I'm going home now," Dottie announced, sliding into her jacket and gathering up her purse. Richard would have been happier if his mother would stick around just a little while longer, but she'd have none of it. "You said it yourself, Sheriff. No suspects. No evidence. No recurrences." She pushed past him. "If I hurry, I can make the morning Mass. I'll see you tomorrow." And out the door she went, bold and brave, full of the bluster only the old and the young shared.

Why is it, Richard wondered, that only the middle-aged are smart enough to be cautious?

Dottie whirled back for just a second, and he feared that she might actually have read his mind. "And no, I don't need you to send over the Cabana Boy to check on me. And yes, I will call if I hear or see anything suspicious." She pulled the door closed before her youngest son could respond.

Danny, however, made the poor choice to snicker, giving Richard a place to vent his frustrations. "Be careful, Cabana Boy, or I'll send you over there anyway and let her eat your gizzards for dinner."

Richard caught a glimpse of Lane in Interrogation Room One. She'd been in there pretending to do schoolwork. Her math book and assignment papers had been carefully arranged to look like she was working. Anybody with a brain, however, knew that the angle of her head suggested she was studying the TV instead

26

of the books. At the moment, she stood in the center of the room, watching the goings-on in Dispatch.

Richard knew what Lane wanted—her eyes wide, her jaw slack. Her grandmother had just been granted a reprieve and Lane wanted to go home, too, back out to the cabin where she could be alone and hide from the rest of humanity. It wasn't like he didn't understand; he knew full well why she spent so much time avoiding contact with other people, how the attack a year earlier had left her man-shy.

Understanding it and enabling it, however, were two different things. He'd been working hard to draw her from her shell, and while he might not be able to contain his mother, he damn well could control his daughter. At least he thought he could...why she's watching TV instead of working off community service is anybody's guess.

His finger poked in her direction, doing his best imitation of Charlton Heston as Moses. The digit apparently had direct control over the girl, because as Richard flicked his finger down, his daughter settled back into her chair. Happy that he'd managed to achieve a fifty percent success rate with women today, he returned to his office.

After an uninterrupted thirty minutes' work, a timid knock drew his eyes to the door, where he found Lane. "What's up?" he asked, setting his pen down and doing his level best to drop his duties and be a concerned, involved parent.

"Getting just a bit stuffy in here. I'm gonna take a walk over to Pearce's."

The emotional half of him wanted to yield, wanted to let her do and have anything she desired, but the sane half refused to give in. He couldn't look weak. He couldn't appear to be letting his emotions run the show. He picked up his pen and returned to his work. "When did you assume command?" He decided to let her chew on that for a while, but he didn't have long to wait.

27

"Oh, for God's sake! Can I just go to Pearce's?"

The tone in her voice angered him, and the pen fell from his hand at the same time his emotions screamed No! Only logic kept him from jumping clean down her throat. Her eyes held a touch of cabin fever; in all likelihood, being restricted to the cell block, the break room, and Interrogation Room One was exacting a heavy toll since she was used to the wide open spaces around Keates Lake. Unfortunately, her eyes held a little more, and that touch of defiance just plain pissed him off.

"What?" He kept his voice calm and even, pushing the anger away and forcing her to consider what she'd just done.

"Look, I'm not six."

"But you are acting like a petulant child, and I am your father. And you'll find this will all be a lot easier if you treat people civilly. Maybe you want to rethink this and come back later when your behavior is just a little more appropriate." He knew in his heart that she was fully aware of what she had done and what he wanted.

It didn't surprise him at all when she flipped around and headed out to dispatch. A quick image of a six-year-old Lane flashed before his eyes, snapping around and tossing her long hair into the wind. He silently admitted relief that her hair could no longer single-handedly dismiss him into unimportance.

A full minute hadn't passed when she was back at the door, knocking timidly. "Getting just a bit stuffy in here. Would it be okay if I walked over to Pearce's? Please?" Her eyebrows rose up to underscore her request, and he couldn't help but feel a twinge of amusement. She wasn't above rubbing his face in the prior discussion, however. "Pretty please? With sugar on top?"

Richard's tone dropped into deadpan. "Don't go overboard."

"Just to Pearce's. Hobble over, hobble back."

"What do they have that we don't?" Richard countered, his displeasure replaced by debate mode.

"Yankee Doodles and grinders."

"Doc doesn't really want you going hog wild on that stuff."

"And fresh air."

"Open a window."

"Crap, man. You wanted me to be civil, and even that's not good enough for you! I been trapped in here forever."

"It's been three days. And I'm trying to keep you safe."

"But there aren't any clues. No witnesses." Her frustration turned her pitch up a notch or two.

Richard's finger waggled a warning. "I'd be a little careful about trying to pull your grandmother on me."

"Come on. Ten minutes. Please?"

He considered it. At least she had asked permission this time. "Will you take Danny with you?"

Disappointment spread across Lane's face, as transparent as dragonfly wings; she obviously hoped to be free for a while, even if she could only squeeze a few minutes out of him to cross the street and get back. But Richard refused to believe that the danger had passed. "Danny goes or you don't."

Lane's eyebrows pinched together as her top lip pulled up. Richard almost wanted to check the floor to make sure she hadn't stepped in a pile of dog manure. "You know Danny's creepy, right?"

"That's my final offer. Take it and go to Pearce's. Leave it and go back to Room One. Oh, wait a minute. Don't you have some work to do? Cleaning bathrooms or something?"

"Well, alrighty, then." The mixture of sarcasm, acceptance, and faux happiness created an almost realistic response. "Can I have some money?"

Chapter 7 – I Gotta Buy Some Stuff

For the third time in his short career, Danny played escort to a member of the Keates family. Despite Lane's different last name, Keates behaviors screamed out at him periodically, reminding him that this girl was in the same category as the department dispatcher, Dottie—someone to whom one should endear themselves for political expedience, but also someone to be mindful of for her connection to the Sheriff.

His charge limped slowly all the way to Pearce's. He'd heard scuttlebutt that Doc hadn't yet cleared her off the crutches, but he hadn't seen her use them at all in nearly a month. He'd also heard rumors that Sheriff Keates pretty much had to drag the girl to physical therapy twice a week.

Despite her reluctance, therapy seemed to be helping. She maybe wouldn't ever have a normal gait again, but she certainly could walk, and determination, spunk, or just plain Keates pig-headedness forced her to get wherever she wanted to go on her own steam.

His college courses and police training gave him sufficient education to know that his attraction to the girl rested in the trauma she had endured and the natural instinct of a person, a man especially, to protect those in need.

She was fragile, the part of her that he'd seen anyway. Other folks talked about the feisty girl who would go toe-to-toe with anyone, but he had only experienced her fear as testified to by the bulk of her decisions back in November. When he and Richard had gotten close to capturing her, Lane had lashed out in terror, smashing Danny in the head. Twice.

Any reasonable human being understood fear-based reactivity. That she'd pulled the stunt on a deputy certainly couldn't be misconstrued as the smartest thing she'd ever done, but he did at least understand it. And just to make sure she understood it, too, Sheriff Keates had tacked extra hours of community service onto her sentence.

Unofficially, of course, but Danny had always appreciated that the Sheriff felt it necessary to impose a punishment on his own daughter for assaulting a Deputy Sheriff, even if said Deputy was technically still a rookie.

The obvious fear had taken a sabbatical, but it hadn't gone away completely. It poked its little head out intermittently in subtle ways: walking arm's length away from everyone whose name wasn't Keates; only going to the restroom or break room if no one else walked the corridor; watching absolutely everything, all the comings and goings of staff and visitors, even the movement of people on the street.

He noted the distance between them now; to test his theory he deliberately stepped in closer to her, careful to make it look like nothing more than a rambling, errant stride. She countered immediately, making no attempt to hide the sideways motion that veered her away from him…she'd keep her three-foot personal space no matter what.

Danny felt sure that, somewhere deep inside her, fear still had her convinced to remain vigilant, guarded, and watchful, as if at any second the bubble might burst and she'd find herself homeless once again, on the defensive, and fighting to survive.

The silence between them was the most awkward, taking on a life of its own, and demanding that someone say something. Since it wouldn't be Lane, Danny acquiesced to ease his own discomfort. "You seem to be getting around pretty good." Lane nodded but didn't bother to speak. "Any likelihood you'll get the rest of your voice back?"

31

A heavy sigh preceded a shake of her head. "Probably not."

They reached the stairs at Pearce's Grocery; Danny hung close, closer than Lane would have liked. A slight ripple of motion in his hand suggested he was about to grab onto her elbow. Lane didn't want or need his help; she pulled her arm from his reach, making no bones about her intentions to do this herself. He entered the store first, acknowledging the grocer but scoping out the aisles for hidden assailants.

Old Man Pearce's face pulled up into a toothless Jack-O-Lantern grin when he saw Lane. "Hey, there you are. Been wondering when you'd get around to coming for a visit."

Lane waved and hooked a thumb over her shoulder, gesturing back out into the street. "I had to get permission from Sheriff Stick-Up-His-Butt."

Pearce chuckled. "Sorta figured. Think you'll be coming back to work soon?"

Her shoulders shrugged up, palms turning forward. "I'll have to ask him, but he's got me doing community service, picking up trash along the highway, painting the bathrooms in the station. You know. Stupid stuff that don't matter 'cause it won't last anyway."

She desperately wanted to be alone, even if just for a few minutes, even just strolling the aisles in the store. Just something independent. "You can wait outside, Deputy. I'll be okay in here."

"Got my orders. Not to let you outta my sight."

Lane rolled her eyes at him, big circular sweeps designed to let him know what she thought about his intelligence. She leaned in closer, lowering her voice. "Gotta get stuff." It was lost on Danny. "Come on, you know. Stuff." He still hadn't a clue. "Tampons?" she blurted, her arms extending out from her sides.

Suddenly Danny understood why she wanted a little privacy; his body jolted as upright as if a rattlesnake had just sunk its fangs into his butt cheeks. "I'll be right outside."

Old Man Pearce watched as Danny beat a hasty retreat. "That'd never work on the Sheriff."

"Don't I know it," Lane said, and headed down the aisle, slowly taking in everything like a tourist on vacation, as if all the trinkets and baubles were vying for her attention and money.

A minute passed, and the bell tinkled its entry alert. Danny's head popped in. Lane turned to find him peering down the aisles in search of her. She waved the little blue box at him, and he ducked right back outside.

She turned down another aisle. "Hey, Mr. Al…no Yankee Doodles?"

He shuffled toward the stock room. "Probably some out back. I been waiting on that Olsen kid to show up and help me unpack. Unreliable toad. I sure hope Sheriff Stick-Up-His-Butt lets you come back to work soon so I can have the pleasure of firing that little bastard. He certainly ain't the man his father is." Creaking on its well-worn hinges, the door swung closed behind him as he tottered into the stockroom.

"Amen to that," Lane whispered. The bell tinkled again, and her eyeballs coursed their sockets in annoyance. Deputy Dawg can't be back already, she thought as she headed back to the front of the store with the little blue box; she pulled up short, finding herself staring into the hate-filled eyes of Jake Olsen.

# Chapter 8 – Richard Ain't Blind

Richard leaned back in his chair, stretching to catch a glimpse of Pearce's store. He didn't know what he expected to find—Lane and Danny had only been gone eleven minutes—but he didn't expect to see his deputy perched against the railing without Lane at his side. Richard pushed out of his chair, stood at the window for a moment, and waited.

Danny poked his head inside, but then came right back out. Then Jake Olsen went in. And still Danny stood outside.

Richard grabbed his hat and gun.

Chapter 9 – But He Is Annoyed

"**W**here is she?" Richard demanded of Danny, who met him at the top of Pearce's stairs.

"Inside. She looked like she needed some privacy."

"You're kidding." It came out more statement than question.

"No," Danny said. "She had to buy some stuff. She seemed a little embarrassed."

Richard thought his Deputy must have lost his mind. "What is it? Too hot for you? Heat stroke?"

"She had to buy, well, you know, stuff," Danny insisted.

Richard's lips pursed, and his hands rose to his hips. The slight lean forward gave him the intimidating presence that everyone in town did their best to avoid. "Tampons?"

Danny nodded, as if he and Richard were both in on the little secret now.

"She's not likely to need those for quite some time yet. And when she does, they're in the ladies' room at the station. When I say "Don't take your eyes off her", I really do sorta kinda mean it." He reached for the door knob.

Chapter 10 – Jason Gets Too Close

Jason, quarterback of the football team, had backed Lane into the freezer case, his face threateningly close to her, his arms blocking her escape as he pressed against her. "Come on. Everybody knows you were selling yourself to survive. Not like every half-baked jack wagon hasn't already been in there."

Lane pushed at him to no avail. "Get away!"

"That's not really what you mean. Just admit it. You miss it. You miss having a man."

Lane saw no way out of her current predicament. Every fiber in her being screamed for a hasty retreat, but her running days lay in the distant past along with memories of her original-equipment-kneecap. The new model never obeyed commands without prodding. And hobbling from one place to the next prevented fleeing for one's life.

She took a deep breath, praying with each passing second that Old Man Pearce would just find the damned Yankee Doodles already. But in the meantime, she had to contend with Jason. Maybe she shouldn't have been so quick to embarrass Danny into the street.

Jason's hand slid down to Lane's waist, then lower to her hip. She swatted his hand away, but he only laughed. "You play this hard to get in them crack houses?"

The bell tinkled, and Lane's thoughts raced ahead. Danny, she thought. Come on, Deputy, come on!

Jason didn't seem bothered that someone had entered the store, and Lane wondered if his cocky attitude or the fact that he seriously outweighed Danny fueled his lack of concern. If they got into a scrape, the odds favored Jason. All Lane could hope for was a drawn gun or enough time to get outside and attract attention.

Jason hunched over her, leaning in close, trying to get a lip-lock while her head squirmed back and forth. He latched onto her chin.

It was so close to what Morgan had done, his hand over her mouth right before he raped her. She had been unable to defend herself then, and rage surged up from her stomach every time someone dared remind her of that vulnerability. And now Jason had tried it.

Jason was a bit too close for her to get a good shot at his solar plexus, but he had maneuvered himself into perfect position for a shot between the legs. She gladly obliged.

He doubled over. "Bitch! That's earned you an ass whooping and a free ride!" Hands cupped around his mangled jewels, he staggered back a few steps, withdrawing from the line of fire. He recovered quickly and managed a single threatening step in her direction before she came completely unglued.

Neither the little blue box smacking him in the face nor the barrage of short, tight punches inflicted any damage. Lane intended simply to increase the space between herself and Jason so she could get away. But Jason blocked the blows and surged forward. He slammed her against the freezer despite the strikes bouncing off of him.

A large, strong hand clamped on his shoulder, breaking his concentration. He whirled on the newcomer, his attitude jumping out as if he had every intention of beating the tar out of anyone who had dared interrupt him.

Chapter 11 – And Dad Ain't Too Happy

Smoldering eyes stared down at Jason, eyes hot enough to singe clean through his brain and out the other side. Richard stiff-armed him into a nearby shelf while keeping Lane at bay with his other hand, preventing her from pummeling the crap out of the boy.

Richard couldn't deny that his daughter was one feisty little bugger when she got going, but he couldn't adequately address the strapping eighteen-year-old male and fend off Lane's mindless anger at the same time. "Danny!"

The Deputy appeared at his shoulder. "Which one?" he asked, with nothing but seriousness pasted on his face.

Richard could only shake his head. Maybe his buddy Wes had been right. Maybe Danny was going to get him killed one day. Not like other Sheriffs hadn't died because of some rookie's mistake. Not like his own father hadn't met his fate that way. "I've got Romeo. Just watch Juliet's knees."

Richard's hand shifted closer to Jason's neck, and he steered the boy toward the front of the store, not at all concerned about any difficulty Jason might have walking. The gesture might have been construed, to any one entering the store, as an expression of camaraderie and friendship.

Of course, they'd have been wrong. Richard knew full well the power of intimidation, and he held a Master's Belt. The gesture said "think twice about doing anything else stupid, what with your neck at the beck and call of an annoyed father, one who just happens to be wearing a badge and a gun."

"Look, Sheriff, I'm…"

Richard raised a single finger to his lips and shushed the youngster to silence. "You were just leaving."

"Yes, sir."

"And you're never coming back."

"No, sir." Jason's head shook back and forth. "Wait—I work here."

Richard didn't balk at the revelation. "Then you won't be coming in here if she's here." His thumb hooked back down the aisle toward Lane.

"Yes, sir."

"You're never bothering my daughter again."

"Never."

Richard released his grip on the boy. "If you do, you do know what I'll do to you, right?"

"Hunt me down and shoot me?"

Richard's head pulled back, his lips pinching together in mock surprise. "That would be illegal. No, I'll tell your father."

Jason's head shook vigorously. "Just leaving. Never coming back. Never bothering her again."

"Good boy." And he watched Jason struggle his way from the store like a rabbit from a fox. He turned to Lane, who was still trying to get away from Danny. Richard caught her eye and watched as his dismay registered on her face. He motioned for Danny to let her go and waited as the deputy excused himself from the scene.

Richard stared down at his daughter as she hobbled up the aisle toward him. "You and I need to have a serious talk."

Chapter 12 – You or Me?

Dottie, Richard, and Ray stood at the monitor, trying to figure out what "it" was. Danny stretched to see over their shoulders, but Richard wasn't finished punishing him for being stupid on the whole tampon incident; he turned slightly and glared down at the deputy, who quietly oozed back to his own desk without so much as a whisper.

Dottie zoomed the camera in, tighter and tighter. "That looks like a tee shirt to me," she announced finally. "Or maybe a towel."

"You or me?" Ray asked.

Richard's hands slid into his pockets. "I sort of have to give her a lecture soon, so this is definitely your turn."

Ray headed down into the cell block. He knew his mother and brother would be watching from the monitor, so he tossed a wave over his shoulder as he passed under one of the security cameras.

At the cell door, he found the makeshift lock to be a pillowcase, wound tight around the bars and tied to keep the door shut. He didn't have any trouble untying it, but what it lacked in functionality it certainly made up for in creativity.

Sitting on the edge of the cot, he gave Lane a pat on the back of the leg to rouse her. A groan rumbled around her throat, and she threw a two-second glance over her shoulder before hunkering closer to the wall, pressing herself against the cold concrete until there wasn't enough space for air to pass between flesh and stone.

"Want to talk about it?" he asked.

A slight shake of the head answered him, so slight that it created no sound, not even the rustling of her hair against the pillow.

"Okay, then. I'll talk. You listen."

She didn't acknowledge him; instead, she spent her time studying the insides of her eyelids.

"Richard is worried about your safety, as are the rest of us. I was once told by some wise man whose name eludes me at the moment that sometimes you just have to trust that Richard's right. Hard as it may seem, sometimes he actually is." His chuckle echoed around the concrete cell. "Even I hate to admit that. As for Jason," his fingers splayed open, "he's just always been sort of a jerk."

Lane whispered over her shoulder. "Does everybody think I was selling myself to survive?"

"Jason said that?" he asked. Lane nodded, but she didn't turn to face him. "No, only Jason thinks that. And maybe his immediate fan base. But since when do his thoughts amount to more than spit in the wind?"

"He's probably spreading it all over town."

"It doesn't make any difference. That's a burden he's going to have to bear," Ray said.

"But it's their looks that I to have to deal with. It's like they're all waiting for me to strip naked and have at every single guy who walks by."

"It may seem that way now, but I think you have to trust that Jason isn't spreading much of anything further than his group of friends. Those boys will listen to him no matter what crap drips off his tongue."

"Boys who look up to him and want to be like him," Lane added. "You think they won't be trying the same thing, just to one up him, prove they're better than him?"

41

"A bridge can't be crossed until you arrive. My bet is most of those boys don't have any need to bully. My bet is you should wait this out."

She flipped the blanket off and scooched to a sitting position, joining Ray on the edge of the cot. "This is never gonna be over. I'm never gonna be able to just live."

"Don't see why not. You survived eighteen years of isolation, twelve years of abuse and neglect, six months of homelessness. You may not think so, but your life has been extraordinary so far. I think if you put your mind to it, you can survive a few months of Jason being an ass."

"But that's just it. Don't you see? There's always something, always some battle to be waged, some war to fight. Something that prevents me from just living my damn life."

She had him there. Her life did appear to be nothing more than a series of twisted struggles. On the surface, anyway. "That's pretty much the way it is for everyone. The battles may be different, but we're all contending with something. Bills, or kids who need braces, or cars that need repairs, mortgages that can't be paid. Groceries we can't afford. That's life. Point A is connected to Point B by the trials we endure. Birth to death separated by the failures and successes of our every day decisions."

Skepticism screamed out from Lane's eyes. Ray hung forward, hands clasped and arms resting on his knees. "I'm not immune to it." He couldn't say he actually wanted to go into it, but he did hope it would help to ease the girl's troubles. "After high school, I went away to college. I spent four years as an undergrad, then another three in law school. Those seven years in Seattle were pretty much devoid of virtue."

When Lane began to squirm, Ray placed a quieting hand on her knee. "Relax. I'm not about to give you any details. Suffice it to say I wasn't with the same girl for more than a few weeks at a

42

time. When I passed the bar exam, my reputation preceded me and nothing really changed. I was stuck in the same cycle. Studying and tests turned into research and trials. Dating students turned into dating interns or paralegals or junior partners. Anything that made me feel good and got me what I wanted."

He rubbed a hand across his chin. "I wasn't a good guy. Then I made probably the worse decision of my life, and it cost me my brother, and it put my mother in the middle of a feud that lasted, well, pretty much your entire life. But it was that event that woke me up, and subsequently I made the best decision of my life."

"You became a priest," Lane said.

"Indeed I did. But even that wasn't the end. All those years of doing whatever I wanted to, whenever I wanted to, made it difficult to live the vows I had taken. I had to battle with the loss of companionship for a long time."

"Do you miss it?"

"Sometimes. But I throw myself into my work and that helps. So imagine how I felt when the Bishop pulled my collar. My trying to help you was misread. I could have wallowed in self pity…actually I did wallow…a little. And I could have just given up. But I didn't. I persevered and took their abuse. And now the Bishop is calling me every week or so to see when I'm coming back to work."

"Except nobody is waiting around expecting you to strip naked and do the dirty at the drop of a hat."

"I wouldn't be so sure." He nudged her with his shoulder, leaning into her. "I used to be a looker. Girls couldn't keep their hands off me."

"Eeewwww."

"No, really."

"Please. Stop."

43

"No, really." He gave her another nudge, leaning way over and tipping her until she had to push him away.

"Great. Persevere. Live to tell the tale. Only wallow for a little while. Got it." She pushed off the bed and shuffled across to the door. "I'm going upstairs now."

Ray followed. "Gee, that was easier than I thought. I should have started out telling you about my sex life."

"Don't make me throw up on your shoes."

"Did I tell you we're going home?"

"No, you left that out somewhere between sleeping with every girl who lay still long enough and becoming a priest."

"Ohhh, so that's how you wanna play it."

"You started it. Just saying is all. I suppose the microphone's been on all this whole time?"

"I imagine so." Ray opened the door for her at the top of the stairs.

"Great. Have fun explaining to Richard how I know all about your sex life."

The squad room turned into a mausoleum, the only sound the ringing of an unanswered phone. The officers' heads snapped toward the cell block door, their eyes riveting on Ray, and their bodies becoming as stiff as plaster statues.

Richard's lips pulled into a tight, thin line as the bristle over his eyes knit together into a unibrow. "You." He jabbed a finger at Lane. "My office."

Lane hobbled off, leaving Ray alone to face whatever Richard had in mind.

Chapter 13 – Really?

"**R**eally?"

Ray balked. "Come on, Rich. You heard the conversation. It's not like I gave her any details."

"No, but she just had to fight out from under Jason's advances, and you decided it would be the perfect time to tell her that you spent your college years as a philandering womanizer. Makes perfect sense to me."

"It wasn't about that. It was about the trials and tribulations of life."

"Oh, yeah, that's right," Richard corrected himself. "And I'm sure that sleeping with every Mary, Jane, and Suzie was a terrible trial for you. I'm sure you just had to do it."

"Are you planning to keep this up all night, or are you just about done?"

Richard tipped back as he appraised his brother. "Just about." He headed to his office.

Chapter 14 – Now You Know

"Now you know why I really want somebody with you." Richard was less than amused by Lane ditching her escort at Pearce's door. At the moment she looked like an animal with a leg caught in a steel trap, pacing back and forth on the short chain and calculating the wisdom of gnawing off her own foot. "Tampons? Really?"

She stifled a giggle, but it broke some of the tension in the office.

"It really isn't funny," he said, but he had a little trouble fighting down a smile of his own. "You know that'll never work on me, right? Next time you want to go for a stroll, I'll send Pete with you. See how far your little story gets you with an officer more than a day or two older than you."

"How long am I stuck here?"

"Until I decide it's safe for you not to be stuck here."

"You let Nana go home."

"No one actually took a shot at her," he reminded his daughter.

"Come on. There's no evidence it wasn't just an accident."

"And none that it wasn't deliberate, either."

"So how long, really?"

He stared at her, trying to figure out if the last few minutes of conversation had actually happened or not, and if so, then why she seemed to have misplaced it all. "Didn't we just go through this?"

She made that tooth-sucking noise that made his skin crawl. The meaningless sound always managed to screw in through his eyeballs and directly into his brain.

"Come on. What if it's, like, a month? I've gotta go to school or I'll get further behind. And it's not like I can do that much community service in here." Her argument proved unconvincing.

"You'd be surprised. You haven't gotten to the windows yet, or the basement. There's tons of stuff for you to do, all within the safety of these walls."

"Tch. Come on. Be serious. When I finish my hours, I can go find a real job." That segued very nicely into, "Old Man Pearce says I can come back to work."

"I am serious. And you have two-hundred and forty hours of community service. It'll be a while before you go back to work for Al." He picked up a pen. "Well, unless he doesn't want to pay you. Then I suppose that could be community service."

"Really? Could we do that?"

The kid couldn't recognize a joke when she heard one. Or maybe he couldn't tell one. He supposed that could be the problem. "No. Just kidding."

"Tch." She grew more disheartened, but her brows furrowed as if a thought had just smacked her in the face. "Hey, no way I've still got two-forty left. I've been putting in plenty of time. Not to mention all that extra crap because of you."

She drew herself to her full height, all five foot six of it, throwing her shoulders back, drawing her hands to her hips, and imitating her father's penchant for barking orders. "Oh, look, go get that trash. Oh, look, go help that guy. Oh, look, go rake those leaves." She did a quick mental calculation. "I gotta be down to one-forty, one-fifty max."

"Actually, it's one-seventy on the books, and you haven't even started mine, yet. So that means we've got months before we have to worry about it, don't we?"

"Come on. You can't just trap me in here."

It couldn't be said that Richard didn't know how to ride a good wave when it presented itself, but he could see the kid's point. If she didn't get back to class soon, they'd have no choice but to parlay her Early College credits into her high school graduation. "Okay. As long as nobody takes another shot at you, we can send you back to school with an escort. And, like Ray said, we'll be spending nights at the cabin again."

Her mouth fell open and her eyeballs bugged out of her head.

He didn't want for a response. "Hey, you're lucky I'm even offering after that stunt you pulled. Go get ready. I'll take you into Shelton for your therapy."

"Can we skip it? I'm not really feeling up to it."

Richard's eyebrows alternated, one up and one down. "You never feel up to it. So no, we can't skip it. And don't even think about making that noise again." Richard thought her eyeballs might pop out of her head from the pressure of holding in that damn tooth-sucking noise, but finally she rolled them about in their sockets and hobbled away.

Chapter 15 – Time to Reflect

Dismissed by Sheriff, King of the Universe, Lane returned to Room One, waiting for Richard to take her to therapy and stewing over the day's unfortunate turn. She had planned just a few minutes alone but had ended up knee-deep in sheep dip with her father, his deputy, and Jason Olsen.

She didn't know why Danny's boxers were bunched so tight. It's not like she twisted his arm and forced him out of the store. She had made a suggestion, and like most men, he flinched at the idea that he might actually have to witness the purchasing of the secret blue box.

Not my fault Dick got all up in his face over it, she mused. Not my fault at all. He's the freakin' deputy. That should be a lesson for him.

But she didn't feel like Danny had been the one tutored today. She felt like she'd been on the receiving end of instruction, and she'd quite nearly flunked. She wondered how far Jason would have gone if Richard hadn't shown up to stop him. Or what Jason might have done to Old Man Pearce if he had tried to interfere. What exactly could Mr. Al have done to help me, anyway? Jason would have just hauled off and cracked the grocer up the side of his head.

Of course, then Jason would be in jail right now, on the wrong side of the bars. But it made Lane feel vulnerable. Again. At the mercy of whoever had a whim, whatever that whim might be. Jason's words played around in her head, twisting around her grey matter, enticing her to find alternate and additional meanings. Whether or not the scenarios held truth didn't matter.

"Everybody knows," he'd said. "Everybody." That meant Jason and his friends, and most likely all the boys in the high school. And probably all the girls registered as "groupies" of the football team. And then those girls would be gossiping among themselves, perhaps deliberately sharing the information with others and allowing still more girls to eavesdrop…in the cafeteria…in the library. On the bus. And texting everyone they knew.

And that really could only mean that literally everybody knew. Their parents would know. Their dentists. Their hairdressers. And since most of the professionals were in Shelton or Hoodsport, that meant the story had a whole new audience, spreading like goose droppings in a mud puddle over there, too. It wouldn't be long before the whole state knew. There'd be no place she could show her face without wondering how much of the latest gossip involved the poor, homeless girl from Mills Valley who had sold herself to survive.

Her stomach took a flop. She knew that pressing her hand on her guts wouldn't keep them from leaping out her mouth, so she calmly made her way to the restroom, hoping not to attract too much attention. Of course, the sound would echo off the walls so everybody would know that, too.

She pulled a full one-eighty in the hallway, deciding to go downstairs to the cell block and use the facilities in the basement. With the door closed, the sound wouldn't be as obvious as if she chucked her cookies up here.

She twisted the door knob and shot a glance back at Danny only to find him staring at her. "Sorry," she whispered, hoping to allay his anger; she didn't really care if it worked or not, since the apology was just for show, anyway. She took a small bit of revenge, leaving the door open as she descended into lockup.

Even he thinks it, she said to herself. It's there every time he looks at me. By the time she'd gotten to the bottom stair, she'd convinced herself that all the men in town eagerly awaited their shot at her. She imagined a long line of paying customers snaking through the squad room and down into the cell block.

Her stomach heaved and the burning taste of bile reached her throat. She slapped a hand over her mouth and vomit squeezed out between her fingers as she raced for the toilet. She didn't even get to enjoy the slamming of the upper door, its echo bouncing off the concrete walls.

Chapter 16 – The Shrink

"**H**ow did that make you feel?" Dr. Peck asked.

Lane knew that Richard had hand-picked this shrink from a field of ten, but she couldn't get over the idea that Dr. Peck had no brain. She shot the good doctor with the infamous dead stare.

"You do know that I'm trying to help you, correct?" Peck made no mention of the look. "It's been two months and you haven't said a single word to me in all that time."

Count yourself lucky, lady, Lane thought. The first guy didn't even have the pleasure of sitting in the same room with me. Lane had walked out of her first psychiatric counseling session within seconds of walking in. The doctor, whose name she couldn't recall, hadn't even said hello, but Lane had no intention of sharing her deepest, darkest secrets with a man who looked like he became a shrink only because his football career fell through. A man the size of Morgan, the one who had caused all the problems in the first place.

As it turned out, she had no intention of sharing her emotions with anyone. It was a private matter between her and Morgan, and he wasn't talking…not any more.

"When you shot Morgan, did it relieve any of your fears?"

I put ten bullets in his sorry ass. I don't really have to worry about him anymore, do I?

"You can just share what you're thinking," the doctor suggested. "Doesn't matter what it is. Right and wrong have no place here. Just whatever you're thinking right now."

I'm thinking you're a freakin' nutjob. Lane stared at the book shelves, the diplomas on the wall, the weave in the carpet…just about anything that didn't have to do with answering questions. When the chime signaled the end of the session, Lane pushed herself up from the chair and walked out without a sound, or a wave, or a grunt. Not even a dead stare.

Richard's Stetson twirled around his hand as Lane returned to the waiting room. She refused to look at him even though he was obviously staring at her, his eyebrows rising up as if he expected she'd throw herself at his feet and tell him everything that just didn't happen in the office.

Looking into her father's pain-filled orbs proved difficult on a good day; doing it after listening to the idiot doctor poke and probe into her most personal secrets was impossible. She was sick to death of the whole event, tired of Morgan's ghost hounding her, annoyed by Richard's assumption that she knew how to live with "regular" people, and less than amused by the pity in his eyes and that look that said "you poor little thing, you got yourself raped."

She took a seat on the opposite side of the room, slouching back in the chair. The crossing of her arms over her chest and her feet at the ankle quite clearly stated that she was all done with this little encounter.

A few moments later, Dr. Peck emerged from her office, her well-fitting suit adding to the persona of professionalism that had aided Richard in choosing her as Lane's psychiatrist.

"Sheriff?" Dr. Peck motioned Richard into her office and closed the door behind him. She offered him a seat and gracefully sat in the chair next to him, a less formal setting for a more personal conversation. "She's still not talking. Are you working with her?"

"Daily. But if I try to talk to her in the morning, she goes to school in a bad mood. And if I try to talk to her at night, she goes to bed in a bad mood. I've tried suppertime, but then she won't eat. I'm sort of at wit's end here."

"Does she wake up in a bad mood if you talk to her at night?"

Richard's head bobbed. "Sometimes. Other times she pretends we never talked at all."

"Does she stay in a bad mood after she gets to school, or is it just a show for your benefit?"

A deep breath, a shake of his head. "I don't know, but I can find out."

"It might be helpful if you talked to a few of her morning instructors. That might give you more of a feeling for when, and when not, to approach her. Getting her to talk to you in confidence is more about getting her to trust you than anything else. Try non-threatening subjects…her plans for the future, how she's doing in school…that sort of thing. And try sharing your feelings. Putting yourself in a vulnerable position may help her to see you as an ally."

The physical therapist's office was only a few minutes' drive away. Since Richard didn't want Erika to pay for Lane's foul mood, he decided against discussing anything with his daughter for the time being. But the PT session ended pretty much the same as the psych appointment: Lane hobbling out and sitting alone while the therapist requested Richard join her in the office.

He couldn't help but notice the look of pain on Lane's face and the depth of her limp. "She okay?" he asked when the door closed behind him.

Erika was just this side of butch, a rugged, handsome woman who, from the look of her well-toned body, loved activity and wasn't afraid to get physical. She had just the right touch of feminine curve to her muscles to soften the "be all you can be" lifestyle. She was also half Richard's age. "She's very stiff. Have you been working with her?"

Richard laughed. "Second time in an hour I've been asked that. She said she could do it herself."

Erika nodded. "She's not, though. You really have to take charge or the mobility in that leg won't increase."

"Well, that ought to go over well. Morning, night?"

"Whatever works best. In a week, move to twice a day."

Richard nodded, and headed for the door. Erika took the opportunity to follow him, her hand sliding casually along his back as if she'd known him her whole life. "Oh, those are tense."

Now both her hands probed his back, kneading into the muscles with deft, appreciative fingertips. "You should come see me yourself sometime. Get those muscles loosened up." A teasing dare simmered in her eyes. "I'm free tonight."

The touch of a woman—a young, willing, and incredibly flexible woman—sent shivers of anticipation through every nerve in his body. And while the angel and devil on opposing shoulders drew pistols and squared off on the issue of Erika's age, Richard's eyebrows fought for independence, determined to reach the top of his skull before his brain insisted on a more appropriate appearance…they lost.

"You're very kind," he offered, avoiding the obvious meaning. "But I've got to get her home and plan out her next few days so we get both PT and psych in."

"I understand. No worries. Just give me a holler anytime. I'll fit you in." She squeezed her business card into his hand, her eyes coursing his body top to bottom as she turned the card over to reveal her private cell phone number.

55

Chapter 17 – The Lecture

A cloud of silence descended as father and daughter returned to the car, Lane limping decidedly more than she had on her way in and requiring a firm hand from Richard to keep her steady. Unable to put a great deal of weight on the knee, she tolerated his assistance, but as soon as they were close enough to the car, her hand went to the rear door handle.

Richard decided against letting her pout in the backseat, thereby avoiding him. He simply inserted his body into her path and steered her to the front door, opening it for her and pushing it wide. His actions gave her only two options: speak and make it clear she didn't want to sit in the front, or get in the car and maintain her silence.

She chose silence, slowly lowering herself into the car and dragging the useless right leg in behind her. She said nothing as Richard climbed in the other side, and she kept her silent vigil going for the next five minutes.

Richard used that time to consider his options. He glanced at her frequently, watched her massage the knee and surrounding muscles. She never looked back at him, preferring the knee and the countryside to his company.

"There's no reason for you to be pissed at me. You're the one not doing your exercises. Tomorrow, however..." He glanced over again, watching road and daughter at the same time. "We'll change that, because Ray or I will be doing that PT with you from now on."

She stared out the side window, her voice reflecting off the glass. "I can do it."

"Yep, you can. But you obviously won't, and I'm not playing anymore. You wanna walk? You gotta work at it."

"It hurts."

"I know. But it'll only get worse if you don't use it. Erika figured that out in forty-five minutes."

Lane's derisive snort knocked his head back as if she'd slapped him in the face with a brick. "What?" he asked, hoping she'd answer. A response was not forthcoming, and he resigned himself to adding another item to the list of "whats" he'd never know. "So, Dr. Peck is a tad disappointed."

"I don't know why I even have to go. Not like she's doing anything."

"We go because Doc Williams says so. And she would be doing something if you let her."

"She's stupid."

At least she's talking. "She's a doctor."

"Well, she sure asks stupid questions for a doctor." Lane leaned against the door, putting as much distance between herself and her father as she could in the small space.

The move made Richard feel as if he had a plague that was physically marching across the vehicle, but he tried to keep her talking. "Like what?"

And then she graced him with the dead stare, the look saying "you're as stupid as the damn doctor."

"She's trying to help you. And to do that, she needs to know what's going on in here." He reached over and tapped on Lane's skull, and since she had pinned herself against the window, she couldn't get away. "Like what you're thinking. How you feel…"

"Oh, for God's sake!" Lane erupted like a volcano.

Richard fought to keep the surprise off of his face. In a matter of seconds, his daughter had gone from a mountain of silent reverie to Pompeii, spewing lava and debris for miles and destroying anything dumb enough to stand in her path. But if she was about to let something out, he had to let it come. No matter how, no matter what.

"How did it make me feel? Like he was stuffing a two-by-four into me, like I was nothing but dirt, like I didn't matter or count. Like I had no say and it didn't matter anyway 'cause I was just there to make him feel good. Nothing at all like it'll feel for Erika after she finally gets you in the sack. Spends the entire time talking about your body, about how "hot" you are, about how "hard" your body is for a man your age. About how lucky a woman would be to have you."

Lane did a complete eye-roll and mimicked her therapist, transforming into a girl on the prowl. "Ooo, don't you just love a man in uniform?" The façade fell away, replaced by Lane's cynical tone. "Aren't you just the most wonderful thing alive?"

You asked for it. Richard guided the car to the shoulder and slid the stick into park, giving him time to decide what to address first, his daughter's pain or the therapist's lust, which was apparently causing even more pain. It had been pretty clear to him that Lane had never had sex before the rape. She hadn't known the good side, so all she had was ugliness. Having the therapist throw sex around like it was a toy had to be tantamount to saying that what Morgan had done to Lane was acceptable.

"I'll speak to her."

"Don't bother," Lane grumbled back.

"I will speak to her," he insisted, keeping his voice firm but gentle. "And if it doesn't stop, we'll find a new therapist. Sex isn't a game. It shouldn't be treated so lightly. It's a serious matter. You know that even if she doesn't."

Muscles worked along Lane's jaw, but nothing else came out.

"You do matter. And you do count. What Morgan did..." Richard had trouble even saying it. "You didn't have a say at that moment. With a decent man, you'll always have a say, but with types like Morgan..." He trailed off, formulated his thoughts. "Morgan hurt you to get even with me. And that's what made him feel good."

"This isn't about you." Her legs pinched a little tighter together.

"I know. But at the time, it wasn't about you. Yes, he used you, but it wasn't you he was looking to hurt. It may not make it any better for you, but you were a means to an end."

"You're right. It doesn't make it better."

Chapter 18 – At Home

The trip ended in silence, Lane staring out the window and Richard believing he'd pushed far enough for now. She tolerated his assistance as far as the cabin door, then she promptly skulked to her room without even saying "hello" to her uncle.

"Hungry?" Richard asked his brother, and the two headed off to the kitchen to prepare a meal. He let Lane have a few minutes to herself, but he wasn't about to let her wallow for the rest of the night. "Hey, Lane! We could use some help in here." Ray's derisive snort suggested that Richard should reconsider his decision to call the girl into the room.

The brothers hustled around the kitchen. Both men had spent the last eighteen years alone, fending for themselves and learning to cook, but both had instantly taken to having help in the kitchen. Even with two of them working, a few tasks remained

Ray assigned himself the tasks of salad making, and Richard began filling a pan with chopped vegetables. Other tasks remained—baguettes to be coated, a table to be set, a pot to be filled with water. "You hear me?" Richard called loudly. He knew Lane heard him, but he also knew she needed a tad more prodding than he liked.

"You're sure about this?" Ray asked.

"Not gonna kill her to help out."

Ray's eyes widened and his mouth fell open, just a little. "Oh, you're right there," he said, coating each word with an extra helping of sarcasm.

Apparently the leg hurt more than Lane had let on, forcing her to use her crutches for the first time in weeks. The sounds of those crutches thumping the floor masked the grumbled vocalizations that Richard was sure he detected just before she presented herself at the kitchen table. "Give us a hand, will you?"

"I'm good with a can opener."

Richard couldn't decide if the confusion on her face was real or simply for effect. "You could set the table. And we need some garlic peeled and pressed. And that pot can't boil until there's water in it."

Lane twisted the garlic bulb around her fingers. "I'm used to eating out of a can."

Richard relieved Lane of the garlic, smashed it against the counter, then loaded one of the cloves into the garlic press. When he was done, he had successfully turned a solid mass into minced and moist goo. "Ray needs a couple of those for the salad, and we need a couple more for the bread. Let me know if you need instructions on how to set the table."

A mound of spaghetti sat in the middle of Lane's plate. Richard sporked a blob of sautéed veggies and dropped them atop the pasta—they slid down the mountain like hot fudge on ice cream.

But when he scooped away Lane's salad bowl and heaped it full of greens, tomatoes, and the works, Lane balked. "I can do it myself."

"Of course you can. But you won't." He pushed the bowl over to her.

"So," Ray said, deliberately interrupting the brewing squabble so he wouldn't have to listen to his brother and niece fight over food again. Spaghetti strands wound around his fork as

61

he twirled it in the middle of his plate. "I've already told Rich…I'm moving back into the rectory."

Lane's fork nearly fell from her hand, but Ray continued as if nothing had happened, not giving her even a second to argue the issue. "I'm thinking we pick a night and get you signed up for something. Like we used to do. What do you think? Karate? Archery? We haven't done those in a while." He jammed the swirl of pasta into his mouth.

"You can't leave."

Ray's head bobbed up and down, and he mumbled between chews. "Have to."

"Why?"

He finished chewing. "Because you don't need me here anymore."

"Yes, I do."

"No, you just think you do." He broke a baguette apart and mopped the garlic and olive oil mixture from his plate. "But I have no intention of standing on the side-lines. Wednesdays might be good. Or Thursdays. I suppose it depends on what else you have planned. Mondays are out, though. I'm going back to soup kitchen duty with Zavier. I sort of miss it. We could join a health club? Or maybe there's something else you want to try. But the sooner we get you out and about, and doing stuff, the better you're going to feel."

Ray had been pressing for weeks, and Lane had been ignoring his suggestions for just as long. "There's just too much going on."

"You have to start living again."

Her tone slipped into curt and defensive. "I will! But I can't take on anything more right now." An awkward silence ensued. Ray studied her carefully, the look on his face never wavering from unconditional love and concern.

Richard's features reflected his surprise, but there was nothing he could interject into the conversation that would make a difference. He changed the subject, rather un-smoothly. "I'm going to do some laundry tonight."

Ray's head remained focused in Lane's direction, but his eyes shifted toward Richard, one brow cocking up in confusion.

"Be easier for me to do it all if I had it all," Richard said.

Ray jumped in quickly. "Got it. I'll get you mine right after dinner."

Lane stuffed pasta in her mouth, slurped the trailing spaghetti in, and wiped the line of olive oil from her face.

"Got any?" Richard asked casually. Lane's head shook in reply. Richard pressed. "I only see one pair of jeans in there. And two shirts. Whole bunch of socks, though."

"That's all there is!" The brusqueness of her answer raised eyebrows around the table and curled Richard's non-fork hand into a tight ball.

Ray eyed his niece, who was doing her level best to avoid the conversation even though the red in her cheeks gave away her discomfort. "That would be my fault," he offered. "Socks come in bags of, like, a gazillion pairs." He dipped into the colloquialisms of teenaged girls to help lighten Lane's mood. "I guess I went overboard on the footwear. What say we go out tomorrow and buy some more jeans? We'll make sure you've got enough to wear while your father ties up the laundry, like, forever."

Richard refused to let the interruption distract him. "How about that mountain of clothes in the middle of the den floor?"

"I thought that was my room."

"Temporarily, which doesn't exactly translate into throw your crap all over the place. And when the leg is strong enough to get you upstairs, don't think for one minute that you'll turn that room into a mirror image of this pig sty." His thumb jerked

63

in the direction of the den. "For all you know, there's something living in that mess."

Ray butted in. "Do we have to do this again? Now?" No one else heard him.

"Just put me back in jail. Then I won't have any stuff for you to worry about."

"Or maybe we could just take your stuff away."

Lane's fork hit the plate and bounced onto the table, leaving a stain in passing. Ray's hand darted out and caught hers as it rose, clamping over the extending middle finger before it could present itself for Richard's viewing. A determined tug on the hand brought her attention to him. "Don't. I've had just about enough." His eyes shifted between his niece and his brother, being sure to include them both in the rebuke. "Don't."

Richard's anger shifted off Lane, but Ray silenced him with a single finger. "Just stop. You," he said, giving Lane's hand a firm squeeze, "clean the damn room and stop worrying about not having any clothes to wear. Whatever you need, one of us will buy for you. And you." His eyes burned across the table. "While you're busy being the jailer, the community service coordinator, and the probation officer, see if you can fit some time in there to just be the father. Now," he released Lane's hand and reclaimed his fork. "Eat, while it's still hot."

———

Ray rattled the pots and pans while Richard took Lane to the mud room to start the laundry. Once he had her alone, he brought the subject up once again, taking extra care to leash his anger. A slow, deep breath, and a tone that had dropped into the realm of calmness allowed his concern for her wellbeing to come out first. "Why are you hiding all your clothes?" The flush to her skin let him know that he was right, but also that she didn't really want to talk about it. "Is it because Ray made off with some of your old clothes?"

She confirmed his suspicion with a shallow nod.

Richard dropped a few colors in the top-loader, glancing out the windows that framed the washer-dryer combo. He often gazed at the scenery when doing laundry, out of boredom or perhaps habit.

Normally he would see nothing of any particular interest in the forest, perhaps an occasional elk or coyote, or the incredibly rare trespasser for whom he'd joyfully don both gun and badge, using the tools of his office to scare the living bejesus out of the interloper.

Tonight, a tiny speck of moonlight glinted off something metal among the trees. He dropped two pair of jeans into the machine, but the sparkle didn't show this time. On his third cycle, Richard shifted to his left before adding several dark tee shirts to the collection in the agitator. Head down as if his attention remained on the clothes, Richard cast his sight to the forest from underneath his furrowing brows. A twinkle of light shimmered in the darkness.

Nonchalantly turning back to Lane, he leaned against the washer, fighting both the urge to duck for cover and the habit of folding his arms across his chest. He opted for a more open stance, sliding his hands to the front corners of the machine. "You do know that sooner or later he'll just go in there and find the rest, right?" Her face scrunched up. "Denying it doesn't mean it won't happen. It's not like we don't know you've got the old stuff hidden under mountains of…" He fought for a better word than crap. "Of all that new stuff that you don't want to wear."

His disarming smile changed to laughter when her eyeballs decided to go all Bette Davis at him. "Look, I'm sorry. I react first. Let Ray take you into Shelton tomorrow. While he's buying you some more jeans, pick up some shirts." He rifled through his

65

wallet and handed her five twenty-dollar bills. "Trust me. There's no need to worry that you won't have any clothes. Or food. Or a home. Okay?"

She nodded again, less timidly this time.

"You know what?" he asked her, pushing himself off the washer. Her eyebrows rose in anticipation, but she said nothing. "I don't really feel like doing this tonight. Just don't tell your uncle we're putting it off." He paused briefly, trying his best to imitate Ray's earlier words and tone. "Like, forever. Deal?"

Lane's lips pulled into a surprised, thin line and her eyes grew wide. Her head bobbed its complete agreement. "Deal." And she left the room, protected by her father's body and never the wiser about his sudden lack of interest in the laundry.

Chapter 19 – Restless Night

Back in December, when the brothers had gone back to Lane's cave hide-out to clean out her ill-gotten acquisitions, Richard had found it immaculate for a dirt and stone abode. The makeshift pantry held an orderly array of food, all arranged by item and size within the milk crates. Even the wood piles screamed of an almost anal need to organize.

Somewhere between starving to death and probation, she seemed to have misplaced the skill. And now he had to kick a pile of dirty clothes out of his way just to find a solid place to stand.

But the hoarding wasn't limited to clothing; food items peeked out from various places—a box of Pop-Tarts on the desk behind her school books; candy bars underneath paperwork in the bookcase; an unopened can of soda on the floor next to the bed. Richard understood why, he just didn't know how to get her to stop.

After Lane went gone to bed, Richard let Ray in on the secret…he'd seen something out the laundry room window but hadn't wanted to alarm Lane. He couldn't even be sure that it was anything to worry about. He called the station to alert the deputies that there might be an issue, and that they should stick close to the radio in case he needed them.

The brothers Keates pretended to go to bed, climbing the stairs to the second floor, turning on and shutting off lights in a sequence that people watching from outside could easily mistake as a normal, nightly routine. Then they hurried back downstairs in the dark, one stationing himself at the front door and the other at the back, both watching the night slip by.

Not an hour had passed before the shadows came to life, gliding down from the forest behind the cabin and converging on the house with such speed that Richard had no chance to call for backup. Ray's signal—little more than a hiss of air forced between his clamped front teeth—sent both brothers scurrying into Lane's room where they now prepared to safeguard the castle, listening intently to the sounds of the intruders as well as Lane's soft snoring.

She lay on her back, bum leg out straight, one arm crushing her pillow to her chest while the other draped across her eyes. Her sleep had grown more quiet in recent weeks—the tossing, turning, and nightmares diminishing with time and medication.

Now Richard watched her, as did Ray from across the room. Sometimes the brothers' eyes would meet, but most of the time they stared at the bedroom door or out their assigned windows, guarding the girl from their hiding places in the study-turned-bedroom.

Lane strolled through the forest; her right leg no longer bore the awkward gait that remained after the bullet tore out her kneecap. She easily stepped over a downed tree, hopped a stream, and strode unhindered to the top of Jensen Ridge.

Her mind caught up with the inconsistencies. Jensen Ridge held no stream; the tributary that fed Keates Lake could not be hopped, nor did it flow from this side of the mountain. The stream dissolved from view, leaving a forested hillside sloping down to the lake.

Ray relaxed in the rowboat with his rifle but no fishing pole, and the rowboat sat in the sand with the oars snug in their locks. Richard leaned against the dock, his hands in his pockets per his normal stance.

The wood creaked. A soft moan, like the shifting of weight. But neither Ray nor Richard had moved. And a shuffle. Like soft fabric rubbing against something. A rough hand grabbed her.

Lane's eyes snapped open and her torso rose from the bed with sudden urgency to find Richard's hand on her shoulder. With a finger to his lips, he pantomimed a silent "Shhh", then pointed out the locations of the intruders: one in the bathroom, two in the living room.

Richard motioned her out of bed and positioned her in the corner behind him, which was partially protected by the desk dripping clothes, books, and papers. He pulled the pillows down into the depression her body left behind and then drew the bedspread back up and over them. Returning to his original position, he took aim at the door, waiting to see if a reaction would actually be required.

Moonlight filtered through the window, casting swatches of light and dark through the chamber. Across the room, Ray stepped further into the shadows. Only the business-end of Remy poked out from the darkness, moonbeams glinting off the metal aimed at the closed bedroom door.

The knob jiggled ever so slightly, then turned. The door eased open, and a black gloved hand led the intruder's way. Ray drew his mark, but he, too, waited. Keateses could be very patient, if they had to be.

Four slugs from a silencer slammed into the pillows, and the hand withdrew. Muffled footsteps receded from the doorway, and a squeal from the stairs assured everyone that the intruders weren't done.

But the Keates brothers sprang into action. Ray hurried to the door, easing it open without even a squeak. Richard pulled

Lane up from the floor, draped her arm over his shoulder and guided her from the room, pointing at the floorboards and cautioning her where not to step. Ray drew a bead on the stairs, taking up the defensive position while Richard backed Lane out the front door. When Richard cleared the house, he spun around and wrapped an arm around Lane's waist, scooping her against his body and carrying her into the forest. Ray followed seconds later.

Lights popped on in all three bedrooms, then yelling, running, and the pounding of feet down the stairs. A light snapped on in the study where, minutes ago, Lane had slept. The family Keates took cover behind trees, the rifles of the men trained on the front door while the youngster huddled against the cold and clenched her teeth together to keep them from chattering.

Richard peered out from behind his tree and eyed his brother. Ray didn't utter a sound, but his lips moved, and Richard knew he was praying, asking for forgiveness for what he might have to do to protect his family.

But Richard never wavered. Had Lane and Ray not been there, Richard would have called out for these intruders to surrender their weapons, then fought it out with them when they refused.

He felt confident of the win based on these yahoos' performance so far. But he wouldn't risk either his brother or his new-found daughter. The cabin door opened, and the Winchester found a perfect fit against his shoulder.

Chapter 20 – Laying Low

Flashlight beams sliced the darkness. From this distance and in the dark, the brothers Keates resembled nothing more than tree branches and shadows, but they were ready to fight back should any of the intruders actually catch a glimpse of flesh or rifle barrel.

The home-invaders closed ranks, spooked by the dark or perhaps by what they couldn't see in it. Their weapons remained trained on the forest, but they eased off the porch and headed down the driveway toward the street.

Twenty minutes of silence passed. "They're waiting," Ray whispered.

Richard didn't need to see Ray's head turning to know his elder brother was scanning the darkness for movement or reflections of moonlight off metal. If Richard could have been certain that the light from his cellphone wouldn't be seen, he would have called for backup. As it was, he had to assume that such a beacon in the dark would draw serious firepower from the men intent on killing off the entire Keates family. "Back door," Richard ordered.

Ray moved the instant Richard spoke, ducking away from the tree and scooping Lane up by her armpit. Once she was back on her feet, she hobble-stepped her way to the cabin, pulling herself along on the trees.

Richard brought up the rear, guarding their retreat, but the road and forest beyond their lake remained quiet. Three men hid out there somewhere, waiting for another chance. The trio would seize any opportunity, be that another attack on the house or ambushing a car if the Keates family made a run for it. He closed the door quietly and found Ray and Lane crouched below window-level.

"If we turn the lights off, they'll know we're back inside." Ray whispered.

Richard nodded. "Which makes the stairwell the only place you can't be seen."

Ray tugged on Lane, and the threesome crawled their way to the staircase, Lane struggling like a spider who'd lost a limb. As the first in the chain, it fell to Ray to check the window angles for shooting vantages; he eased up onto the stairs with his rifle at the ready and waved his niece to join him.

Lane stopped at the gun cabinet, yanked open the door, and reached for a shotgun.

Richard caught her hand. "We're not at that point yet."

"If they get back in, it'll be too late," she argued.

Richard couldn't disagree with her logic, but he had no intention of letting a teenager on probation use a firearm. He tossed a box of shells to Ray before snatching the shotgun from its clip.

Richard motioned them to sit tight as he flipped open the cell phone. When dispatch answered, he said just two words, "Code thirty," and then snapped the phone shut with a flick of his wrist. Code thirty: Officer in trouble. Emergency.

He crawled along the sofa to the far side of the room, scurrying snake-like on his belly, getting closer to the study and putting himself in a better position for crossfire. If it came to it, he could draw the gunmen's fire, giving his brother and daughter a better chance of surviving.

Two minutes dragged by, and Richard had to remind himself that the situation made time stall. He relaxed with the first whine drifting on the night air, growing louder and more insistent as the siren's wail echoed through the still forest.

Moments later, the car spun into view, kicking up dirt and gravel as it sped toward the cabin. It slid sideways and came to an abrupt stop. Danny and Pete jumped out and each took a defensive position, one assessing the house, the other training his weapon on the road, both ready to set the night ablaze with gunfire.

Chapter 21 – A First Step

Pete drove the cruiser back into town since his emergency driving skills were far superior to Danny's. No one made any comments about the nausea-inducing blur of trees flying past, the yellow line wavering back and forth, or the sickening feeling of sliding across the seat as Pete careened around the curves.

Danny rode shotgun, his hand on the twelve-gauge just in case he had to snatch it from its cradle. His right hand held fast to the overhead grab handle and kept him from sliding out of position.

The Keateses populated the back seat, with Lane book-ended by her father, uncle, and their respective weaponry. Hunched forward, she shivered silently in the dark.

"Car's parked back up in the woods on the right, just around this bend," Pete said to Danny, but the turn-off sat empty now, no sign of car or gunmen.

Ray reached behind Lane and gave his younger brother a swat. When Richard looked over, Ray tipped his head toward Lane; Richard just stared at him.

Ray did it again with more embellishment. A head tip, a gesture with his hand, his eyebrows rising. An exaggerated shiver.

Richard drew a breath, leaned forward, and felt his daughter's shaking shoulders. "Come here." He eased her back and toward him, pulling her against his chest.

Across the car, Ray's notorious Cheshire cat grin flashed his approval and earned him the Sheriff's infamous evil eye. In the dark, Richard knew that Ray couldn't see the stiffness in the girl's body, but Richard could certainly feel the distance under his arm.

Chapter 22 – Back In Jail

Lane woke to the gentle pattering of spring rain against the window, a soothing, peaceful beat that begged a long, indulgent stretch while she double-fisted the sleep from her eyes.

The wind-up alarm clock stared at her from the edge of the sink; at nine a.m. on a Tuesday morning, it was clear she wasn't going back to school yet. She eased herself up to the edge of the cot, finding herself once again in a jail cell. It was the same cell Richard refused to return to accepted specs—the cell he threatened to use for re-incarcerating her whenever he didn't like something she said or did. Or didn't do. Such threats usually accompanied him complaining about her learning to live like a civilized human being.

This time the cell was nothing more than a dorm room for civilians in protective custody. The cell door was wide open, and a second cot had been brought in. Nana Dottie slept across the small room, snoring gently.

Lane tiptoed to the shower room to use the facilities there instead of risking waking her grandmother. The events of the prior few days replayed in her mind, tracking back through the attempted murders and focusing instead on the fight she'd had with Richard. "Not like there's any space for me in that damned room. Ton of crap that ain't mine," she muttered.

Doc Williams had called in a specialist to assist with the laryngeal repairs; the two surgeons had done a great job, and speaking had grown easier with continued practice. Volume remained a problem, and her voice seldom rose much higher than a hushed tone; keeping her voice low was rarely a problem. "Freakin' sardine can."

Deep inside she knew she'd elevated the conflict to inappropriate significance, no doubt transposing the importance of some other issue onto the condition of her pseudo-bedroom. The shrink had told her to watch for such occurrences. Now that it had actually happened, the presence of the psychiatrist in her life annoyed her even more.

She pushed it away, focusing on the more pressing situation: someone had broken into the cabin and tried to kill them, making it much more likely that the first incident hadn't been an accident after all. That the intruders went upstairs could only mean they were after the entire family, not just the one with the Harris last name.

A ghostly image of Morgan floated across her eyes; nine tight shots to the chest oozed blood as a tenth shot to his cheek tore away part of his face. The apparition didn't provoke the response it once had, but his sneer suggested that he would win, even in death. The phantom turned its head, the torn away fragments of skull revealing Morgan's shredded brain. Lane raced for the stainless steel throne and yakked for all she was worth.

Nana waited for her at the sink and wrapped her up in the grandmotherly version of a bear-hug. "Are you okay?"

Lane nodded. "Sorry. Didn't mean to wake you."

"Don't be silly. Bad dream?"

"Morgan." Lane cupped water in her hand and washed away the bitter taste of bile.

"Have you told your father yet?"

Lane shook her head slightly. Although she really wanted to avoid the conversation, she could find no civil way to tell her grandmother to butt out.

"Your uncle then?" Another shake of Lane's head. "You really should let them help you with this."

"Can't."

Dottie's eyebrows rose, the way they did sometimes when she couldn't believe what she was hearing. It made Lane smile because it reminded her of her own well-known dead stare.

"If I pick one, then I hurt the other. I don't want to hurt them."

Dottie reclaimed the girl and squeezed tighter. "Oh, dear. It's not about picking one over the other. It's about extending your envelope to let them both in."

Chapter 23 – New Deal

The interview room hadn't changed since Jenna's last meeting with Barnett, with the exception of a nostril-offending smell in the air. Jenna couldn't be sure if the body odor was left over from the last inmate in the room, or if Barnett had brought the aroma with him "I would have thought a million per would have been sufficient to make my problems go away." Jenna's annoyance raked across Barnett's faux civility.

"Most of that paid for my services, my dear. With what was left over, I barely had enough to seduce two more of those unemployed mill workers. Serious talent requires serious money."

He watched for a moment before pushing more emotional buttons. "Of course, we can just wait until the trial if you think you can convince the jury that you were an unwilling participant. I do, however, believe the child will be more credible than you. And then the entire Keates clan will show up to say goodbye and wish you well. Maybe they'll put together a little care package for you. Perhaps some toothpaste and Chap Stick."

Jenna glared across the table. "If you get them all, I'll pay you ten million dollars. But for that kind of money, the rules change. I want to be there. I want the satisfaction of watching her face when she discovers that I won after all. And I want the brothers to know that, too. She goes first, then the brothers, and I get to watch."

"To get you out of prison, I'll have to get you back into the general population. That is likely to be dangerous for you. Not to mention painful."

"Look at me…I think I know what to expect. We'll just add the new scars to the old and call it a day. How do you plan on getting your new employees to do their jobs?"

"I don't. I have connections to a big firm in New York City. They can be here tonight, and they can tie up our loose ends while they're at it."

Jenna was back in her element, running the game and playing strategies. "I don't care what you have to do or what it takes. I want out of here. I want to have the run of my home again and sleep in my own bed. I want to live like a civilized human being again, coming and going and doing as I please, with whomever I please to do it. Taking tea on the patio, or getting my hair done. Being pampered at the spa, or dining at Xinh's Oyster House. And I want those damn Keateses to pay for taking all that away from me."

# Chapter 24 – I Need a Haircut

Lane stared into the mirror. Her nerves had begun unraveling when it became apparent that someone was actually trying to kill her and her new family; now one last thread remained, ready to snap if anyone so much as put a foot on that bridge.

Her face had filled out some. Eating regularly could do that to you. The black circles under her eyes faded nicely to a more pleasing skin tone. But her hair. God. She raked a hand through the tangled mess. "That's gotta go."

She hobbled out to Nana Dottie's desk, tossing a slight incline of her head to Danny as she went by. "Nana? Do you have any scissors?"

"Of course, dear." Dottie rummaged through her desk, pushing aside her notepads, pens, and files. "Looks like somebody beat you to it. Sheriff probably has them." Lane gave her a dead stare, but Dottie answered it with her normal jailhouse professionalism and just a tinge of frustration. "He's your father, Lane. Just ask him."

Lane didn't really want to talk to Richard, but she did need those scissors. She knocked on his office door.

Richard looked up over his glasses, then pulled them off and used them to gesture Lane in. "What's up?"

"Got any scissors?"

He nodded. "Yep. What do you need them for?"

Today was proving to be a good day for dead stares...another one slipped out and nailed the Sheriff. "To cut something."

"What?"

"Does it matter?"

Richard dropped his glasses on the desk and leaned back in his chair. "I think we both know what you're going to do with them. You get nervous, you hack off your hair. You get upset, you hack off your hair. You have a bad day, you hack off your hair. Get the gist of it? Besides, you just cut your hair." He flipped through his desk calendar. "Three weeks ago."

"You're keeping tabs on my hair cuts?"

The slight twist of a smart-ass reply pulled at her father's lips. "I'd really rather you had a professional do it."

The volcano returned, bubbling up from deep inside Lane's gut. "What freakin' difference? Why do you even freakin' care?"

Richard stared across the room. For a few seconds nothing happened, and then he simply repeated himself. "I'd really rather you had a professional do it."

The tactic threw Lane off the assault. Her tone simmered, and the lava ebbed back into the abyss. "Too expensive."

"I think I can afford a haircut."

Lane's hand waved in the air. "Takes too long. Have to make an appointment. I can just do it myself."

"I talked to Dahlia a couple weeks ago. She says you can go down anytime and she'll squeeze you in."

"Dahlia? Marigold's sister, Dahlia? You're kidding, right?" Lane's eyebrows rose high on her forehead.

"Come on. She does a pretty good job."

"Um, no. She really doesn't."

"We just won't let her near the Miss Clairol. She even does my hair."

"There's a glowing recommendation."

Richard threw her a half-hearted evil eye, but said nothing about the jab. He rose from his desk, snatching up his keys. "Come on. I'll take you."

"No, that's okay. It's not that bad yet." She turned back for the door.

He dropped his keys and called after her. "Okay, but all the scissors in this building are locked in my desk."

Chapter 25 – Just Eighteen

Watching TV in Interrogation Room One wasn't all bad. Nana and Ray had been re-sequestered, and Lane enjoyed their company for the most part. She absently massaged the dull ache in her right knee, her fingers kneading along the scar-line as she munched away at some microwave popcorn that Danny had made for her.

"For her" being the operative phrase. Ray and Nana had been playing cards at the table when Danny strolled in and deposited the bowl of white puffs in Lane's hands. Apparently, he'd forgiven her for the whole tampon issue, and he left without even looking at the two adults.

Dottie's eyebrows laughed their mischievous little smile while Ray did a double-take. "What was that?" he asked his mother.

"Oh, I think you know."

Ray's eyebrows rose slowly, mirroring his mother's for height but reflecting none of her amusement. He leaned closer. "She's five years younger than him."

"So?"

Ray's head popped back as if his mother had suddenly turned into Moe Howard and poked him in the eye. "What?"

"So what she's younger than him? I was seven years younger than your father."

"That's different."

Lane's interjection slung sarcasm all the way across the room. "My hearing works just fine."

Dottie ignored her. "Don't see how. I was seventeen when we met, and we married a year later. You popped out sometime after that. And then what's-his-face with the broomstick up his butt."

"Dick?" Lane offered.

"Yeah, that'd be him."

Ray shushed his niece. "You better not let him catch you calling him that."

Lane glanced around, peered around her fellow protected civilians to see their joint custodian busy in his office. "Yeah. His hearing ain't that good."

Ray drew a card from the stack. "So, uh, you and Danny do popcorn often?"

Lane cast him the dead stare. "Danny and I don't "do" anything." The answer didn't prevent her skin from skipping the lighter shades of embarrassment and jumping all the way to fire engine red.

Ray flipped a card onto the discard pile. "Make sure it stays that way." Lane mumbled something unintelligible in response.

Dottie rummied out, again. "You owe me dinner. Of course, that depends on whether or not we ever get out of protective custody again." She headed for the door but planted a kiss on Lane's head before leaving. "Don't you worry. If it's meant to be, it will. If it's not, it won't. Simple enough. Do you think I need an escort to take a powder?" She learned the answer quickly. Danny dogged her all the way to the restroom.

Lane snatched up the remote and began flicking through the channels. Ray pulled a chair closer and took over the knee massage. "Have you decided what you want to sign up for after I move out of the cabin?"

"I don't want you to move out."

"I know. But right now, I think my presence is hindering more than helping. I think you're both relying on me too much.

84

You two aren't getting acquainted anymore, and now I'm just the tool you both use so you don't have to deal with each other. And I don't like being a tool."

Lane fought to keep the smile off her face, wondering if her uncle understood her amusement. His raised eyebrow assured her that he did. "Even for you. So what do you want to do? Besides guns, that is…you're sort of banned from them for a while."

Her head waggled. "Not really up to it."

Ray's fingers continued working on Lane's sore knee. "Sounds to me like you just don't want to. Any particular reason? Have you outgrown me?"

Lane scrambled for a response, her skin once again turning scarlet. "That's not it."

"What, then?" He took her hands in his.

She had not intended to hurt him, but she also knew that her hesitation could be interpreted as mistrust. A tear crested her eye and trickled down her face, but no other tears followed. "She's gone, Ray. I'm not that person anymore. I can't run. I can barely walk. I'm…not her."

Ray leaned closer, but Lane refused to meet his gaze. "It'll take time. But you have to start somewhere," he assured her.

"I don't think time will help. I feel like…I've gone…silent…inside. You know? Empty. I can't hear the wind anymore. I can't smell the trees. I'm just not her anymore."

Ray pulled his niece into a deep hug. "You have to trust that this will get better. No one can say it'll all go away, and no one can tell you that in X months everything will be fine. And yeah, it's gonna require work on your part, not the least of which is opening up and telling this stuff to your shrink." He released her and went back to work on the knee. It quickly progressed to physical therapy, and he motioned her closer to the edge of the couch so he could help her with the range-of-motion exercises.

But she remained silent, a delaying tactic she commonly used when deciding how best to broach a subject. She knew her uncle would figure out something was up, and it took just three extensions of her right leg before he pressed her. "What's on your mind?"

The hesitation continued for a moment, but Lane knew that if she really wanted some insight from someone, Ray sat at the top of a very short list. "So, you've," she took a deep breath, "been, um, intimate with someone."

Over the years, she and Ray had plenty of casual conversations about sex, mostly the repetitious "why to wait until you're married" speech. And although he had used his college years to draw a lesson for her, she didn't know if he would actually spill any details about his own sex life.

"We sort of discussed that. I wasn't always a priest." He slowly drew the leg out from the couch, extending it as far as it would comfortably go. When Lane cringed, he immediately stopped and reversed the motion, flexing it back toward the sofa.

Lane nodded. "Was it ugly?" She hoped the question would give her uncle a better sense of the conversation, the whys and wherefores, what brought it up and why she needed to know.

"No."

"For her? Was it ugly for her? They were her, right?"

The knee therapy ended abruptly, but Lane was too embarrassed to look up. She listened as Ray sucked in a long, slow breath.

"Yes, they were her, and no, it wasn't ugly for any of them. They were mutual encounters." Lane fell silent. "We've gotten this far…" Ray said.

"I think it's always going to be ugly for me."

He took her hand and leaned into her line of sight. "It may be. It also may not be. Love, physical love, can be the greatest gift two people give to each other. It can also be the most

86

horrendous weapon one uses against another. Only time and healing can determine how this will impact your future, but it's not something you have to work through alone."

She nodded. Ray's guidance usually eased her concerns, at least in the short term. This issue, though, was a long term problem, one that required her to address it directly, and that was something she just didn't want to do.

"Have you talked to your father about this?"

Lane shook her head.

"Why not?"

"I don't even know what to call him."

"What are you? Kidding me?"

She screwed up her face at him. "Well, what happens if I call him Dad?"

"What do you think's gonna happen?

"What if he doesn't like it?" she pressed.

"Why wouldn't he like it?"

It hit. She cast him the dreaded dead stare, nailing him square in the eye. "Answering my questions with questions isn't answering at all."

"Of course it isn't. It's a dialoguing tool. To get you to think about what's really the issue."

"Thanks, Doctor Phil."

"And you're evading. Why wouldn't he like it?"

"I dunno, maybe because he just found out."

Ray gave her hand a gentle squeeze. "He doesn't seem to be having any trouble being your father, if you ask me. He does seem to have a little problem relating to you, but not with being your dad. Why don't you just try it and find out?"

Lane shrugged. "What if I just call him Dick?"

"Reconsider that. Please."

"So, what if he doesn't like it?"

Ray and Lane paid little attention to the goings on around the station once the sex conversation started. Danny hadn't yet returned to his post, which suggested that Dottie was hiding in the bathroom. Pete managed the front office, handling incoming calls as well as making outgoing calls to find per diem officers able to drop everything and come to Mills Valley to help. So neither Ray nor Lane saw Richard coming until he spoke. "Like what?"

Lane clammed up tighter than a frightened mollusk. "Nothing." For a moment, she thought Richard might actually laugh at her.

"You do remember I'm the Sheriff, right? Sees all, knows all?" He waited a second, but no reply came. "So, now that we've settled that, you can call me Richard, or Rich, or Rick, or almost anything but that other word you've been known to use."

Lane's skin flushed hot as she wondered if he'd heard her "Dick" comment, but he didn't allude to it further.

"But I'll tell you what will happen if you do call me Dad." Lane glanced over, waiting for him to finish his thought. "Once you do, you can't ever go back to calling me anything else."

Chapter 26 – Eavesdropping

Lane rummaged around the break room for something edible. She jumped a little when Danny called to her from the doorway.

"What can I get you for lunch?" he asked. Lane shrugged and kept searching. "It's no trouble. I'll be heading down to Marigold's soon to pick up lunch for everyone. Might as well tell me what you like so I don't come back with some chicken liver pâté."

Had the cabinet door been made of living tissues instead of wood, the dead stare may well have killed it. Obviously, the dope didn't know how good chicken liver pâté could be. Or else he didn't know who he was talking to. But Lane relented. "Mac and cheese."

"Good deal. Sheriff still wants me to keep an eye on you, so if you need anything, be sure to let me know."

Lane's eyes rolled back to an appropriate position before she turned to face the young deputy. The way her head bobbed up and down would have said, "Get away from me, you freak," to just about anyone else in the world.

It didn't seem to faze Danny, and a smile spread across his face. "Great. That'll make it easier…if we're both on the same page." But he didn't leave.

"I'll be okay. I'll stay right here. And when it's time to find another boring place to plant myself, I'll let you know." He didn't take the hint. "And I really could use a little alone time right now." That argument didn't work much better, but he did appear to consider it. "I just have to sort some stuff out."

With that Danny walked fully into the room. "I can help."

Lane hadn't expected that. "Uh," she said as her mind raced, "girl stuff."

"Not falling for that again." He took a seat, no longer squirming at the notion that someone might ask him to actually touch that little blue box of tampons. His eyes settled on hers, waiting for her to join him at the table.

Crap. Lane just couldn't seem to get away from all the do-gooders trying to help. "It's stuff I can't share with you."

"Sure you can. I'm all ears."

Lane's anger swelled toward the surface, and while she managed not to rip the deputy's heart from his chest and dance on it in front of him, she couldn't keep her annoyance out of her voice. "Uh, no. Richard's probably where I should start, but I don't seem to be able to do that. And you ain't Richard. What makes you think that you can get through if he can't?"

Lane glared at him, her narrowed eyes daring him to answer. Danny rose from the table. "You're right. Maybe I can't help. You should talk to your father. Or your uncle." He left, and if Lane was very lucky, she'd find something to eat before he returned with the mac and cheese. Then she could claim to be full, take a nap, and leave Deputy Dawg to eat with Nana and Ray.

A box of crackers sat alone on the shelf over the sink, tossed up there and forgotten. Only God knew exactly how long they'd been there, and only God cared. Lane pulled them down.

She popped open the fridge and peered into a paper bag clearly marked Pete. "Wonder how pissed he'll be if I steal his lunch?" She decided against it. But the six yogurts on the top shelf were Nana's, and she definitely wouldn't mind.

Yogurt and crackers. Good enough. The yogurt didn't last long at all, easing down her throat without so much as a tickle. The dry, stale crackers were another story altogether, scratching all the way down. Lane's throat felt as if she'd swallowed a live hamster that now desperately wanted out—four glasses of water pushed away the last tickle of fur.

Satisfied for the moment, she disposed of the trash, or evidence depending on how one looked at it, washed and dried the spoon, and headed out into the squad room.

Danny held the receiver to his ear, jotting notes as he watched her progress, but Lane didn't acknowledge him as she opened the door to the cellblock. Instead, her attention was drawn to her family, all three of whom were clustered around the dispatcher's desk.

Nana Dottie's tone held a great deal of indignation. "Why?"

"Because I can't worry about you and her at the same time," Richard said. "With you both here, I won't have to worry about either one of you."

"If it really is her, she doesn't want me, Richard. She's after witnesses. That's you three, and as long as you're all in here, you're all safe. I can best be of use bringing you some clean clothes, doing your laundry, and fetching you some home-cooked meals so that Marigold doesn't turn you all into little blimps."

"Maybe, but I'm Sheriff, and if I have to arrest you in order to protect you…" He fell silent with a touch of Ray's hand.

"Mom, there's something you need to know," Ray said. "Whether it's her or not. Based on what happened at the cabin, it looks like they're after Lane first. It looks like they want the rest of us to know she's dead before they kill us. And they can use each and every one of us to draw her out."

The look on Dottie's face spoke the volumes in her heart. It was the first time Lane had seen her grandmother stammer, but it provided a suitable place for Lane to insert herself into the conversation. "It's Jenna, isn't it?"

Three stunned faces turned to find her, and they cast glances of chastisement between themselves. Richard shook his head, a clear attempt to dismiss and diffuse. "Nothing to worry about."

Lane persisted. "Is it? Is my mother trying to kill us?"

The three adults remained quiet, Nana coming around the desk to secure her most precious possession. Richard shifted, still avoiding the discussion.

"Ray!" Lane screamed, the escaping air making her sound more like a punctured basketball than a desperate human.

Ray acquiesced. "We think so."

"But she's in jail!"

Richard took over the conversation. "Yes, but that doesn't mean she isn't in contact with people who aren't in jail. We called County to see who's been visiting her and if we could get transcripts of conversations. But it looks like only her lawyer has been to see her."

Ray chimed in. "And that means the meetings are confidential."

"Which I pretty much hate right now," Richard added.

"Not debating you on it. Fact is fact. We can't know what she's been saying to her lawyer, or if he's been passing info to others."

Dottie didn't like this any better than the first time she had been sequestered under protective custody. "So we're trapped in here, worrying about our lives, until, what? We all die of natural causes or she does something to implicate herself?"

"Only until I find the gunmen. I expect when we spell out that Washington State still employs the death penalty, they may be willing to shed some light on the attack."

Ray balked. "No death penalty for attempted murder."

"No, but there is for killing a cop, or for a contract killing. Had they succeeded, there's no doubt they'd buy the farm for it. And I won't mind scaring them with it." He turned to Lane. "So, like I said, nothing for you to worry about." And with that, he dismissed the subject entirely. "You ready for some lunch?"

Emotions struggled along Lane's face as she shook her head. She would have liked to scream in anger and pull her mother's hair from her head. But she had felt the sting of Jenna's betrayal before, and it made Lane want to cry, as well. Her head sank, her eyes focused on the floor, and she retreated to the safety and isolation of the cellblock.

Chapter 27 – Getting Closer

Lane let herself out of lock-up six hours later, after a nice cry and a three hour nap. When she couldn't sleep anymore, she watched two ants play peek-a-boo, coursing along the inside of the cell window, dodging out through a tiny crack and then back in again.

Five hours into her self-imposed isolation, the door at the bottom of the stairs had opened and the jingle of keys skittered along the concrete walls. Forewarned by the noise, Lane pretended to be sleeping just so they wouldn't make her go upstairs and socialize.

With her back to her cell door, she couldn't tell exactly who it was, but she was sure the individual was not related to her by blood. She would have recognized the footfalls of her father and uncle, and Dottie wore hard-soled loafers that clacked along the floor as she walked. She decided it was Danny because Pete, a no-nonsense kind of guy, would simply have awakened her.

The last hour of her self-imposed exile drifted away. As the sun shifted further west, shadows lengthened along the floor. Little noise reached the cellblock, but occasionally the laughter of pedestrians managed to squeak through the window casing, or the rumble of a truck shook the cellblock foundation.

More often than not, the only consistent sounds came from birds, some squawking in anger when intruders wandered too close to fledglings, others just happy with the day and making the most of the sunlight.

Lane listened to them, identifying each by their assorted whistles and calls, trying to figure out if they were in the trees or

94

rummaging the ground for snacks. In her spare time, she ran through the next few hours in her head, thinking of what she'd have to say and do to appease the assorted people upstairs.

Except for Ray, everyone had their pissy little behaviors. Richard's anger had a way of sticking around a while but suddenly vanishing without explanation. Nana Dottie's attitude sometimes imitated Ray's light and easy-going behavior, but if she was really angry, hellfire and brimstone could be seen bubbling up from the depressions of her footsteps.

Deputy Pete walked with his shoulders so far back that both of his feet entered a room before his brain. When he got annoyed, the bow in his spine relaxed, bringing his shoulders forward so that he could loom over his quarry.

And Creepy Danny was just…creepy.

But Pete and Danny will be gone by now, she thought. Richard probably sent them home to get some sleep. A couple of daily hires would be hanging around upstairs, being all macho and what all.

Her stomach had long gotten over the yogurt and stale crackers, and it growled its displeasure. She would have to face everyone sooner or later, so she decided that she might as well get a meal out of it.

She stiffed-legged her way up to the squad room and found three Rent-a-Cop officers in crouched positions, two with their hands on their guns, one with the weapon fully withdrawn from its holster and pointed at her.

Richard's voice called from his office. "That's the daughter, gentlemen."

Lane eyed them as if they had food stuck in their teeth, catching their name tags in the process. Santos, the black-haired Hispanic, hid a shy smile, probably caused by the embarrassment of being spooked by a teenaged cripple.

Quick-Draw, whose real name was Bailey, had a cockiness that suggested he was above all this small town drama. The sidearm did eventually make it back to its holster, but it happened slowly enough to make Lane wonder if he would shoot her just to avoid admitting he'd been wrong to draw the weapon at all.

Only the tall bald guy, Eckert, recovered without reaction. As the three rose up from their mock-ape stances, Eckert was also the only one who acknowledged the girl standing before him. "Miss."

Lane cast a silent nod in Eckert's direction and headed to the break room.

"Door!" Richard called from his office, and Lane dutifully gave the cellblock door a push before rounding the corner and sidling past Room One where Nana and Ray had started up a new game. Neither seemed to notice Lane, and nothing about their behavior suggested they were angry. Lane kept moving, unwilling to address any issues they might have just yet.

Her vat of mac and cheese was extra full today, no doubt dished up by Marigold herself. Everyone, it seemed, tried harder these days. Some did their best to be forgiven for being such jerks when they thought she was Morgan's kid. Others found little ways to express their pity, like double-packing the take-out containers. Lane settled down at the table and shoveled up a spoonful of pasta.

Richard strolled into the room. "Pete found an abandoned car out near Highway 101, almost to Shelton. Turns out to be stolen, but we're thinking it might be the getaway car. If we're lucky, we'll get some fingerprints out of it." He pulled the container away while the spoon was in Lane's mouth and dropped it into the microwave without uttering the words, "Wouldn't you like that better if it was hot?" But he did give her a poor excuse for an evil eye. "Feeling better?" he asked.

Lane nodded, but was sure the look in his eyes meant he wasn't really buying it.

Richard leaned against the counter, waiting for the microwave to finish heating the leftovers. "You know, it's okay if you're scared. I think we all are. Well, except maybe your Nana. She seems more angry than anything else."

When the microwave chimed, Richard set the now heated food back in front of Lane, along with a package of Yankee Doodles that he'd managed to smuggle into the room without her seeing them. He drew them out of her reach when she went for them before her dinner.

"Later… this isn't one of those new-fangled places where you get to eat dessert first." He pushed the mac and cheese closer to her, and she dug in, only remembering to thank him after the gooey noodles slid onto her tongue.

"You're welcome. So," he said, sitting at the head of the table and dialing his tone down a notch or two, or four, until it came out lighter and friendlier. "Danny tells me you want to talk about something."

Lane fought down the look of horror she was sure had just crossed her face. From where her father sat, there'd be no hiding it, and all she hoped for was that he wouldn't bring it up. Had he been sitting next to her, he'd have missed it altogether.

As if reading her mind, Richard gave up his chair, moved to the one next to her, and tried his awkward best to recline in it. A smirk emerged and a brief flash of curved lips graced Lane's face. Once again she found herself fighting to keep her emotions hidden.

"So, what do you want to talk about?" Richard asked.

Lane scrunched up her face, not for a second contemplating telling him what was really on her mind. She found a whole new topic to discuss. "Danny's giving me the creeps."

Richard snorted as he laughed. "He sort of has that affect on some people. Your Nana called him a "perv" for following her to bathroom."

Shoveling the food in quickly gave Lane a reason not to speak too much, but that didn't stop Richard. "She's also seriously bent with me for locking her up in here."

Lane put the spoon down. "Do you think Jenna's gonna get outta jail?"

His eyebrows furrowed on his forehead for a second. "It's possible. I hear she's paying a fortune in legal fees."

"I should leave."

Richard misunderstood the statement. "You can't be tired already?"

"No. I mean leave town. If I'm not around, they won't be able to carry out their plan."

"Don't worry about that."

Lane cut him off, her voice just barely clinging to the civil side of surly. "I'm not worrying. I'm just stating facts."

"It makes sense, but it also lacks long-term durability. The trial could take months. Are you willing to go into witness protection for the next year?"

"If it'll keep you all from getting hurt."

Something flashed across Richard's face, a quick glimpse of pride or maybe admiration. "I don't want to lose you again. Eighteen years of not knowing keep wrestling with six months of knowing. You'll be graduating and heading off to college, and I'm not ready to let you go yet. If we decide to do WitSec, we all go together."

A slight flush of her skin preceded her eyes dropping back to the table. All in all, she enjoyed hearing it and knowing that he'd miss her, but now was as good a time as any to spill her guts on a subject he had just brought up.

"Richard." She paused, toying with how best to proceed. "Richard, what if I don't want to go to college?"

His head tipped slightly to the side like it did when he was surprised, or proving a point, or seriously considering something. "Are we talking for the time being or ever?"

Lane shrugged. "For the time being. But maybe ever."

He didn't press her. Lane assumed the shrink was getting through to him, showing him how to steer a conversation rather than drive it. "Okay," he said.

She turned to meet his gaze, a bit of confusion overriding her prior moment of surliness. "No…fight?"

He shook his head and waited.

"Ray's gonna be upset with me."

Richard's burst of laughter bounced around the tiny room and took Lane by surprise. "What would that be? The first time ever?"

"Not funny."

"Yes, it is. He'll get over it. Your life is yours to lead. If you want to hold off on college, fine. If you want never to go, well, so be it. We may be disappointed because you won't have all the opportunities you could have." He leaned closer, nudged her with his arm the way Ray did, a gentle affectionate closeness that wasn't overbearing or demanding. Obviously he'd been watching his brother's interactions with her. "But I'm not going to complain if it means you stick around a while longer."

She smiled and went back to her mac and cheese, even offering him a spoon. He declined with a shake of his head. "Uh, no. But I got the idea from Danny that you wanted to talk about something more serious."

Lane's face burned red again. "I was just trying to get him outta the room."

———

After dinner, the Sheriff and his daughter retired to Room One, joining the rest of the Keates clan. Richard took a seat at the table and watched Lane fess up. "Sorry for skipping lunch. I just needed some alone time," she said.

Dottie rose from her chair instantly and wrapped the girl up in a hug. Richard felt a twinge of jealousy when Lane reciprocated, but he pushed it away, hoping that one day his daughter would grow that comfortable with him.

"Sorry," Lane said to her uncle.

Ray smiled. "Accepted…playing cards or watching the tube?"

When Dottie's skin-scorching glance hit Richard, he acknowledged that she would continue to resent his insistence on protective custody, regardless of the logical sense it made to him. As mad as she was at Richard, he could see no evidence of it in her treatment of Lane; she ushered the girl toward the sofa and settled in to watch television for a while.

"TV, then," Ray said, scooping the cards into a neat pile, and then joining the women on the sofa.

Ten p.m. came and went, and the two eldest Keateses finally gave up fighting to keep their eyes open. They headed out of the room, stopping by to give Lane a peck on the head before departing. Ray even took a moment to whisper a bit of uncle-ish advice to the girl, but it was just loud enough for Richard to hear. "Trust is earned, but you have to let him try."

Lane hunkered into the arm of the sofa, wedging herself up with a pillow. With vacant space on the sofa, and his mother no longer slicing the flesh from his body with her eyes, Richard sank down into the upholstery and leaned against the opposite arm, kicking his feet onto the coffee table.

If he had been Ray, Lane would have made herself comfortable on him rather than on the sofa arm. She wouldn't ask; she'd just do it. Reciprocally, if Ray entered the room, he wouldn't ask, either. He'd just make himself comfortable near her, enticing her to relocate.

He reached over, nipped the edge of the pillow between his thumb and forefinger, and pulled. It slid ever so slowly, and she eyed him warily before picking up her head and simply letting him have the pillow.

His mouth fell open. Try again, he thought. He wedged the pillow against his body and twirled his hand around, inviting her over. He couldn't tell if she was looking or not, but she wasn't responding at all.

He leaned over again, this time hooking his finger into the belt loop on her jeans and tugging, moving her just an inch before she sat up and eyed him. He whapped the pillow, twirled circles with his hand again, and cocked his head to the side, beckoning her to join him.

She did. Sort of. She leaned across the sofa and reclaimed the pillow, slapping it back into her corner without a second glance at her father.

"No, huh?"

Lane wiggled her head into the pillow; she cast her father a sidelong glance as if an idea had just buzzed in through her ear and impacted with her brain. She stretched out her legs and draped them across Richard's knees.

It was a small step in the right direction, and a smile crept across Richard's face, small at first, then broad. And visible in reflection on the TV screen when it blacked out for a commercial.

"You look like Ray when you do that."

"Is that a bad thing?"

"He looks like a dork when he does it."

"And me?"

"You look like Ray when you do that."

"That's just cold."

"Just saying, is all." Lane flicked the channel, looking for a late night movie.

Richard dug in his pocket and pulled out a traffic whistle. "Found this for you." He dangled it in front of her. She twisted a little to see it and gave him the dead stare. "It's so you can call for help if you need it."

"Isn't that what Creepy Danny is for?" she whispered.

"Just in case Creepy Danny's in the john." He jiggled it until she took it. "Now we're even for calling me a dork."

Chapter 28 – Harris Mansion

Barnett made himself at home in the Harris Mansion. With his brother murdered and his sister-in-law in jail, someone had to look after the place. It pleased him that the house staff, Camilla and Anton, took to his presence without hesitation, not balking at any of his orders, nor resisting any of his changes. Well-trained, he thought. Hard to find that in help, these days.

He had also taken over the master suite, helping himself to those of Morgan's clothes that fit his own personal tastes and instructing the servants to give the rest to whatever charity had a box in town. Goodwill Industries won big that day.

The two men sitting opposite him in the large, well-appointed office wore off-the-rack suits. Barnett made a reasonable attempt not to hold it against them, but decided they had gone shopping together, specifically to find something suitable to wear to this meeting. He leaned back in his chair, listening to his guests while puffing on a fat stogie and appreciating his dead brother's expensive habits.

"If you're dead set on the girl going first, we could miss lots of opportunities to take out the rest." Jack's decidedly Jersey accent held just a hint of sarcasm. The rest of him held no stereotypes; his hair was not greased back, his shirt was not two sizes too small in order to show off amazing pecs. In fact, the skinny geek didn't really look like a hit-man at all.

"The girl goes first." Barnett blew a smoke ring toward the ceiling, watching it rise and disassemble itself. "Payment for all of us depends upon it."

Angelo, on the other hand, was a walking stereotype. His round belly, born of spaghetti and pizza, pressed against his belt and the limits of good taste at the same time. His dark eyes looked like portholes to Hell, and the muscles in his arms and chest rippled beneath his tee shirt. Even the wrinkles on his face screamed the experiences he'd had and the pain he'd caused. "Don't make sense," he said, the low growl a threat in itself.

Barnett flicked the cigar ashes onto the Oriental rug, adding unnecessary patterns to the colorful mosaic. "It hardly matters that it makes sense to you. The client is paying for a service. If the terms aren't satisfactory, tell me now and I'll find someone else."

Jack smiled a shallow, grim line that would have scared the crap out of a bull mastiff. "No point in being snooty. We'll let you know if the terms are acceptable once we hear all the requirements. You want her first, she's first. What else?"

"She dies in full view of the brothers. And the client wishes to be present at the proceedings. When you have the targets, call me."

"Does it matter how they go?" Angelo asked.

"Not at all, though I expect she'd like it to be painful. As long as the brothers watch while the girl dies, I doubt the client cares if it's by gun or knife or with your bare hands. Indulge yourselves if you've a mind to." Barnett's hand waved in the air, dislodging more ashes off the end of the cigar.

"And the brothers?" Jack asked.

Barnett watched Jack's eyes flit around the room. The potential assassin seemed to be looking for something, perhaps gauging Barnett's worth by the physical surroundings, or perhaps just evaluating the man willing to purchase death. Barnett didn't mind. "One's the current Sheriff, the other a priest, I believe, though from what I'm told, he actually hasn't served in that capacity for quite some time." Barnett noted the frown on Angelo's face deepen.

"You care what order the boys go in?" Jack asked.

"Shooter's choice," Barnett said, deferring to them on that one issue.

Angelo's growl rumbled up from his stomach. "And the old woman?"

A slight toss of Barnett's cigar hand dismissed her. "No payment for her. If she's in the way, take whatever steps you deem appropriate."

Angelo's dark eyes burned, but he shifted onto his elbow, leaning heavily against the arm of the chair.

Angelo drove back toward Shelton and to the no-frills hotel he and Jack had booked. The place sat on the high end of okay, and it wasn't very far from the casino, which had an abundance of women to entertain them. But it wasn't the kind of place that screamed "high-roller" or "whale", the kind of thing that would attract attention. Nor was it the kind of place that a highly paid assassin would rent. Mostly, it hosted businessmen and families, the kinds of folks looking to get the most for their money, the kinds of folks no one remembered after they checked out.

Angelo's growl returned, his grip on the steering wheel turning his knuckles white. "Those are stupid requirements. Too many things can go wrong."

"What difference? It's not even that big a deal. We nab 'em, sit on 'em, and then do 'em for the lady. The money more than compensates for the logistics," Jack said, surveying the countryside. "What a turd mound. Nothing but trees. Now I know why I've never moved out here."

105

Angelo couldn't have cared less about the trees. He cared about the targets. "Popping 'em long distance would just be easier. Head shot." His thumb and finger cranked an invisible bullet through the windshield. "Splat. End of discussion and drive out of town. Then we wouldn't have to worry about unknown variables, like that old woman."

Jack's thin-lipped smile turned to meet Angelo's stare. "We ain't getting paid for her, so unless she's stupid, she'll live."

Angelo's head shook side to side. "Grandmothers tend to be more protective than stupid. Mine was. Yours was."

"And it got them both killed, didn't it?"

Chapter 29 – Angelo and Jack

Smoke rose toward the ceiling in elongated swirls, dissipating long before it arrived but adding to the haze in the darkened casino bar. Angelo surveyed the room, eyeing every woman that sauntered by all strapped up and decked out for a high night on the town. He had his requirements, and he'd take his time to meet them, making sure he found just the right entertainment for tonight's festivities.

Watching them brought its own pleasure, studying them, noting their idiosyncrasies, musing over the differences between men and women. Women moved in tandem with each other, groups of two or three moving in unison everywhere they went— the bar, the bathroom, the dance floor.

Men had no such compunction. They went to the john themselves. Got a drink without moral support. And though a man might dance with his beer, the odds were against him taking to the dance floor with all his male friends just so everyone would have a good night out dancing.

As he scoped the room, Angelo avoided lingering on women in jeans. Some of them had tight bodies stuffed into those jeans, but a lot of them were hiding imperfections by wearing loose fitting trousers and tops. He didn't want to select a product and discover he'd been a victim of the old bait-and-switch.

Similarly, women without makeup held no interest for him. Several of them were incredibly attractive, wholesome country girls who didn't need anything additional to make them alluring. That lack of concern over their looks overshadowed a lack of attitude, and Angelo certainly had little use for a down-to-earth country girl. Maybe for marrying her and settling down on a ranch in the middle of nowhere to breed the next generation of made-men, but not for the kind of fun he had planned for the next few days.

A couple of retirees shuffled by, clutching their purses as if the tiny bags held millions of dollars. One of the blue-haired beauties cast a glance into the shadows, meeting Jack's eyes with a steely glower of her own.

"That one?" Jack asked. Angelo didn't even respond, his eyes already moving on to the next group of tandem walkers coming down the aisle. The first two weren't much to look at—a timid, mousy brunette who seemed completely out of place in the bar, and a tall blonde who hadn't yet mastered walking in the heels strapped to her feet.

But the third one, a raven-haired beauty with the kind of blue eyes one only got from contact lenses, caught Angelo's attention immediately. Her clothes fit like transplanted skin, tucking in and sticking out nicely on all the appropriate curvatures, and those curves screamed "Look at me!"

And Angelo obliged. "Have a seat, girls. Rest those pretty bones and have a drink with us." The mouse looked to her compatriots and uttered a respectful, "No, thank you." The blonde fell off one of her heels. But the girl who resembled a bird of prey made Angelo's heart leap for joy. She looked down her perfect little nose at him and courted her own death with a derisive "as if" snort. To compound the insult, she'd eyed him up and down, then shifted her gaze to her perfect breasts, her hands gliding along her torso, across her ass, and then down her hips before she walked away with a booty shake broad enough to sweep a Volkswagen off the street.

As Angelo's hand wrapped around the neck of his beer bottle and squeezed, Jack smiled broadly. "There she is. And a fine specimen, too. Any plans on how we get her away from her posse?"

"Won't have to. They'll be heading home soon. Blonde's feet are killing her, and the mouse was partied out before she got here." Angelo's eyes burned with an intensity to match the black depths of Hell.

"What if they go home together?" Jack asked. The partners seldom took more than one victim at one time, but seldom didn't mean never. It just meant more planning.

"Too bad for them."

Chapter 30 – Her Way

Richard stretched awake at six a.m., feeling the vacant space beside him and assuming Lane had gone to bed sometime during the night or early morning. He didn't mind sleeping on the sofa, his daughter beside him, her feet across his lap or pushing into his thigh as was the case at different times during the night. She'd fallen asleep a half hour into the late-night movie, but he didn't mind that, either. All in all, he thought, I rather liked it. He scruffed his hair and headed down to lock-up.

Ray, pulling on a tee shirt, met him at the bottom of the stairs. Together, they strolled down to the cell shared by Lane and their mother. Soft snoring from Nana confirmed she was still asleep, but Lane's cot was empty, the sheets all tangled and balled up. That in itself meant little, since the girl never made a bed without actually being told to do so.

He strolled to the shower room and felt free to enter when no sounds ushered forth. No Lane. Nerves jumped to the front of his brain. A strange tightening in his chest preceded the tingling that shot down his arms and legs. "Mother," he said as he jostled Dottie awake. "Where's Lane?"

Dottie threw the blanket off as she rose. "I thought she was with you."

All three headed back upstairs, Richard in the lead. "Lane!" His voice echoed off the concrete walls and up the stairwell. Bailey met him at the top of the stairs, but Richard brushed past him. "Where's Lane?"

"Thought she was with you."

"You thought? When was the last time you saw her?"

"She went to the head, what, about two a.m.?" He sought confirmation from Santos.

"Yeah, 'bout that," Santos confirmed.

But by the time the three words emerged, Richard had already dismissed him and headed for the facilities. "Lane!" He threw open the door without regard for her modesty, but she wasn't there.

Curtains rustled in the breeze from the open window.

Chapter 31 – The Bow

The cruiser had barely stopped when Ray jumped from it and raced to the cabin door. Richard jammed the stick into park before chasing his brother. "I've got the gun, Ray!"

The second cruiser slammed to a stop just behind the first and Danny, pressed back into service with a phone call, positioned himself between the two vehicles, training his weapon on the lake and driveway. Santos mimicked Danny's actions, coming around from the passenger side and shielding himself from possible gunfire with the cruiser's hood.

Richard entered first and swept the room quickly before allowing Ray to join him inside the cabin. Open cabinets and drawers pointed to Lane's motives. "She came back for supplies," Ray said.

Richard pointed to the wall over the fireplace. "And the bow. How good is she with it?"

Ray threw open the closet door and rummaged around inside trying to find the quivers of arrows stored there but coming up empty. "If it were close enough, she could take it down. Beyond fifty feet or so, she couldn't hit Oregon. She's got about six dozen arrows."

"Broadheads?" Richard asked, gauging the killing power of the weapon.

"Half-dozen Razorbacks. The rest are target and field points. Maybe a couple fish points, but sailing from a sixty-pound bow, they're all going to do some damage." Ray continued around the room, reading the signs of Lane's passing. "Two-way's missing."

Richard whipped the second radio from the charger, thumbed the button and shouted into the mic. "Lane!"

Ray slid in next to him. "Be calm, Rich."

Richard acknowledged the advice, taking a deep breath, letting it out slowly, and thumbing the button again. "Lane, please. Talk to me." He waited, but silence ensued. "Lane. Please."

The radio crackled to life. Lane panted heavily into the radio as she breathed a single word. "Hi."

Ray clapped Richard's shoulder and both brothers exhaled a sigh of relief. "Where are you?" Richard hoped she'd tell him, but he felt it was a long-shot at best. She didn't respond. "This isn't the way. You're putting yourself at risk, and the rest of us who are out here looking for you, too."

"You're wrong," she whispered back. "If they can't get us all together in the same place at the same time, we're all safer. They won't kill any of us unless all of us are there. This is the perfect solution."

"You're safer if you stay with us, in the jail, where I can protect you." Richard pleaded, but he knew he'd lost the battle.

"Sorry. You think you're right. But I think I'm right. And I have to do this. I can't stick around knowing they're trying to kill me to hurt you."

"Lane! You do this and I swear to God, I'll ground you for life!"

"As long as nobody dies, I can live with that." And the radio went dead.

Chapter 32 – Nana's Out of Control

Richard wondered why it was that he, an officer of the law, tall, muscular, and exuding the confidence and authority of his office, couldn't verbally control the two women in his life, and why it always came down to physical force to subdue them. "I'll lock you in the cell if I have to."

Dottie pushed against him, slapping at the steel-band arms that held her like vice grips. "I have to find my granddaughter!" Obviously "no" wasn't a word to which she had become accustomed.

"Mother, everybody here is looking for her. Half the town is on the watch for her. Even Marigold is offering a reward."

"A reward? Free dinner for a week isn't that much of an incentive." Sarcasm hung in the air like mist in the forest.

Richard didn't let the criticism take control of the discussion. "The high school teams are out combing the forest. Vic's paying his two employees to look for her instead of fixing cars and pumping gas."

She thrust a finger in his chest, deliberately jabbing him with the nail. "You should be out looking for her."

"I have been. And Danny, and Pete."

Dottie craned around him to eyeball the Rent-a-Cops, one of whom had unwittingly let her granddaughter crawl out the bathroom window. She studied them all, including the Asian guy who'd shown up today. Four strapping examples of manhood, just standing around.

"Don't even look at them," Richard said. "Only one of them is from the area. If we send the other three out, we'll end up spending our time trying to find them, too."

"Is there no one else you could bring in? Deputize Vic. And Jake. And that mean boy of his. And Ray. And…"

Richard didn't let her continue naming every able-bodied male in Mills Valley. "And grind the town to a halt?"

"This is an emergency. You have the power."

"I know that, Mother. Please. Let me do my job. We'll find her. I promise. Why don't you go downstairs for a little while? When this melee is over, I'll send someone down for you."

"You're trying to get rid of me. I should be at dispatch doing my job."

"Ordinarily, there's nobody I'd rather have there, but you are too close to this situation, and I think you need a break from it. Perhaps just a little one, but you need to bring your objective self back to the front and forget, as hard as that's going to be, that you have a vested interest in this particular girl."

"Is that what you're doing?"

"Giving it my best shot." In an uncharacteristic move, he draped his arm across his mother's shoulders and steered her toward the lock-up door.

At the threshold, she pulled away, planting her feet like tree roots and refusing to move one inch closer to the stairs. "You swear to me you'll find my granddaughter."

Richard kept the concern from his voice and from his face. He knew he might not find Lane, and that the killers might get to her first. He hoped his daughter's theory might be enough to protect her, at least in the short term. But he had to get his mother under control right now. "I'll find her."

With one last flesh-rending glare, she headed down to her basement cell, and Richard closed the door behind her. He pulled

Danny over. "Give it five minutes, then go down on the pretext of doing rounds. Make it look good. And then lock her in."

Danny's head pulled back as if the Sheriff's word had developed physical form before arriving at his face. "You want me...to lock up...your mother?"

Richard stared down at him, his annoyance no longer restrained. "Is that a problem for you, Deputy?"

Danny had matured a bit in the last few months. Normally Richard would have thought that a good thing. The young Deputy no longer feared the Sheriff, nor was he always sucking up. But as he'd relaxed, he'd developed a rather casual streak. "Uh, yeah. She's your mother." Danny thrust the keys away.

Richard fought the anger, reminding himself his daughter was in danger and his mother in the way. He pushed the keys back to Danny and leaned closer. "That's an order, Junior." He strolled away, leaving Danny at the cell block door, but he called over his shoulder. "If it makes it any easier, tell her that her protective custody has just gone code orange."

Ray stretched the phone line to its max and relinquished the creaky desk chair as Richard entered the office. "Thanks, I'll let you know just as soon as I hear anything." He dropped the receiver back on its cradle. "Zavier hasn't seen her, but he's going to check with the other churches. I asked one of the new guys to take a current photo down to him so he can send it to his contacts in the Diocese. Hope that's okay."

Richard nodded. "Danny sent her picture off to Detective Glenn, who helped us out with the plea deal. But I didn't think of the churches. Good idea." He motioned his brother toward the chairs across the room.

"No, thanks. I've got more work to do."

Richard called him back before he got fully out of the office. "Ray, I'm locking Mother up."

Horror washed Ray's face. "What? Why?"

"Because if I don't, she's going to be running around town making herself a target."

The howling of a mad woman split the air, winding up from the basement stairs as Danny threw himself out the cellblock door, slamming it behind himself and pressing his body against the door to keep the monster below at bay. He'd messed up his hair, pulled out his shirt tails, and loosened his tie.

All in all, the effect made him look like he'd been attacked by a grizzly bear, or maybe even one of those werewolves that one so often read about prowling the forests of the peninsula. At first, the new officers shifted nervously toward him. Pete's roar of delight let them in on the joke.

Richard shook his head in disbelief, but a smile tugged across his face anyway. "Any other questions?" he asked Ray.

"I guess not. And me?"

Richard's head did that tip thing, cocking toward his shoulder as he considered the issue. "Depends on you. You stay inside the station and you're free to move about as you like. But you make one move toward the exterior door without a bodyguard, and you'll end up behind a locked door faster than you can grant absolution to a two-bit whore in New York City."

"I can live with that."

"I thought you'd see it my way. You're so much more practical than Mother."

"I'm also so much more male than Mom. Women tend to use their emotions more."

"Women." Richard shook his head in mock disgust.

"So, can I borrow Danny and go pick up some clothes and things? We can swing by Mom's, too, and get her some stuff."

"That's the kind of thing anybody can do. Make a list for me."

"You're going?" Ray asked.

117

"No. I'm the Sheriff. I'll hand that off to one of my deputies. I've got more important things to do than worry about whether or not you've got clean clothes."

Ray laughed. "Like finding my niece."

Richard shook his head. "Nope. Like finding my daughter. So I can ground her for life."

Chapter 33 – Back in the Woods

Lane shivered against the morning dew, her breath rising as billowy clouds of steam in the cool air. The forest invigorated her, calmed her, and protected her, but at the same time it reminded her of the night Morgan had attacked her, the months of fighting to survive, and Richard's bullet ripping her right knee from her body.

Despite the negative occurrences, she conceded that she was more comfortable here, more relaxed, less tense, and completely free. Living with people was proving far more difficult than living without them.

She had spent a great deal of time with Ray over the years—vacations, Sunday dinners, and the occasional night or two during the week—but those were more like treats, something to be savored but not taken for granted.

Now they shared the same house. Ray spent every free minute pushing her to get back on the proverbial horse even though Lane wanted nothing to do with that pony. And when she dug her heels in, he'd pry into her emotions to try to get her to talk about her feelings. Just like the shrink.

Then there was Richard who, somewhere between probation officer and father, couldn't quite grasp the idea that an eighteen-year-old didn't need to be told when to get up, when to go to bed, when to eat, brush their teeth or make their bed.

I'm an adult, she thought, thoroughly indignant with Richard's intention of governing her every waking moment. She'd been running her own life since she was six. "Six!" she said aloud.

"And I don't need somebody telling me what to do all the freakin' time."

She hadn't taken much gear on this particular trip. Her game plan was to throw off pursuit and swing back to the cabin to stock up on long term essentials. The items she had taken had immediate survival use.

The bow in her hand felt heavy and awkward. She hadn't picked it up in years, and had never been particularly good with it from a distance. Within fifteen yards or so, she could get fairly close to the bull's-eye, but at serious distance the target had to be the size of an eighteen-wheeler.

Three quivers of arrows slapped against her back in rhythm with her footsteps as she trudged north through the woodland, easing over downed and rotting tree trunks.

The rest of her supplies sat protected inside double layers of black trash bags. Even if moisture seeped into the first bag, the second bag would keep all her things dry until she needed them.

Among the supplies she had appropriated were the radio, on which her father had already tried to convince her to return, and a set of binoculars. Both items would keep her abreast of her pursuers' movements, hopefully before they showed up and slapped her in irons.

And, because very shortly she'd be soaking wet, she had swiped some of Richard's clothes to change into, partly because Richard wouldn't expect to find his daughter in his clothes, but also because all of Ray's clothes seemed to be stuck in limbo, which God had apparently created in the Keates' laundry room.

On top of that, she had grabbed an extra pair of shoes, the mini-flame thrower and some Wetfire Tinder Cubes for starting fires, two leftover bagels still in their sleeve, and one of the water-filtering canteens that could clean river water and make it drinkable. At least that's what it was supposed to do—remove particulates, Giardia and Cryptosporidium and turn impure water into potable. She had never actually tested it, so if it failed to do the job properly, she would have the worst case of diarrhea in the history of the world.

And with a bulletproof vest to protect her against any gun shots designed to strike center mass, she'd be pretty safe for a while…provided that the killers didn't try for another noggin buster.

Hopefully, she wouldn't have to worry about that. If Ray was right, the killers' intentions revolved around live capture and group execution. Given that Lane planned to evade all of humanity for as long as necessary, Sheriff Stick-Up-His-Butt would have plenty of time to figure out who the shooters were and put them in jail.

Whether her destiny held a long-distance shot to the head in isolation, or an up-close-and-personal slug to the back of the skull while her family watched, the immediate situation required the fine art of elusion. Lane pushed on, struggling through the pain raging in her leg. As its range of motion decreased, she found herself stiff-legging her way through the brush and up and down hills.

Stopping for a rest might relieve the discomfort; it would also allow anyone tracking her to catch up. And as sure as bears did their business in the woods, Lane was certain that pursuit had already begun. If not her father, then one of the deputies, or maybe even those guys in Shelton with the hound dogs. The sooner she threw them off the scent, the better.

The tree trunks provided protection as she scanned the river banks for hunters, fishermen, police, or even something more dangerous like bear, moose, or elk. A mule deer's head twisted at the shoulder to watch her; its return to drinking screamed its lack of concern with the human. Moments later it strolled off into the forest, leaving the river and surrounding shores devoid of other guests.

Lane slipped out cautiously, still expecting to hear Richard's voice bellowing at her. If he caught up with her now, her plan would be ruined—she couldn't possibly escape dragging a leg behind her.

But no one stepped out and shouted, no one charged as she moved closer to the water. Gingerly testing the river with her fingers, she realized that this had to be the most hair-brained idea she'd ever had, even more stupid than crawling out the bathroom window and scraping the sill down the length of her right leg.

"Like I ain't cold enough already." She didn't bother whispering; her voice wasn't loud enough to carry.

She pondered the question for a moment, looking north and south down the river, hoping to find a better location for her crossing. Nothing jumped out at her, nothing screamed, "Hey, wait, over here. I'm only a foot deep."

As rivers went, this particular flowing body was nothing more than a trickle compared with a river like the Mississippi. Spanning little more than twenty feet across here, this channel would be an easy cross in the summer, but not right now.

Ripples along the surface indicated submerged rocks and other obstacles, debris that would be fully visible in another few weeks after the runoff from the mountains slowed down. If Jenna had chosen a more opportune time of the year for her endeavors, Lane might have been able to utilize those now-hidden rocks to cross the river, and might not have to get freezing-her-ass-off, dripping-water-for-a-mile wet. "Thanks, Mom. Really."

But it wasn't a very deep river, averaging depths of no more than ten or twelve feet most of the time. Enough to sink in, and certainly enough to drown in if you couldn't swim or had a bum leg that couldn't kick.

Lane's plans didn't include breathing water. She expected to get neck deep and then throw herself forward, letting momentum do the work and coasting to the other side. At least that was the idea. She stepped out into the water, shaking as the first cold slosh of water slipped into her shoes. She hunched forward against the cold and willed herself onward.

The water churned around her legs, wicking up higher still into her dry clothes. It slapped at her, whacking her with tiny whitecaps and swirling around her in miniature whirlpools.

At knee-deep, she decided to chuck the trash bag toward the other shore while she still had enough strength to throw it. It arched up and landed with a plop on the far side, two feet up on the bank. It slid back down, snagging on a rock and settling.

There was little she could do with the quivers draped over her shoulder. Getting the arrows wet would impede their ability to fly until the fletching dried out, but throwing them to the opposite shore would have them strewn about along the bank. Worse yet, any unfortunate enough to land in water would instantly orient themselves downstream and speed along with the flow, lost to her forever. Lane slipped her arm through the bow and nestled it against her side, pushing it back as far as she could to keep the quivers lodged against her back.

Her shivering grew violent, but she scuffled forward, slowly lest she step carelessly and find herself floundering and unable to get the bum leg back underneath her.

Five feet from shore, then six feet. Headway was slow, and the frigid water sucked warmth and energy from her entire body. She slid her foot forward, trying to whittle away at the distance to the opposite shore without placing herself in any more danger than need be.

Nine feet. Ten. Waist-deep now, she expected the bottom to fall away soon. She slid the foot forward, and again, and a third time. Neck-deep and shivering like a puppy in a thunderstorm, Lane pressed forward. Seven or eight feet lay between her and the far shore. Odds were the river wouldn't get too much deeper before climbing back up to dry land. But with her strength nearly gone, she had to get this trek over with.

She threw herself forward, kicking the one leg that worked and dragging the other. While one arm beat a crazy windmill against the water's surface, the other pressed the bow and quivers tightly against her body. Thirty seconds later she floundered, completely spent. With one last gulp of air, she sank into the water...all three feet of it.

She lurched forward, exploding from the water, and crawled hand-and-knee out of the river. "Jerk," she muttered. Her face sank to the ground with her butt still in the air as she caught her breath, but she knew she didn't have time to relax. She quickly stripped off her outer clothes, leaving them in a heap on the river bank.

The trash bag yielded its cargo. She dressed quickly, donning Richard's jeans and shirt, folding up the sleeves and legs until her shorter appendages stuck out. Topped off with his sweatshirt, she'd be warm enough once she started moving.

Saran-wrap had protected a sandwich from the watery trip, keeping it nice and dry even if its maker wasn't. Lane opened it carefully, avoiding all skin contact with the bread, and dropped it near the pile of wet clothes. Three additional sandwiches joined the first, randomly strewn about the area. The food and a sprinkling of talcum powder would confuse the dogs for a short time at best, but that would be good enough.

It didn't really matter if the dogs were air trackers or scent trackers, for the odds favored them, anyway. Unless a sudden storm came up and washed away all evidence of her, all she could do was throw the beasts off her trail long enough to find a place to hide.

Except for her hastily arranged decoys, the forest would remain as pristine as when she arrived. She clipped the radio and canteen to her belt, hung the binoculars from her neck, and stuffed the fire starter, spare shoes, and other survival items back in the trash bags. All loaded up and ready to go, she stepped back in the water and followed the river south.

Wading through the frigid water was delicate work—one careless foot placement could cut her soles from stones, branches, broken bottles, or other debris and put an end to this journey. Of course, frostbite was another concern, and taking the time to watch each footstep kept Lane in the water much longer than she would have liked.

Her feet screamed their displeasure with the icy needles digging into her flesh and searing the nerve endings. When she could take the pain no longer, she stepped out of the river and stamped around on the banks. The skin was red and tender, but not yet in imminent danger. Frostbite would no doubt set in soon if she continued her watery trek, but she needed to delay the dogs as long as possible.

While her feet thawed for a few minutes, she wove back and forth across the bank, going in circles and crisscrosses and leaving scent in a tangled mess for the dogs to sort out. And though her feet could have used some more dry time, she stepped back into the water and pushed on. Hopefully her appendages wouldn't fall off before she found a suitable place to exit the river for good.

Chapter 34 – Jenna Gets Out of Solitary

With the metallic scrape of key against lock, the door to Jenna's cell swung open, freeing her to the general population, the one place she didn't really want to go. Solitary may have been boring as hell, but getting jumped by a gang of angry women was certainly no way for a genteel socialite like herself to spend her days. Unfortunately, Barnett had said it was a prerequisite to getting her out of jail altogether.

"Get your stuff. Move." Neither of the guards had paid her much attention during her stay in the bucket. Jenna, on the other hand, had nothing but time while in Iso, and had spent more than a few hours analyzing the corrections officers and their behaviors.

The man was on a career path, probably hoping to rise to Captain, maybe even all the way to Warden. His clothing was always clean and crisp, his back always straight, his behavior always professional, though occasionally gruff to inmates who didn't listen to him. Jenna disliked him intensely, but only because he reminded her so much of her ex-fiancée, Sheriff Richard Keates.

The woman guard was a tier-lifer. She had no wish to climb the penal system's version of the corporate ladder and was more than content to spend her duty hours strolling the tiers. Her hair was always swept back off her face and into a tight bun, pulling her skin as tight as a well-inflated balloon. Wrinkles and stains marred her clothing, and an inch of skin poked out between buttons where her belly fat refused to be contained by the ill-fitting shirt. As much as the female guard looked down her nose at Jenna, she couldn't compete with the look of disgust that Jenna gave her.

"Sometime today," the female guard snapped.

Jenna gathered up her meager possessions—a couple magazines, her toothbrush and toothpaste. A change of clothes. She left the Bible where it sat untouched since her arrival in the isolation unit.

The march back to her cell did not go unnoticed. Word spread quickly that the Princess from the Peninsula was on the walk. A group of not-so-well wishers followed. The male guard barked at them to be about their business; they fell back a little but continued to dog Jenna and her escorts from a more respectable distance.

Cat calls and wolf whistles echoed off the cellblock walls. There'd been a time, all dressed up in her finest, that such attention would have made Jenna smile, reminding her of just how desirable she truly was.

Now the sound was vile, nothing more than the vomit served on the plastic, beige trays in the chow hall at mealtime. Her body shuddered involuntarily, just like that morning at the mansion when she'd seen Lane again for the first time in six months.

She dropped her things on her bunk. The top bunk. The bunk hardest to get into—the fish bunk. She even hated the term fish, knowing on the surface that it meant she was the new kid in town, but knowing also, deep down, that it held a sexual connotation.

Her dreadlocked cell mate jumped off her own bed and to her feet instantly. "Hell, no."

But the guard jabbed a warning finger in her direction, and then he and his partner walked away.

"Alright, that's alright." She stripped the bedding off her lower bunk, balled it up, and stuffed it under the bed—pillow, blanket, sheets, and all.

"They're coming for you," she said, her finger just inches from Jenna's face. "They're coming for you, and they're gonna beat your ass. And then they'll get to the good stuff. Don't you mess my bed." Her head shook back and forth, and she got even closer to Jenna. "Don't you do it."

Jenna tried to stand her ground, tried to act tough and aloof and above all this violence.

"You ain't messin' with Bopper's girl, are you?" The voice came from the cell door.

The owner of the lower bunk dropped her hand, whipped around and left, stepping past the posse of six on the walk. "Wouldn't even. She all yours." She didn't even look them in the eye as she headed away.

The gang entered, all swagger and the female equivalent of machismo. Jenna knew immediately that she was in serious danger. She tossed an attitude, determined to maintain her dignity and silence them with her power and presence.

One of the intruders snickered. Two of them grabbed her hands. Another jammed a sock into her mouth to keep her quiet. The fifth produced the broken end of a broom handle from inside her clothing and handed it to the interim posse leader.

The first few blows were intended to remind Jenna where she was, who she was, and who her betters were. The beating continued about her torso, front and back, and her legs until she could no longer stand on her own.

The two women hanging onto Jenna's arms dragged her to the bed, forcing her face down on it, holding her so she couldn't get away, and laughing as her eyes grew wide with terror. Their leader joined Jenna on the bed, descending on her with the broom handle. "I hope you're ready."

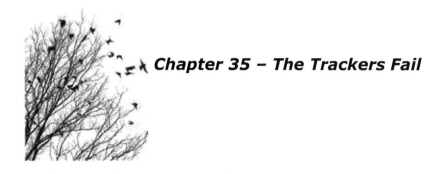

Chapter 35 – The Trackers Fail

The dog handler dropped the pile of wet clothes on Richard's desk. "She changed clothes, left sandwiches for the dogs, sprinkled some kind of smelly powder all over the place, and stayed in the water. Ain't figured out where she come out yet. We'll go back out in the morning and pick up where we left off. I'll need something with a fresh scent. And remember not to handle it." He left as abruptly as he had entered.

Richard's eyebrows sank into a deep wedge as he swept the wet clothes into the wastebasket and took them to the outer office. Ray sat in the dispatcher's seat, pondering something or other. Richard didn't know what Ray had assigned himself to do, and he wasn't sure he cared as long as his brother remained in the station. He set the wastebasket on the floor near the desk.

Ray leaned over, peered inside. "What's that?"

"Her clothes."

"They found her clothes? Are you telling me she's running around naked?"

"God, I'm praying not. Looks like she planned this out pretty good, though. Did enough to confuse the dogs for the day. Next time you head down to the restroom, drop these in the washer for me?"

"Sure thing."

"Dan," Richard called, and the young Deputy promptly dropped what he was doing and joined Richard at the dispatch desk.

"S'up?"

The Sheriff's spine straightened a bit, pulling his shoulders and head back. That casual streak in the young deputy was really starting to bend Richard clean out of shape. "Need you to run to the cabin and pick up some of Lane's clothes. If you can't find any in the laundry hamper in the bathroom, just check out the den. Tons of them in there. All over the floor. Use gloves so you don't get your own scent on them."

"Dogs lost her?" Danny asked, his surprise registering in his voice.

"Not exactly."

Danny's eyes popped wide. "Not exactly?"

"Dogs didn't lose her. She eluded them." Richard headed back to his office. "For the moment. And while you're there, pick up something of Ray's, just in case she decided to switch clothes and leave someone else's scent all over the mountainside."

Ray chuckled. "Should I go with him?"

"Nope," Richard said as the office door slammed shut behind him.

Chapter 36 – Nana's House

With her back pressed against a tree, Lane watched Nana's house for over an hour, looking for anything that might signal the house was under surveillance by either police or criminals.

She kept an eye on the most likely vantage points: the embankment behind the Sheriff's Office, Vic's gas station, and the church. Situated just a short walk from her job as Dispatcher, Dottie never drove to work, and that closeness put Lane so near Richard that if he knew, he would no doubt be chasing her down right now, dragging her to a cell, and locking it behind her…forever.

But the countryside held no visible threats. She slipped down to the house, using trees and out-buildings to conceal herself from the Sheriff's Office windows and consoling herself with the belief that if the killers were hiding nearby or in Nana's house, they wanted her alive for the time being.

The back door was locked, but that hardly mattered. The casing was original equipment, boasting its full one hundred years, and the door shrank and swelled with the seasons. Lane gripped the handle and lifted the door up and toward its hinges. It didn't shift much, but that half-inch allowed the striker to swing nearly free of the well-worn catch plate. Like a bear shouldering its way through brush, Lane popped the door open and let herself into her grandmother's house.

Heat escaping the registers created an eerie sound as Lane tiptoed around in the shadows. A slow and cautious snoop through the house revealed no hidden intruders. Other than me, she thought.

A quick peek through the curtains revealed calm at the Sheriff's Department, no deputies on the stairs, no marksmen in the windows. That didn't faze Lane; she wouldn't let her guard down just because she didn't see anyone. They were certainly in there, puzzling about, assigning patrols; even with the sun drooping low and shadows lengthening in the forest, Richard and Ray would still be up, prowling the station trying to figure out where to look for her next.

So far, hiding out from her father and uncle had been fairly easy, except for the cold water crossing, and relatively safe. For now, she'd keep the lights off to prevent drawing attention and bide her time. Another opportunity would present itself sooner or later, just like the one that had popped into view this morning—right after Richard fell asleep. I wonder what happened to Officer Insenstivity? she wondered. "I am sooo grounded."

Even though she believed she had bought herself some time, she knew she had to remain vigilant. She had to do what she had come to do but still be ready to leave at a moment's notice. If someone showed up unexpectedly, her plan to rest and recuperate here would be shot to hell.

The first thing she needed was a quick and easy meal, and Lane slapped together a Bologna sandwich—one meant for her and not tracking dogs. Doc Williams' repairs helped her voice a little, but improved her ability to eat tenfold. She still had to chew completely, and she tended to avoid scratchy foods if possible, but she could eat like normal folks and finish in a reasonable amount of time. A second sandwich joined the first soon after, and she washed it all down with a tall glass of milk.

After her dinner, which she ate peering out from behind the curtains of assorted windows, Lane headed to her grandmother's bedroom, stripping off Richard's clothes and replacing them with some of Nana's. The matriarch's build better approximated

Lane's, so her clothes fit more appropriately. Style didn't matter much, but thankfully, Nana had a cool streak wider than both her sons put together. She had jeans and sweatshirts, even sneakers. A hip lady. At least when she wasn't working for her straight-laced, broomstick-up-the-butt youngest son.

As she folded Richard's clothes, Lane surveyed Main Street. Four cars occupied spaces at Pearce's Grocery, another sat in front of the Post Office, and the Sheriff's Department boasted a full complement of cruisers. The people she saw, however, had purpose. They completed their errands, not lingering around town any longer than necessary.

Lane set Richard's folded clothes on the bed. She didn't bother exchanging her shoes for some of Nana's because this would be the last place to which the dogs could track her. The yappy little beasties would pick up her scent again in the morning and show up here. Lane, however, had plans for a scent-free escape and would be long gone before their incessant baying wound its way down from the forest. Her smile lit the hallways as she made her way to the garage to make sure her plan could be brought to fruition.

Lane popped open the door and stepped into the garage. She walked a slow circle around Grandpa Rainier's 1971 Jeep Commando, her smile growing broader with each step.

A window of opportunity would present itself between midnight and dawn for her to slip away without being seen. Patience and a careful watch on the Sheriff's office would pinpoint the exact time. Fortunately, Grandpa Rainier preferred an automatic transmission; had he favored the stick, Lane would have found herself all dressed up with places to go but no way to get there.

Chapter 37 – Jenna Wakes in the Hospital

Barnett sat stoically in a guest chair, feeling too large for it and very uncomfortable in it, like a rhinoceros at a tea party. He flipped through a copy of Newsweek that he had appropriated from the waiting room, and his foot tapped a rhythm with the gentle beeping of the heart monitor. When Jenna finally woke, he spoke over the top of the magazine. "The news is all bad, I'm afraid."

He didn't want to waste any time on this woman. He and Morgan had been fierce rivals, and under other circumstances, he might indeed have liked to bed his brother's wife. But not now. Not anymore. He wasted no pity on her. "You were raped. Five of them have been placed in solitary, but their ringleader seems to provoke serious loyalty. They won't give her up even if it means they get harsher sentences."

Jenna's lips split apart in shock, leaving a dark, cavernous slice across her face. Anguish, or perhaps shame, seeped into her eyes, but Barnett couldn't decide if the emotions Jenna displayed were real or simply her best attempt at real. "They had to transfer you here for the hysterectomy," he said. "The damage was much too severe to be repaired. I suggest you register high on the pain meter whenever the nurses ask so that you can prolong your stay here."

For the distress on her face, Barnett would have expected her to cry, but all Jenna could manage was a solitary tear. He wondered if perhaps that single drop of grief had been the only one to survive all those years of Morgan's sadism for no others followed it.

"I thought you were going to get me out of there." Jenna's words dripped with the venom for which she was known statewide.

"I did. They can't keep you in isolation indefinitely, and you obviously can't be in the general population. The plan didn't quite work as expected, but now that you're out, I've got some options. How does house arrest sound? You'll have to wear an ankle bracelet so the police can monitor your whereabouts. But Morgan had some, shall we say receptive, contacts. I'm sure I can convince them to listen to reason."

"You're enjoying this," Jenna said.

"My dear, I'm looking out for your best interests, which just so happen to be the same as mine. We need to pull in those offshore funds. We need to consolidate them, and use them for a greater good. It might be all well and good to save them for your retirement on the islands, but I think we should consider spending some of it now. Let's just call it an incentive to a sympathetic judge."

"You just want to get your hands on the money."

"Of course I do. And you just want to get out of prison. You make the decision. I can take what I have and leave you in jail if you prefer."

"Get me a piece of paper," she growled. "Unless you want me to carve the number into your forehead."

Chapter 38 – Hiding Out

The Jeep's headlights dimmed to black long before Lane pulled onto Harris Lane and coasted into the driveway of the first house. It had been on the market for as far back as Lane could remember. Morgan had wanted it, and he tried to buy it the first day the sign went in the yard. But bad blood flowed between him and the owner, who summarily refused Morgan's very generous offer. He preferred to pay taxes on an empty house than see it end up in Morgan's greedy hands.

Morgan reciprocated; he called in or bought sufficient favors to prevent the house's sale. Eighteen years and counting. But then Morgan died, and Lane remembered the recoil of the pistol in her hand as she squeezed that trigger ten times, sending her tormenter to an early but well-deserved grave.

All favors fell away, and the house had been shown dozens of times since his death. A bidding war ensued; the bank continued to show the house because all that could possibly do was drive the price higher. A hide-a-key box had been installed on the breezeway door to allow entry to all vetted buyers.

And just about anyone else with a brain. Lane punched in the listing number stamped prominently on the "For Sale" sign, popped the front off the box, and helped herself to the key inside.

A breezeway attached the garage to the house and had been staged with simple patio chairs, but Lane's first order of business required hiding the Jeep. She wasn't sure what would attract more attention—the dark green Jeep with a white cap, or a car being there at all. Securing it inside the garage was the best solution.

With the door closed, casual passersby wouldn't notice the vehicle, though anyone who approached the house would. Not much I can do about that. Maybe they'll just think that's staging, too.

Once she had the vehicle inside the garage and screened from sight, she investigated the rest of the house. The door on the other side of the breezeway opened into the kitchen, which had been neatly orchestrated with a small table that served only to magnify the amount of space. Eight chairs and a table twice that size would easily fit. Big enough for a large family, quaint enough for a small one.

The fridge was plugged in but nearly empty. The realtor had placed a few long-term keepers in there for effect: a bottle of Coke and a box of Fruit Loops for the kiddies, a bottle of red wine for the lady of the house, and a six-pack of Dos Equis beer designed to catch the eye of any guy who wanted to be the next most interesting man in the world.

The glow from the fridge faded away as she closed its door. Lane quickly realized that the light, peeking forth in the middle of the night and illuminating the kitchen, would certainly shine through the windows and shout to the Olsens next door that the house that had been empty for nearly two decades was empty no longer. That would certainly bring their prying eyes. Or even those of the local constabulary. Richard was sure to be bent clean out of shape, and though he'd get over it eventually, there could be little doubt that Lane would spend the rest of this little emergency behind a locked, barred door.

She pulled the shades down over all the windows in the kitchen and parlor, blocking the tattle-tale lights from streaming out through the glass portals. But neither the front nor rear doors had any provision to cover the glass panels built into the wood. She'd have to find a way to block them to prevent any light from escaping.

The living room was longer than it was wide, and the far end held a sixty-inch flat screen TV, properly secured to the wall and definitely appealing to the sports fan in every potential purchaser. That and the leather recliner made this the go-to room for any man visiting this house.

A hallway stretched back from the main living areas, past the bathroom and four small bedrooms, and ended in the master suite, which had its own bath. Lane pulled all shades and drapes along the way to prevent any accidental exposure, and the towels intended to make the lavatory pretty became makeshift curtains, wedged between door and frame to cover the glass panes in the front and rear entrances.

With the building secured, Lane relaxed. The heat was on, just enough to keep the pipes from freezing, but that would certainly keep her from freezing, too. She took a second tour through the house, more slowly this time.

Three of the four smaller bedrooms hadn't been staged at all, left to fend for themselves as possible buyers imagined who or what might fill each of the rooms. The fourth had been staged as an office; a cardboard PC sat on a small desk, and a pair of bookcases sandwiched a large window that looked out onto the fenced-in back yard.

The master suite was fully decked out, though—matching armoires, dressers, and bedside tables, a small sitting area by the front window, a walk-in closet with several suits and dresses hanging from the rod, and a king-size sleigh bed. It may have been the only bed in the house, but it also had bedding that, combined with the heat, would make an overnight here quite cozy.

A few pictures lined one of the dressers, no doubt intended to alert the woman of the house to the home's family qualities. Infants, toddlers, high school graduations, a sharply dressed marine at his boot camp graduation, grandkids playing in the yard…and Old Man Pearce and Mrs. Al sitting on the back porch, surveying their earthly kingdom.

"Well, that certainly explains the bad blood, doesn't it?" Lane set the picture back down and padded quietly to the master bath, pleased that the faucets still produced water, which grew warmer by the second. "Richard is gonna be so pissed."

With her hair wrapped in a towel, Lane headed down to the basement armed only with the box of cereal she'd appropriated from the refrigerator. Munching away on a few of the colorful O's, she eased along the cold, concrete floor. Moonlight cast enough light for her to see that nothing remained in the cellar except the forced hot-air furnace and a washer/dryer set. A ring of small windows lined the walls at the top of the foundation; she'd been smart to leave the lights off.

Twin oil tanks stood along the front wall, no doubt placed there to make fuel deliveries easy. Lane inspected them, finding the fill pipes and the oil level gauges. With one tank full and the other three-quarters full, there was little to worry about in terms of a surprise visit from the oil man. As long as she didn't get careless, she figured she'd have a peaceful night, and hopefully enough time unmolested for Richard to catch whoever was trying to do her in.

Chapter 39 – The Dogs Pick Up Her Scent

After a false reading on the riverbank during which the dogs ran in circles for the better part of ten minutes, the trackers finally picked up a good whiff of Lane's boots about a mile from where she'd left her clothes on the riverbank. They set off at a fast clip, determined and eager to catch their quarry.

Pete had been assigned to dog-duty, partly because of his hard-earned experience on the force, but partly because Creepy Danny made Lane uncomfortable. He thought Danny's inexperience held the blame, making the young deputy push too hard to earn his place in the Sheriff's Department.

A boost to Danny's confidence would most likely curtail some of his stupid antics, and his creepiness, but limited opportunities existed. The Sheriff certainly wouldn't put the kid out in front...not in the near future. Not with the kid's new penchant for saying "S'up." And Pete sure in hell wasn't putting himself on the butt end of Richard's mood without a damn good reason.

Lane's trail clung to the ground, vibrant and thick, and the dogs had no trouble following it, their noise echoing through the morning forest. After a sudden turn that led the group south toward town, Pete stood on the ridge overlooking the church. The dogs bee-lined straight for the house half-way between Pearce's Grocery and the rectory.

Pete thumbed his radio. "Sheriff."

The response came immediately. "Go ahead."

"Send the newbies over to your mother's house."

Richard ran from his office, grabbing Danny and two of the new guys. "Dottie's!"

Danny led the way, running like someone had painted a target on his back and an entire hive of angry hornets were determined to hit it. Richard leaned out the station door for a quick peek, careful not to linger too long in case someone out there had the urge to take a shot at him.

Dottie's garage lay in full view, the door up, and the vintage '71 Jeep gone.

Down in lockup, Richard's footsteps foretold his arrival long before he stood at the bars. Dottie glowered at him. "Let me out."

"No can do. I need not to worry about you while I'm worrying about her."

"I swear to God, Richard, when this is over..." She met him at the bars, letting the threat trail off. "Have you found her?"

"She spent the night at your place."

Dottie sighed, her relief that Lane was currently okay masking her fears as to her granddaughter's future status.

"By any chance, did you ever tell her she could borrow Dad's car?"

Dottie frowned, and Richard knew all he needed to know. Not one prone to emotional displays, Richard nonetheless let himself into the cell and gave her a hug, holding her close as tears streamed down her face. "Where do you think she's gone?" she asked.

He shrugged. "I don't know."

"Do you think she's gotten far by now?"

"I don't think she's running, Mother. I think she's eluding. She outwitted the dogs long enough to get away, and that means she can pretty much stay clear of me indefinitely."

"You found her last time."

"Only because Ray had an idea of where she might be. If he hadn't, or if I hadn't gotten there when I did, she'd have been long gone. Now I've got nothing. She could be anywhere."

Chapter 40 – The Money

Barnett scoured the house, top to bottom, looking everywhere, leaving no cushion unturned, no book unopened. Somewhere in the Harris Mansion, Morgan had hidden his passwords, passcodes, and passbooks, the keys to all the money he had stolen.

Even though he had been unable to convince Jenna to trust him, Barnett had managed to bushwhack her into giving him one account number. After checking with the Swiss Bank Mirabaud & Cie and discovering just fifteen million, he decided to find the rest himself. He knew there was more. Deep in his bones, if he knew his brother at all, he knew there was enough money hiding somewhere to drown in.

For the life of him, he couldn't figure out how Morgan had let his personal affairs get so out of hand. Gunned down by his wife's bastard daughter. His U.S. assets all tied up. The known overseas assets under investigation. But this was Morgan after all—a man who had spent his entire life squandering other people's money—he was too smart to not have funds hidden away from the government. And Barnett still had time to find it before Jenna was released to house arrest.

If he hadn't found it by then, he would just follow her around the mansion, see where she nested, what she took interest in. Sooner or later, he'd catch her with her fingers in the jar, and then he would relieve her of the entire cache of cookies. Best of all, he'd have no further use for her and could discontinue his association with her, preferably utilizing the Jersey Boys already in his employ.

Unfortunately, he hadn't found much of use, hadn't even been able to find codes for the small wall safe in the master suite or the larger one behind that ugly picture of Morgan and Jenna staring down from the wall in Morgan's office. And he had a sneaking suspicion, since they appeared to be the only places he hadn't looked, that one of those safes housed the information he so desperately wanted.

"No matter. Jenna will open them." If not, then Barnett would just call the manufacturer, provide whatever notarized documentation they required, and he'd get into the blasted safes then, even though it wouldn't be as soon as he preferred.

But he had time. Plenty of it. And as soon as the fertile end of the Keates family was wiped out, he'd have plenty of time to gloat, too. The thought of celebrating Lane's death sparked another consideration. "I wonder if the kid knows anything."

Chapter 41 – Skill Set

Richard stared at the neatly folded pile of his own clothes, his chin perched between his thumb and forefinger, his head turned slightly to the side, looking like a bird eyeing a breakfast worm.

Lane had been in the cabin; he and Ray both knew it. She had taken survival gear and the bow. No secrets there. And then she'd taken Richard's clothes to deliberately throw the tracking dogs off her scent.

"I would have bet good money she'd have taken your clothes," Richard stated, tossing a glance at Ray, who leaned against the window sill with his arms folded across his chest, an uncharacteristically closed position for him.

"Have you done any laundry lately? Seems to me I did the grocery shopping and the dishes, but ain't no laundry coming out of the mud room. The only clothes of mine that are clean are my blacks," he said, referring to his priestly garb that had been hanging in his closet, unused, for several months now. "That's probably why you can't get Lane to give you any dirty clothes...because they never come back."

"Yeah, like she doesn't know who walked off with all her baggy jeans. I can't believe she figured out how to elude the dogs."

Ray shrugged but remained quiet, contemplating the situation and focusing all his energy on a spot on the floor.

"That kid's got quite the criminal mindset."

Ray snorted out loud, and his eyes snapped up, refocusing on Richard. "I always thought she had your mindset.

Independent. Analytical. Problem solving. Always trying to stay one step ahead of the situation. I think you're having trouble because it's like trying to catch yourself."

Richard hadn't thought of that. It brought him closer to the desk, creaking forward in his chair and leaning both elbows atop the blotter, his brows furrowing in thought.

"Any word on the car?" Ray asked.

Richard's head shook. "Nothing. Got the whole state watching for her, and that Jeep is too damned hard to miss. That tells me she hasn't left town."

"Well, she's not in town or somebody would have seen her."

"Which means she's holed up somewhere on the fringes." Richard raced from his office, followed closely by Ray, and went straight to the glass-encased tactical map on the wall behind dispatch. Pete joined them there.

Using a black dry-erase marker, Richard crossed off areas where he didn't expect to find Lane hiding. The first line separated the entire peninsula in two parts; above the line was the national forest, and he was pretty sure from her evasive behavior that she hadn't gone back that way.

Below the line sat Mills Valley Township, and he drew a box around it, enclosing everything between Shelton on the east and Humptulips on the west and ranging north/south from the national park to Deckerville. If their premise was right, Lane was hiding somewhere relatively close by.

Ray took the marker and crossed off the church and rectory. "She wouldn't go there with Zavier still in the house. She doesn't trust him at all anymore. Ratting people out puts them on edge." He proceeded to cross off spots in town that would put her in jeopardy of discovery: Pearce's Grocery, the Plaza, Vic's Gas Station, Marigold's Diner, Doc Williams' clinic, and the schools.

Richard popped the cap off another marker and scribbled lines through the neighborhoods behind Main Street. "Too many people. Too much chance of discovery."

He drew an X through another cluster of houses that Ray pointed out. "Danny's folks."

Richard snickered. "And Danny. Living in their basement, from what I hear. Do you know if my per diems are staying in town?"

Ray nodded. "One for sure. Staying in the motel. Heard him complaining about the free coffee."

Richard X'd off the motel, as well, but circled the campground. "I will be so bent if she's broken into my trailer."

"And all the rest of the empties?" Pete asked, with just a bit of innocence infused in his words.

"Yeah, I'll be bent about that, too, not to mention that it'll really screw up her probation. One more reason to get her back in here before she does something else stupid."

Ray pointed to another cluster of houses on a cul-de-sac a mile outside of town. "I think two of these are up for sale. And the old Raeford place." He tapped on the map where a solitary farmstead stood against the foot of the National Park.

Richard exchanged his black marker for a red one, and then circled all three houses. "Who else is for sale, foreclosed, or abandoned?"

"There's some hunting cabins up in here," Ray said, drawing his finger along a dirt road. "A lot of foreclosed houses butt up against the resort land." His finger traced another line along Whistler Road. "This one, this one." He stabbed at little specks on the map. "But these are all too close to town, I think. Too many other people around to see her come and go."

Pete eased in, his hand sliding to the east side of town, stopping on Harris Lane. "That one on the corner's been empty for years."

Ray balked. "I suppose it's possible, but it's awful close to the mansion. And the Olsens."

Richard disagreed. "Jake tells me that he and Lane are "peeps" now. Jason, on the other hand…" Richard's eyes rolled. "Some bad blood there, but he won't even think of trying anything with his old man around."

The brothers and Pete worked their way from one end of the cordoned-off area to the other, circling or crossing off houses or complete neighborhoods, depending on whether the location could or could not be a potential hiding spot for one errant, teenaged probationer. When complete, the map looked like something a three-year-old had taken his crayons to, but the jumble made complete sense to the men who had created it.

"Alright, Pete. Lay out a plan and start checking them out. I'll call Wes and have him put together a list of all the empty campers."

Chapter 42 – Breakfast with the Jersey Boys

Marigold craned to see out the porthole in the kitchen door, studying the two men sipping coffee and gorging on a late morning breakfast in a booth along the front windows.

For the most part, the locals had all come and gone, hitting the diner much earlier so they could have a quick, home-cooked meal before heading off to work or whatever else it was they saw fit to do with their day. Aside from five old-timers who usually took up residence at the end of the counter and spent three hours each day rehashing the previous night's televiewing, the two strangers were the only patrons left.

The body-check mirror hung on the wall inside the kitchen, placed there nearly twenty years ago but used several times daily to make sure the "body" in question looked appealing in case a certain small town Sheriff walked in. Marigold double-checked now, smoothing down her curves, hoisting up her breasts, and fluffing her hair into place. Once satisfied, she popped out of the kitchen, grabbed the coffee pot, and headed over to her newest customers.

Marigold put her best face forward, and the smile that she normally saved for Richard, though he never noticed, graced her lips. The two men moved their cups closer so she could refill them. "So, what brings you boys to town? Come for the hunting or the fishing?"

She watched them as they continued to eat, eyeing each other across the table. When the skinnier of the two looked at her, she felt like she'd walked into the cooler butt-ugly naked and turned into an unwrapped, freezer-burned slab of meat.

149

Finally, the larger fellow set his fork on his plate and graced her with his attention. His dark eyes simmered like pools of hot oil and screamed his displeasure at being interrupted, or perhaps interrogated. She knew she was fishing for information and trying to assist the Sheriff, even if just a little, but she'd done nothing inordinately obvious, nothing she wouldn't have done or said to any other customer, local or transient alike. These two gentlemen couldn't possibly know her intentions; she held her ground.

"Contractors," Angelo grumbled. "Doing a job up to the Harris place."

"So you'll be around a while?" Marigold's eyebrows rose up, doing her best impersonation of Perry Mason.

"Week or so. 'Spect we'll be in here quite a bit. Unless you're gonna wanna play twenty questions every time we walk in the door."

Marigold walked away, taking the coffee pot with her. She could feel the blustery Italian's eyes on her as she filled the cups of the old-timers on the other side of the diner, but she refused to look back, returning instead to the counter where she quickly prepared the bill for her less-than-civil guests. She slapped the check on their table without even thanking them for their patronage.

An hour later, they still hadn't left. They watched and studied, eyeballing everyone who walked in or out, noting cars passing on the street, and occasionally craning around to see further up the road. Maybe they were lost, or maybe they were looking for someone. Or maybe their employer simply expected them to be working, unaware that they were padding hours on the bill. Of course, it was just as possible that they were lying about their business in town.

She headed back over. "Anything else I can get for you gents?" The icy feeling rose up her skin again when the skinny one looked at her; he shook his head in reply.

150

Angelo grumbled some more. "No. Just leaving." He dropped two twenties on the table and headed out. Creepy guy stared at her for another few seconds before following the bigger ape. Something in his eyes suggested that she maybe shouldn't have charged them at all for their meals; maybe she should have given them a freebie just to get them to leave.

Jack caught up with Angelo at the car. "What do you say? Snag that one to replace the bimbette?"

Angelo's sneer said more than his words could. "You kidding?"

"Nah, she'll do. Not like she's gotta be a looker to end up dead."

"I pick 'em because how they look is important to me. Perv that you are, you just want to ride them to death, but me, I want to wipe that smug "I'm better'n you" look right off their hoity-toity faces. Somebody already beat me to that one."

Jack shrugged. "Well, find one soon, okay? I'm working up a powerful desire."

"Bimbette's still breathing."

"Which pretty much makes her uninteresting for me...unless you're getting tired of her?" Jack's eyes sparkled with a glimmer of hope.

"Relax, psycho. I'm just about done with her. Take your time with her though, because once it's done you should probably lay low 'til we find that kid." He pulled Lane's picture from the folio Barnett had given them. "Ain't nothing in those eyes saying she deserves it. Sorta looks like whatever Harris' brother did to her pretty much wiped out any possibility that she'd end up like her mother. But we gotta job to do, so might as well take our pleasure in it."

The engine roared to life, and Angelo pushed aside a picture of Ray. "A priest...nothing there at all. But this one." He flipped the picture of Richard at Jack. "This one could use some bringing down...I bet some of that's his job. But I tell you," he said, and pulled one final picture from the folder. "I wouldn't mind having a go at this one. The kid's mother. That woman's screaming for a come-down party. Maybe when Barnett gets her out of jail. Something tells me Harris won't be interested in keeping her around if he finds the money without her."

Chapter 43 – Open Channel

Bright and early the next morning, Pete was on the trail of empty houses again, driving through town with Bailey riding shotgun for him. Pete didn't dislike the guy exactly, but he didn't really like him, either. Bailey had a bit of an attitude, the sort of bravado that said "I'm from the big city, and I'm here to help you, country boy."

Pete kept their conversations to a minimum, constantly steering Bailey back to business rather than letting him pry into Pete's private life. "Are you married? How long? Kids? Lived here your whole life?" The sort of questions a new partner might ask, and Pete simply refused to think of this man as his new partner.

The guy was in the middle of a diatribe about his exploits on his high school football team, the games he'd single-handedly won, and the girls he'd scored. Pete rolled his eyes and grabbed the mic from its holder. "Hey, Danny. Come back." The crackle of static didn't stop his rider from explaining how simple women were.

"Go 'head, Pete."

"Where you at, Junior? I'm gonna put you to work today. No more sitting behind a desk answering phones."

"Well, unfortunately, Sheriff's got me sitting behind the desk answering phones right now."

"Hike your gun up, boy. I'm heading out to Raeford's to check it out. Be there a while checking the outbuildings and all. Why don't you head on over to Harris Lane. Check out that empty house on the corner. Then swing by the Olsens and see if they've seen anything."

"Got it. When the new guy gets back with the Sheriff's coffee, I'll head over. Want me to swing by the mansion? Marigold says she doesn't trust the two guys working up there."

"Might as well. Marigold's as good a barometer as any other. Take somebody with you, though. No solos until we get this resolved."

Lane gathered up her meager possessions, including the radio that had just announced that Creepy Danny was on his way to her location. Setting the house straight involved a quick run-through, putting the empty box of cereal back in the fridge, making the bed, opening blinds and drapes, and folding towels she'd used. Minutes later she bolted through the breezeway and into the garage, thumbing the garage door opener so she could move the Jeep into the driveway.

She yanked on the overhead door, giving it a pull and letting its weight and gravity handle the rest. It slammed shut, rattling the windows in their casings. With one final check for obvious evidence, she locked the breezeway door and restored the key to its hide-a-box, then jumped in the Jeep and sped away, heading toward Shelton to avoid running into Danny coming out of Mills Valley.

She slowed down and pulled a big U-turn in the street coming to rest in the pull-off she and Ray had so often used, the same pull-off in which Morgan had attacked and raped her.

A shudder swept through her body, and once the stick shift was in park she leaned over and slammed her hand on the passenger door lock. The one on the driver's door got the elbow treatment, but with both doors locked, she felt a little more comfortable. It didn't keep her eyes from shooting back and forth, nor from becoming close friends with the rearview mirror.

She put the car back in gear in case she needed to make a quick getaway, but she knew there was no way to evade Danny in his cruiser. She couldn't hope to drive fast enough or well enough to get away from him.

Her head bopped back and forth between her shoulders. "But if you come outta those woods, baby, I am gone." She jabbed a finger in the direction of the mansion, then hooked her thumb over her shoulder for emphasis.

From her vantage point, she couldn't see the road from town nor Danny turning onto Harris Lane, but with her confiscated radio, she did at least have a clue. The radio crackled to life, and Danny's voice squawked from the box. "We're at One Harris. Investigating the empty house."

Finding nothing suspicious at the empty house, Danny strolled across the yard to the Olsen place. Jason answered the door. "Hey, Dad!" the young man called into the house.

The deputy nodded to the young man, a strapping example of virility with the sort of physique Danny probably should have worked harder to build. Jake strolled up, towering over his son and blocking out the door. "Been listening to the scanner. I wondered when you'd get up here."

Danny acknowledged the man with a tip of his head. "Mr. Olsen. Just wondering if you've seen anything out of the ordinary in the past day or two. Maybe somebody sneaking in next door."

"Kinda funny how that girl give y'all the slip again."

Danny smiled. "Sheriff don't think so. He's hopping mad. Sorta thinking he's wanting to take a switch to her butt."

155

Jake laughed. "Somebody oughta. But it won't be Richard, that's for sure. So you're thinking she's hiding next door here?"

"She's driving Sheriff Rainier's old Jeep. Not in the garage now, but doesn't mean it wasn't, or that it won't be. Appreciate it if you'd keep an eye out, and give us a call if you see her."

"Sure thing. You want I should catch her for you?" Jake's tone suggested he was mocking the police force.

Danny rose to the bait. "Hey, if you think you can, go for it."

Chapter 44 – Danny Meets Barnett

The door of the Harris mansion swung open with slow deliberation, and Barnett stepped into view. Danny nodded greeting to the man whose physical stature was at least as intimidating as Morgan's, perhaps more so. "Good morning, Mr. Harris. I'd like to talk with you if you can spare a few minutes."

Barnett swept his hand through the doorway, gesturing the two officers inside. "Certainly. Please, the office is right over here." Danny remembered it, a quick look around revealing that it hadn't changed since the last time he'd been there. Barnett motioned to the chairs in front of the desk, but both officers remained standing. "How can I help?" he said, relaxing into the well-padded desk chair.

"We're wondering if you've seen anything suspicious in the last day or so— a girl, a strange car. Maybe more than one strange car."

Barnett's fingers splayed open and steepled before him. "I've got a couple of contractors doing some work for me here at the house. In fact, they should be arriving any time now. You're welcome to speak with them, of course."

"Thank you. And her?" Danny showed him a picture of Lane taken by her grandmother right after her release from jail.

"Not recently, except for her picture in the paper. Terrible thing. I didn't know Morgan had that kind of anger. I suspect no one did. He was several years older than me, so I didn't really know him. But I must say she looks like she's doing quite well."

The doorbell rang; seconds later Camilla showed two men into the office. She refused to make eye contact, keeping her eyes focused on the floor. She didn't wait to see if Barnett even wanted the newcomers; she swept them into the room and departed without a word.

Barnett motioned them in. "Gentlemen. Please. Join us. These deputies are investigating, I believe, the disappearance of a local girl."

"Geez, dat's too bad. Skinny little thing, ain't she? She get kidnapped or run off?" Angelo said, studying the picture of Lane as if he had never seen her before.

Danny recognized the accent as east coast, Jersey or New York most likely, but he skillfully evaded answering questions put to him and focused on obtaining information from the only strangers in Mills Valley. "When did you arrive in town?"

"Yesterday," Jack offered. "We swung by that diner in town to get some breakfast this morning. Daisy? Maisy?"

"Marigold's." Danny jotted notes in his pad.

"Yeah. Pretty good food. The waitress is kinda nosey, huh?"

"I'm sure she's just trying to help us out. How long will you be in town?"

"Three, four days. Maybe a week. Really don't expect it to take very long."

"What's the nature of your business?" Danny made an open-handed gesture designed to entice the two men to relax and be straightforward with their answers.

"We're security consultants. Mr. Harris is concerned that the house may not be as safe as it could be."

"You staying here while you do the work?"

"Shelton. Little place right off the highway." Angelo dug around in his wallet and found the receipt. "Here it is."

Danny read it over, jotting down the pertinent facts before returning it. "Thank you for your cooperation. If you should see her, please be sure to give us a call," he said, handing out his business cards.

Chapter 45 – Professionals

Richard leaned against the doorjamb of his office, arms folded across his chest. The vantage point allowed him to see a great deal of the goings-on in the station, but he focused on Ray, sitting alone in Interrogation Room One with his elbows perched on the table top and his fingers pressing deep into his skull.

Richard didn't have to be Sheriff to know that Ray's problem right now hinged on one particular teenager who for the life of her, didn't seem to want to take orders from anyone. He pushed off the door frame and joined Ray in Room One, dropping into an empty chair. "Any ideas?"

Ray looked up. "It's enough to make you bleed out the eyes."

"Do you mean that spiritually or literally?"

The question brought a weak smile to Ray's face, but did little to lighten his mood. "Her intentions really don't count here, do they?" Richard's head waggled back and forth, but he declined to actually speak. "I know she thinks she's helping. And I almost believe she might be right." Ray looked up to find his younger brother staring at him with a look of amused benevolence on his face. And Ray nearly hated it. "Don't."

Richard's hand twirled in the air. "There's a "but" in there somewhere. I heard it."

"But these guys are professionals. And the best person to deal with this is also a professional. If she were any other kid, this wouldn't even be an issue."

"We'll find her. I just need to get through to her. Any suggestions?"

"Try remembering she's not a child. She's done more, and had more done to her, than probably ninety percent of other kids her age."

"That sounds more like a parenting lesson. As far as that goes, I figured I'd just do what you do."

Ray shook his head. "You can't become a cheap imitation of me. Well, ok, maybe not cheap. Still a copout. She'd recognize that as you trying to win her over by being me. That won't get you anywhere."

"You've had what, twelve years to get to know her and develop a relationship with her? I haven't. I'm doing this by the seat of my pants."

"Most parents do."

"Please don't psych me."

Ray smiled and pulled himself out of the chair. "What would Dad do?"

Richard balked. "Dad? Considering that she's an awful lot like you, Dad would tan her hide."

Ray's smile grew deeper. "Yeah, probably. But I'm really talking after that." And he left the room.

Richard pondered it a while, thinking about his father. He had always thought his Dad ran a tight line between authoritarian and benevolent protector.

Rainy had been Sheriff in his time, a ramrod-straight man who never wielded his power unduly but never took guff from any man. He offered wisdom and counseling as easily as he turned the key on a cell. And he'd been killed in the line of duty.

Richard's intention had always been to follow in his father's footsteps, and he did his best to emulate the man in everything that he did. Rainier was a king among men, a quiet, powerful, respected example of the heights to which a single human being could rise.

He'd seen his father angry any number of times. Mostly he was angry with Ray; Richard had made it his life's goal not to run afoul of Dad's mood, and he avoided the authoritarian by walking the straight and narrow path. But Ray had been a classic teenaged boy; underage drinking, sneaking into movie theaters, even getting caught playing doctor with, of all people, a Deputy's daughter.

Dad's anger often found its way out in spewed words. Ray had always been duly apologetic, but it never stopped him from getting into as much trouble as he could find.

Dad had never actually yelled at Richard. But that one time Richard followed Ray into the movie theater, Dad had been so disappointed that Richard never got over the look on his father's face. He chuckled out loud, wondering what Dad might have thought about Lane. He'd probably speculate on how she got to be so much like Ray, but that was an easy question to answer: Ray had been her mentor.

Now it was up to Richard to be her father. Ray had stepped in when the kid had no one else to whom she could turn, and Ray's counsel didn't need to be modified—he had done a fine job with the little he had. Richard had to take over, carry on, and be the force in her life that guided her toward maturity. Like his father had been for him. If ever there was a moment that Richard needed to be Rainier, this was it.

He pulled his radio from his belt and thumbed it alive. "Lane. I know you're listening, but I don't want you to respond. Just listen."

Chapter 46 – Just Listen

Lane pulled the radio closer and listened intently as her father spoke.

His voice was calm. Alarmingly so. And softer than she'd ever heard it. Soothing, almost. But it maintained its firm authority.

"We've got us a bit of a problem here, don't we? I want you to take directions, but you've sort of outgrown the "I need a parent" stage of your life."

He sounded tired over the radio, worn out. Lane nestled the radio against her belly and stared at it, as if she were conversing with him face-to-face. This was actually easier for her than a personal conversation, because she didn't have to look at him, didn't have to seen the pain or pity dripping from his eyes.

"I'd like to say this will all just change overnight, and we'll both wake up tomorrow different people. But we both know that's not true. Time got us to these places we find ourselves in now. Only time and determination will get us out and get us to a point where we can deal with each other…on common ground."

His words held more than a bit of truth. Lane had been fighting to survive since as far back as she could remember, discarded by her mother and Morgan as unnecessary baggage. She couldn't help but wonder if Jenna's treatment of Richard had turned him in on himself, as well. After all, she'd discarded Richard, too, just not as brutally as she'd tossed Lane away.

"I'm going to make a conscious effort not to expect more than you are able to give. I know you and Ray have a special bond." His voice cracked a little, and he cleared his throat. "And

I know I haven't earned that. But I am willing to try. Doesn't mean I don't expect you to clean your room."

A sheepish grin twisted Lane's mouth up on one side.

"But we've got time to work on all that. Right now, you're in danger." The grin fell from her face, but he moved smoothly into a rebuttal, as if he'd been expecting a retort. "You think you've done the smartest thing, keeping away from us to throw a wrench in their plans. But these guys are professionals. Sooner or later, they'll just kill whoever they find wherever they find 'em. And if they find you first, and there's no one there to help you," his voice cracked again, and the radio went silent for a moment.

"We both know your uncle and grandmother will be devastated. What you don't know is that so will I." A tear brimmed in Lane's eye and trickled down her face. "I'd like to think you'd come in now, the whole safety in numbers thing. But just in case you don't, I'm going to give you some advice. Walk away from Grandpa Rainy's car. It sticks out like a sore thumb. And we're going radio silent. We're not sending out any more open air communications. That just serves to give both you and the shooters a heads-up as to where we are and what we're doing."

He cleared his throat again, and she could barely make out the scratchy sound of his hand rubbing across his chin. "If you need me, go to the nearest occupied house and ask them to call me on a landline. Stay out of sight. And please...don't do anything to screw up your probation."

His voice changed, and she pictured him throwing his shoulders back, squaring them off and drawing himself to his fully intimidating height. "It may not seem like it at times, but I do love you. More and more every day."

163

Chapter 47 – Others Are
Listening, Too

Jack squealed with glee. "Oh, that was just beautiful. I've got a tear in my eye."

Angelo glowered out the car window, fixing his stare on the streets of this pissy little community. "Ain't funny."

Jack pulled back in surprise. "Of course it is. What's the matter with you?"

"They've wised up. You didn't hear him because you were too busy laughing. Radio silent. They ain't broadcasting their plans anymore."

"Don't matter."

Angelo's scowl grew deeper. "Really?"

"I got it all figured out. Let's just wait 'til dark."

Soul searching was the kind of thing that priests were good at. And since he had been unable to sleep the last few days anyway, what with someone trying to kill his niece and her vanishing into the wind again, he sat in front of the TV blindly watching whatever drivel was on.

Out in the squad room, Bailey kept guard with his feet propped up on the desk and the newspaper spread open in front of his face. Nyugen was making the rounds through town, looking for suspicious activity. Pete, Danny, and the other two borrowed officers had gone home for a few hours' sleep shortly after Marigold delivered supper for the staff and guests trapped in the building overnight.

Richard was downstairs with their mother, spending some time with her to ease the terms of her confinement. No doubt, Ray mused, he's getting an earful. He decided to take a stroll through the office, giving his itinerary to the on-duty officer.

"Yeah, just don't crawl out the window like the kid did."

Ray drifted down the hall to the restroom. The door swung closed behind him, sealing him off from the station, the glare of the TV, and the callousness of the jackass on duty who had earned the nickname, "Officer Insensitivity".

He took his time, relishing a few minutes of solitude without input from anything or anyone. He lingered, splashing water on his face, scruffing a hand through his thinning hair, and staring at his own beleaguered features. The lines on his face seemed deeper these days, and the tightness in his chest reminded him of the heartache he'd endured after Lane's attack and disappearance the prior year.

This time was different, though. This time she'd voluntarily left, and for a split second he felt better about her departure. But he couldn't think about her flight without thinking of the reason for it: hired killers were after her and the rest of the Keates clan. "She'll be okay. She's smart. She'll stay safe." Ray's head bobbed up and down, assuring his mirror image that he was absolutely correct, but his eyes rose heavenward. "Please keep her safe."

With a deep breath of composure, he headed back to Room One, casually glancing toward dispatch to find the newbie waving him over, the phone clutched in one hand. "Yeah, I'll get him." He called to Ray. "It's some priest looking for you."

Ray hustled over and scooped the phone away, hoping Zavier had some good news for him. "Zavier, you find her?"

There was an odd pause on the other end of the line before a gruff voice spoke, not Zavier's at all. "If you ever want to see her again, you'll keep quiet and do as you're told." Immediately, the hackles on the back of Ray's neck rose and his legs grew heavy with fear. "I see that you're taking me seriously. Good. Treat this call as if this Zavier dude were really on the phone with you."

"Okay." Ray nodded.

"You need to find a way out of that building. You've got ten minutes before we leave here without you. And if we do, she'll pay for it. Now say thank you as if you mean it."

Ray continued nodding. "Thank you." If it hadn't been for a tiny crackling of fear, it might have sounded sincere.

"Now say goodbye and figure out how you're getting out of there without attracting attention." The caller hung up.

"Goodbye." Ray dropped the receiver onto its cradle.

"Good news?" Officer Insensitivity asked.

"Not really." Ray stood motionless, head reeling and fear choking out logic. For a moment, he thought he might actually retch right there on Officer Insensitivity's newspaper.

"You ain't looking so good. Who was on the phone?"

Ray waved him off. "Zavier didn't find her." His hand moved up to his stomach. "Not feeling so good." Ray returned to the lavatory, knowing his only way out right now was to follow his niece out the window.

Chapter 49 – The Pick Up

A Ford SUV drove up and a lanky man jumped from the vehicle as it pulled to the curb. Ray affirmed to himself that he'd give his life for his niece and strode toward his destiny, meeting the man at the sidewalk. "You're here to kill me." He spoke with a calm finality that spoke of faith and resignation rather than fear.

"Eventually," the man said, drawing the rear door open wide and waving Ray into the backseat with a chauffeur-like sweep of his hand. As Ray bent forward to get in, a whack to the back of his head sent him sprawling into the vehicle, and the man jumped in behind him, pushing Ray's legs out of the way.

Pain throbbed at the base of Ray's skull, dragging him close to unconsciousness. His captor zip-stripped him into submission, binding the priest like a steer at both the wrists and ankles. Ray gagged on the cloth forced into his mouth, but he could do nothing to prevent it.

Blurry images greeted Ray when he managed to squint his eyes open, and he watched the thin man squeeze himself between the bucket seats and joined the driver in the front. The man twisted back, and Ray tried to get a good look at him, but the man grabbed him by the shirt, dragged him off the seat, and forced him onto the floor.

Ray had only conjecture and dialog to fill in the missing blanks. The car pulled away from the curb slowly. The driver, a heavier set man, was apparently trying not to attract any attention. No doubt getting a ticket now would stymie the duo's brewing plans for multiple executions.

"So, Einstein, where do you want to take him?" Ray didn't recognize the driver's voice. Despite capturing one of the Keates family, the man didn't sound at all pleased.

"I don't know what your problem is. We got one, didn't we? Just two more to go. And maybe we can use him to bring the others to us. Just go park at the gas station for now. We don't want to be the only car on the road when they figure out he's gone missing, too."

Chapter 50 – Fury and Flurry

Richard paced the room like a caged lion, but most of his anger churned around his stomach, turning inward at himself. The evidence spread before him like the newspaper on the desk—Bailey hadn't been paying full attention to his job.

But Richard had been the one who left per diem officer alone. Richard had been the one who spent the last hour socializing in the cell block. And Richard knew full well to whom the largest share of the blame truly belonged.

"Again? You let two protectees climb out the freakin' bathroom window? Maybe I should bring my mother up here so she can try it, too," he bellowed.

Richard had called Dan, Pete, and the other three officers back to the station house. He put together a game plan on the fly, one designed to protect the one person he still had in protective custody as well as find the two he'd lost when Bailey chose the daily news over his duties.

"Danny, I know this is gonna burn you, but you're grounded to this station twenty-four/seven until this is resolved." Richard tossed the young deputy the keys to the kingdom, including the gun cabinet. "Get yourself a shotgun and plenty of shells, and then take up residence in the cellblock. Afford my mother as much privacy as you can, but if anybody gets by us, and I do mean anybody, I expect you to hang their hide on the wall."

He handed Danny a fresh radio off the charger rack. "Grab a couple vests, and make sure she puts one on. I'll send someone down to spell you so you can get some sleep later. And I'll put Marigold on lockdown duty."

Danny was still technically their rookie, but he knew his weaponry. He snatched the semi-auto eight rounder and two boxes of shells. "Have her send the coffee ASAP." But Danny snickered as his eyes danced in Pete's direction. "When she has time, of course. She'll probably want to make sure you're okay first."

Richard's brow descended toward the bridge of his nose, and his gaze shifted between his two deputies. Pete's lips cracked apart, the closest thing to shock that Richard had ever seen on the senior deputy's face.

Danny persisted. "You should probably just ask her out on a date. Not like the whole town doesn't know she's got the hots for you."

If it hadn't been that Richard needed all hands on deck during the crisis, he might well have unleashed his anger at the young man playing matchmaker, perhaps suspending him for a day or two to remind him who the boss was. He needn't have worried about anything so subtle. Pete reached out and gave Danny a whack in the head.

The impact had the desired effect...Danny's mouth shut. As he slipped quietly down to lock up, Richard turned his attention to the rest of the squad. "Pete, anybody seen the Jeep?"

"Not a soul," Pete said, zipping up his bullet-proof vest and sliding on his leather gloves to keep his hands from sweating during what was expected to be a long night. "Plenty of places to hide it, though."

Richard nodded. "Take two of the guys out with you. Sweep the north side of town for hiding places. Behind houses, in barns, access roads, hunting cabins. Flush out whoever doesn't belong there."

"What if she's not out there?" Eckert asked.

171

"She's not the only one you're looking for. You just might spook the shooters. If no one budges, just keep sweeping back toward town. If we're lucky, we'll find that Jeep."

Pete interrupted, just a speck of confusion escaping with his voice. "She won't be with it."

"True…if she listened to me. And if she did ditch that beast, there will be one helluva trail what with her dragging that bad leg behind her."

"She still got that bow?" Officer Insensitivity piped up.

"Your job is to find her, spook her, drive her downtown. Don't try to apprehend her unless you can do it without a battle."

"So she does still have the bow."

Richard whirled and stood toe-to-toe with him, daring him to butt in again. "She isn't the criminal we're after, so an arrow better be zipping by your head before you even think of unsnapping that firearm again." A short-lived staring match ensued; Richard won.

Pete inspected his firearm, making absolutely no attempt to hide the smirk carving his face. But he did step closer to Richard, lowering his voice. "Thinking I should take three guys and two cars…make a bigger display. You keep Eckert here with you, and I'll get the dimwit out of your hair for a while." His chin inched toward the man responsible for the loss of two Keateses.

Richard agreed. "We'll lock down the station, and then I'll call the State Police. But announce yourselves when you get back so I don't want to shoot you."

Pete smiled. "Radio?"

"Silent unless absolutely necessary. Let her see your lights but not hear you. That'll unnerve her because she won't know what you're up to."

Chapter 51 – The Plan is in Motion

Angelo had parked the rental car among the used vehicles for sale at Vic's, though he suspected that at least two of the beaters were destined for the repair bays.

Now he and Jack watched and waited. Hunkered down so that their heads barely extended above the dashboard, they didn't have to kill very much time before two cruisers, lights flashing through the darkness, sped down Main and turned north on Mill Road.

"That seems pretty pointed. You think they found her?" Jack wondered.

"I think they're looking…her, him…" He hooked a thumb over his shoulder. "Or us. Of course, they don't really know it's us, per se. They're probably looking for those three yokels who hit the cabin. But if they should trip over her and get her back into custody, we're back to square one."

"Well, it'll certainly be easier for us if they don't find her, but we still got the priest. And according to dear old dad, Uncle Ray here is special. We ought to be able to use him for something." Jack couldn't help but let out a giggle of excitement.

"Better be, 'cause this whole gig looks like it's going south. I knew we should have just taken them out from a distance. That woman's worked up one powerful vendetta to risk it all just to see this go down her way."

It took several cold hours for the cruisers to make their way back downtown, and Angelo had been forced to leave his car window open so the breath of three people hiding in a single car didn't condense on the windshield. Once the deputies parked and the officers disappeared inside the station, Angelo fired up the car and headed into the forest.

He drove slowly, as if he had no particular place to go, out past the plaza and the campground. When no further houses were in sight, he turned off the road and dragged Ray from the car.

Chapter 52 – Ray Doesn't Yield

Blood dripped down Ray's face, some of it soaking into his clothes, the rest spattering into the dirt. The stinging on the bridge of his nose suggested a gash, perhaps from broken cartilage. A break would certainly explain the congestion and his inability to breathe normally. He gulped air through his mouth, cradling the ribs that his adversaries had worked so hard to crack.

"Done turning the other cheek, Father?" Angelo heckled.

Muscles rippled under his clothing, reminding Ray that Angelo was more than capable of beating him into submission. But the massive paw spun casual revolutions in the air, suggesting that Angelo preferred actually fighting, exchanging blows and testing his mettle against another man to determine which of them was the superior force. Ray rested on his knees, wondering what about his performance so far had been misconstrued as fighting ability.

Angelo dragged the priest back up to his feet, and Ray's midsection screamed its displeasure long before the next punch. When it did finally hit, pain seared along his ribcage, stabbed into his lung, and sent him back to the ground.

"Just want to know where she lives, Father."

"You lied to me," Ray wheezed, spitting blood.

"You shouldn't be in such a hurry to die, but I'll say an extra Hail Mary," Angelo said. "Where does she live?"

Ray refused to divulge the information. Angelo pulled the priest back to his feet and wound up for another punch.

Chapter 53 – Disposing of Multiple Problems

Angelo and Jack had been partners for quite some time; they knew each other's preferences and idiosyncrasies, though the rest of the world may well have called them peculiarities. They had refined the art of secrecy that kept them in business, free to come and go and do whatever they pleased.

Just after the Port Angeles Marina opened for the day, the Ford SUV pulled into the parking lot, and Jack sought out the dock master. He returned quickly with the keys to their private charter.

Angelo dragged Ray from the vehicle and swung open the cargo door, revealing four bulging duffle bags, the kind that would easily fit underneath airline seats. He grabbed two of the sacks and carried them down to the appointed slip. Jack slammed one bag against Ray's chest.

Barely able to stand on his own, Ray wrapped both hands around the handle of the tote, perching it against his hip as he struggled to follow Angelo. Jack took the final bag himself and brought up the rear as he kept an eye out for witnesses, cops, or other issues that might put an end to the day's plans.

When they arrived at their boat, the rest of the charter party was already waiting. Jack introduced himself by first name only, then introduced Angelo. "And this would be one of the Keateses you were having so much trouble with." His hand swung in an arc toward the beaten priest.

The three newcomers to the party maintained a wary and aloof distance. Jack smiled at them, then at his partner who stowed the duffles near the stern rail and came back for the priest. Angelo, however, focused on the work, tying Ray to the stairs that led to the pilot house before climbing up to the wheel to prepare for departure.

"Coming? We got work to do." Jack untied the vessel, spurring the three men to hop the rail. He offered his guests a beer and watched the dock shrink away as Angelo piloted the boat out into open water.

Chapter 54 – In Deep Water

The vessel idled down to a loud purr before the engine cut off completely. The boat bounced around on the waves, riding the swells and drifting with the currents, with no particular direction, goal, or deadline.

Angelo descended the stairs to the deck and took up a flanking position that kept him out of Jack's line of fire but easily capable of backing up his partner.

The names of the three men held no importance for him. Jack had called one of them "Lee", and one of the losers had come right from work wearing a uniform emblazoned with his name—Frank. But the other guy could have been President of the United States for all Angelo knew or cared.

Jack popped the top off another beer, tipped it back, and then directed a fairly general question into the air, making it free game for whoever chose to answer. "So, what went wrong?" Waves lapped at the boat, and the flag whipped at attention in the wind, but otherwise, there was precious little noise at all.

Reaching under his bench, Jack pulled out the cases, and slowly zipped one open. He took his time pulling the ends apart, peering inside, looking at the three men and gauging their emotions. They seemed a little edgy, nervously sucking off the longnecks while trying to look cool and casual.

Jack reached into one bag, prolonging the suspense as long as possible. His hand twirled around something and then eased out of the bag, withdrawing the severed head of a dark-haired young woman, her face badly contused, her eyes wide open. One of her pretty blue contacts had come dislodged during the fracas that killed her, leaving her with mismatched irises—one eye bright blue and the other brown.

Ray hurled on the deck. The no-name guy made it to the rail before tossing his lunch. Retching noises escaped Frank, but no substance issued forth. He backed away, his forearm covering his mouth. Lee struggled to remain calm, his eyes narrowing on Jack, focusing on the man without acknowledging his apparent handiwork.

Jack set the head on the bench next to him, addressing the girl as if she was still alive. "Sit tight, babe." He withdrew another body part from the bag, a delicate, thin-fingered hand with chipped and broken nails, thrusting it in Lee's direction. "Gimme a hand, will you, Lee?"

Ray vomited again. Frank refused to look, neither at Ray nor Jack. No-Name had yet to return from the rail, so what he was doing was anybody's guess.

Jack tossed the appendage over the rail. It slid beneath the waves and sank quickly. "Snack time, fellas," he said, taking the bag to the rail and dumping the contents into the water. He turned back to Lee. "So, what was it that went wrong?"

Lee remained stoic, but he did at least speak. From the color of his skin, Angelo decided that Lee's stomach had moved closer to his throat, but he did a good job keeping it from jumping clean out of his body. "They were ready for us."

Angelo leaned against the rail, resting the bulk of his weight on one elbow, his legs crossed at the ankle. His casual demeanor downplayed the coming violence. "How's that possible?"

Lee shrugged. "Couldn't tell you. We got in, popped the girl, or at least we thought we had. Went upstairs to get the brothers, and that's when we figured out they weren't there."

"Why did you go in if they weren't there?"

Lee's hands splayed open in frustration. "They were there. We saw them go in. They had supper, watched TV, did some

179

laundry, and they went to bed. All three of them. But before we got in, they figured it out. Nobody was in bed. They slipped out while we were upstairs."

"Gotta wonder why you weren't watching better," Angelo ventured aloud.

"Didn't expect them to split."

Jack dumped another duffle of body parts into the water, emptying the contents before releasing the bag. "I thought you guys knew the Sheriff."

"Yeah, we do. But sometimes the unexpected just happens."

"You're absolutely right about that." Jack drew his gun and popped off a single round, nailing Frank in the head and spinning him over the rail. The swells enveloped him quickly, swallowing him into the depths. Ray hollered, trying to rise but getting nowhere, sliding on the deck in his own vomit.

Lee reacted instantly, reaching for his gun. Angelo clocked him in the back of the head, sending him sprawling, and Jack relieved him of the weapon.

No-Name inched along the rail, heading for the bow. Angelo stalked after him, lifted him bodily, and heaved him off the ship. The waves washed him further away with each undulation.

Ray screamed, his voice going hoarse as he pulled against his bonds and struggled to get free. No-Name hollered for a minute, slapping futilely at the millions of square miles of water until he spent all his energy and slipped beneath the waves.

Angelo caught sight of a couple of fins. Perhaps No-Name had help descending into the abyss. He pointed a finger at Ray. "Don't be in such a hurry to join him, Father."

Another duffle of body parts ended up in the drink, and Lee scuttled across the deck to the rail. Off the edge beyond him, more fins signaled the "fellas" were grouping en masse.

With just one duffle left, Angelo knew he had to get busy. He gave his handgun to Jack, stripped off his jacket, and motioned for Lee to join him center deck. "You win, you live. It's that simple."

Of course, Angelo thought, it's not true. If you're lucky enough to punch my ticket, Jack'll just feed us both to the sharks. "I, for one, ain't looking forward to swimming with the fishies today."

Chapter 55 – It Is Done

Jack dumped a pail of water on the deck and tossed the bucket back into the sea for more. Angelo push-broomed blood, vomit, and bits of flesh to the stern and swept them out through the sea gate. Another bucket of water splashed onto the deck, making the sweeping that much easier.

Lee sprawled on the planking in a pile of chum, his face badly swollen, his hands raw from fighting for his life. "What do you want? I can pay it." His voice barely reached Angelo over the sound of the broom's bristles scraping against wood.

Jack just laughed. "I heard you're on the brink of losing your house. Not that it matters. Money's not an issue. We've got plenty of that."

"Please. There must be something you want?" Lee implored.

"We want you to help us catch some sharks," Angelo said.

Lee knew where this was headed. He tried to rise, pushing himself up despite badly bruised ribs. Angelo's big foot kept him down.

Jack tossed over a rope, and Angelo quickly and efficiently tied a line around Lee's body and up under his arms. He placed the slack in Lee's hands. "Hang on tight, now."

Jack tied the free end to the rail using a knot that he had learned during one of their many outings. Angelo two-fisted Lee from the deck, hauled him to his feet, and pushed him off the boat.

Lee clutched the line and tried to draw himself back to the vessel, but Angelo had already climbed up to the wheel and engaged the motors. The boat headed back toward shore, the wake slapping at Lee and making it even harder for him to claw his way back to safety.

Jack called over the railing. "We call this "trolling for sharks". Catch us some big ones, now, ya hear?" He needn't have reminded Lee of the predicament he was in. The first hit flipped him over in the water, and his scream rose above the sounds of the engine.

Ray cried, slapping against Angelo's bulky arms as the big Italian untied him and hoisted him upright in a single smooth move. The first punch sent him back to the deck.

"So, now you know how bad it can be. You also know that we're capable of getting the job done. But I'll make you a deal," Angelo offered. "Tell me what I want to know, and we'll just kill you simple. Nothing like this. No pain. No suffering."

Another scream from Lee drew Ray's attention. He struggled to the rail and tried to haul the helpless man back to the boat. The rope burned the skin from Ray's hands as a shark grabbed Lee and pulled him under.

Ray's mind tore into three factions. Two of those factions now screamed for control, one yelling to yield while the other lamented that doing so was tantamount to treason. The third sliver at the rear of his brain remained silent.

The priest dove inside that tiny piece of gray matter, wrapped it around himself, and bathed in the glowing, soothing calm he found there. And in the midst of pain and turmoil, God suggested he surrender.

Angelo's meaty right hand clamped onto Ray's shoulder and spun him around to face the other paw, already drawn tight into a bone-crushing sledgehammer ready to shovel-hook the priest's ribs once again.

Ray's hands rose, slowly, his brain not quite accepting the defeat but completely aware that his body couldn't take any more abuse. "Fourth street after the campground."

Angelo smiled. "Could have saved yourself a ton of trouble," he said, then delivered the bone-crusher despite Ray's compliance.

Ray lay on the deck, his eyes squeezed tight against the pain. He barely had the strength to breathe, let alone speak. "Why was it so important?"

"Because everybody always tries to get home. It's just a matter of time."

Chapter 56 – Target Practice

The arrow thumped into the ground a good nine feet from its intended target. It joined two dozen others of assorted colors, markings, and construction scattered way left of the makeshift bulls-eye—concentric circles drawn on a piece of paper and impaled on a broken branch.

Lane moved closer. She had earned a trophy once in the fifty-foot range, though from her showing today the award could have been nothing more than a concession to a talentless child. Perhaps proving that she could still shoot from a shorter distance was a better place to start.

Four arrows zipped past the target tree and embedded themselves beyond it, but at least she had gotten closer to the ball park. The next three arrows pierced the edges of the paper and boosted their shooter's confidence. Another set of twelve quickly followed, each striking on or very near the target.

But when she moved back out to seventy feet, the arrows strayed off course once again. Lane compensated right, at what she thought was an impossible correction. Reasonably it made sense to keep practicing; otherwise she'd have to get right on top of whatever she intended to shoot before she had even the slimmest chance of hitting it. But she'd have to keep an eye on these corrections, too. As her aim improved, she would have to decompensate for those adjustments.

She spent another twenty minutes retrieving her arrows, prying them out of trees, rooting around in the brush for them. Cheery shafts of white, yellow, and red carried brightly colored yet mismatched feathers, purple and green, orange and blue, white and pink, making them easier to find among the browns and greens of the forest. Six of them had shattered beyond further use. A seventh proved irretrievable despite Lane's attempts to pry it loose. She snapped the wooden shaft off as close to the tree as possible so that the bark would have an opportunity to grow around the wound.

The hunting arrows consisted of dulled, earth-toned aluminum and graphite shafts with black fletching. They had been constructed for stealth; they wouldn't give away the position of the sportsman even by something as minor as sunlight glinting off the silent missile. They knew their job, and they did it well. The locations of three remained a mystery; the arrows were permanently lost to the mountain.

Another round of practice left both shoulders sore, one from holding the bow out stiff from her body, the other from holding the string in a tight, kissable position. The second set, though, held a tighter pattern, all were retrievable, and only two broke upon impact with rocks.

The third set started out fairly good, but precision hit the road the instant her shoulders went from complaining to screaming. She simply couldn't draw the string far enough for a decent shot. All in all she wasn't horrendous, just seriously out of practice.

Calling it quits for the time being, Lane packed up her arrows and headed off through the forest, one arrow nocked in the string just in case she ran into something more dangerous than a squirrel. Spring was probably the worse time to roam the woods alone; the hungry bears alone were enough to scare the stuffing out of serious mountain men, let alone teenagers with bows they couldn't draw.

There were also young animals getting their bearings, and their nervous parents would be ready to intercept trespassers. Cougar, bear, elk, and deer had been known to freak if a human got too close to their offspring. Hell, even birds would dive bomb anything venturing too close to fledglings stuck on the ground.

The sun had long since hit its zenith, and shadows had begun to stretch along the ground. Night would soon claim the forest. Careful observation, both visual and audible, would prevent a great many problems; the bow would be her only defense should she stumble upon anything when rounding a corner or cresting a rise.

Not that she'd be able to kill whatever it was. Not unless she was smack dab in its face. And at that range, it would probably get her before she could draw the string. Even if she did manage a shot, the odds favored the beast. Wounding it would only serve to enrage the animal rather than stop it, and a bear was ornery enough without an arrow sticking out of its butt.

The biggest problem, however, wasn't the possibility of running headlong into something with teeth, claws, or hooves. The biggest problem was the lack of mobility in her right leg. Dragging the limb up and down hills, over logs, and across streams took a heavy toll, burning more energy and causing more sweat than any of the physical therapy sessions she had thus far endured.

She limped to the top of Jensen Ridge, her short-term strategy being the acquisition of dinner and supplies before heading back into the forest before nightfall.

The visit would also give her the chance to hunt out something to dull the ache in her leg. The pain started in the hip, which bore the brunt of her awkward gait, then extended to the thigh, those muscles screaming from doing extra duty lugging around the rest of the leg.

The discomfort traveled to the knee, the joint resisting all requests to bend in a normal fashion and reminding the rest of her body that it, after all, had been the one cleaved by a bullet.

187

Even the lower half of the leg ached down along the calf muscles and into the ankle. It wasn't likely to get any better in the near future.

She wheezed, hands resting on her knees as she tried to catch her breath. The cabin lay at the bottom of the ridge; all she had to do was stroll on over and have some dinner. A couple ibuprofen. Maybe one of those hydrocodone painkillers Doc Williams prescribed if she could just figure out where Richard had hidden them.

Three steps into said stroll, her ankle twisted, caught by something hidden in the leaf litter, and she plunged headfirst down the hill.

Chapter 57 – Too Late For Dinner

The quick trip to the cabin didn't go quite as planned. The throbbing in her head woke her, and she found herself prone on the slope with her feet higher than the rest of her body. Apparently she'd used her head to stop a runaway tree, which accounted for the fact that her heart beat louder through her ears than anywhere else.

The sun gracefully descended to sleep, and night sounds strung throughout the forest. Crickets, tree frogs, the fluttering and buzzing of flying insects. The scurrying of mice. The wind whispering along the newly leaf-lined branches.

There had been a time when those sounds would have reminded her of her independence, of freedom, of her love for the forest and the mountain. Now they tortured her, laughing at the vulnerable predicament she had landed in.

She lay still for another few moments, assessing the situation, deciding she couldn't have been out for more than a few minutes. No lights shone forth from the cabin, no one lurked nearby in the dark. Behind her some fifteen feet up the hill, the bow had become entangled in the scrub.

The quivers, however, had made the trip downhill still attached to her, and several of the wooden-shafted arrows had snapped during the foray; she was lucky she hadn't been impaled by one of them. The rest of the arrows and the bow looked none the worse for the uncontrolled plunge.

Lane wiggled her fingers and toes, stretched her arms, flexed her legs. A bruise on her hip groaned its displeasure. Scrapes and scratches down the length of both forearms stung when she dragged them against the ground. Her brain pounded against the inside of her skull, and the knee that had already endured so much seemed to be screaming "Are you freaking nuts?"

She decided to give a go at getting up from her awkward "all smashed up against the tree" position. Funny, she mused, remembering how that tree chased up the hill toward her while she was sliding down, that it didn't bother to get out of the way.

A motion caught her eye and she eased back to the ground, searching for the source. A tiny, orange spark of light grew brighter, then eased in intensity. It dropped a few feet, hovered there for a moment, then rose again. The whole process repeated anew with the orange glow burning brighter.

Someone was smoking a cigarette on the far side of Keates Lake.

Chapter 58 – Free to Move About the Country

Just before dawn, the smoker gave up his wait. He simply stood up like he didn't have a care in the world and headed off toward the road, vanishing from sight rather quickly once he got to solid footing. Instinctively, Lane knew he had to be one of the hired killers. Richard would freak to know she had been so close.

Hovering at ground level, peering out from behind trees and scrub, Lane wondered what happened to the other two guys, if these were even the same guys that had invaded the cabin, or if perhaps there were multiple teams of assassins roaming the countryside trying to find her. The forest, after all, was a tad larger than a few guys could adequately cover in a week.

This particular executioner was gone now, though Lane waited another ten minutes to make sure he didn't double back. Obviously, he thought someone might show up at the cabin. If his timing had been better, or hers worse, he'd have caught her there.

Lane pulled herself up the tree with which she had so recently become intimate, using it as a body-block just in case the hit-man actually had doubled around. After recovering her weaponry, she snuck to the rear of the cabin. No one popped out of the woods, no trip wires introduced her to the dirt, and no one hid in the house, leaving Lane free to gather up a few more things with which to make her time in the forest more comfortable.

Despite the fact that men with guns wanted her dead, a reality that left adrenaline surging through her blood while her ears listened for the slightest sound that might suggest one such man was in the house, Lane felt oddly detached from the whole experience.

The position in which she found herself wasn't exactly new. Morgan—a man whom Lane refused to refer to as anything more significant than her mother's husband—had attacked her in Mills Valley and left her to die in Seattle. From the moment the hospital released her, she had been on her own, scrounging for food, sleeping in any dry space she could find, making do with whatever was at hand. And dancing on the wrong side of the law whenever her circumstances required it.

The three-fold increase in stalkers meant nothing. In fact, precious little about the situation bothered her. It wasn't like she had to do anything unsavory, immoral, or illegal this time to survive. The cabin contained everything she needed to spend time alone in the forest—food, bedding, clothing, weaponry—things she hadn't had when she had been forced to go solo last May.

The possibilities of what these men could and would do to her weren't lost on her, but the promise of solitude in the forest held its own reward. No one to please, no one to worry about, no chores, no hassles, no work, no problems. Just the relief that comes from surviving by the skill of one's own two hands. And perhaps just a little help from God.

Lane smiled. "But you never shout at me." Her eyeballs shot briefly toward heaven as she rummaged around the closet in the study-turned-bedroom for her backpack. She dumped its contents on the floor, adding to the disarray.

Her sleeping bag had been dry cleaned, sealed in a plastic bag, and tucked into the recesses at the top of the closet. She jabbed at it with an arrow, pushing, pulling, prying at it until it finally slipped free of its neighboring storage items and dropped into her waiting arms.

In the kitchen, she popped open the pantry door and helped herself to the box of Pop-Tarts. Not the half empty box, but the full one. A couple cans of vegetables made the cut, too. Corn. Peas. But the lima beans remained exactly where she found them.

She also snagged the spare hand crank can opener, the one Richard hated and wanted to throw away. The one Ray insisted they keep just in case of emergency. "Like me." She stuffed it in an outer pouch along with a handful of plastic spoons. And while she was right there, she nabbed the scissors from the junk drawer. She'd get her haircut one way or another.

Hemming and hawing hadn't had a place in her life until very recently. Now she had the luxury of making decisions based on personal preferences. The cans of stew and soup stayed behind with the lima beans, but three cans of corned beef hash relocated to the backpack.

A tent would have been nice. Real nice, she thought. A small fire nearby for warmth and to keep wild animals at bay, serving double duty to heat the hash. But that was before she knew the killers were in the forest with her. Staying in one place would be difficult but not impossible, but that meant no permanent fire or anything else that would draw unwanted attention.

She would rig small fires when she could to warm supper or to give herself a few minutes of warmth, especially at night. And then she'd hole up somewhere, using whatever was handy for insulation and camouflage, and praying that the lack of a fire wouldn't entice wild animals to check out the inviting smell of fresh human.

The last thing to catch her eye before heading back out into the forest was Richard's old leather jacket. His new jacket, the crisp, clean, polished one, represented his professional side, and he always wore that one to work. But this one, the old beater he'd grown up with, was the one he was most comfortable in, using it when he was hunting, fishing, or hiking. Or just sitting around outside with a beer in one hand and his feet on a stool.

She would try to get word to Richard about finding the killer here at the cabin, but that had to wait until she was safely away. She snagged her father's jacket and shut the cabin door.

Angelo sat on the west edge of Jensen Ridge, hunkered down against a tree with his gun, a bottle of beer, and a pair of binoculars that the priest had so willingly told him how to find. In the marsh on the far side of the pond, he watched the amber glow of Jack's cigarette, thoroughly expecting anyone else in the woods to hone in on that oddity and not look for any other.

Jack had strolled over to the driveway and out to the road over twenty minutes ago, but still Angelo searched the hillside for movement. He was just about to give up on the idea of catching the girl here when he caught movement on the hill behind the house.

His quarry, laden down with a pack full of supplies, climbed into the forest.

Chapter 59 – A Night in the Woods

The day had been glorious. After snagging survival gear and supplies from the cabin, Lane had scoped out the forest for a suitable hiding place, deciding that this spot had the best resources and opportunities. Numerous large boulders littered the landscape around Tippett Point, left behind after the last great Ice Age. Several convergent streams joined forces here before heading south.

The boulders provided a natural shelter, and Lane had spent a few hours cramming logs and rocks into the far end of the space formed by two of them resting against each other. When she was done, the back side was nearly impenetrable. At least to small animals. Odds were against a raccoon getting in, or a skunk or fox.

A cougar, on the other hand, or a bear, would keep at it until they broke down the wall, and they had the claws to do the job quickly. But they would make a lot of noise doing it. In those few moments, the human hiding inside would have the opportunity to either poke them with an arrow to make them think twice, or to simply shoot them at close range, which would increase the possibility of killing the creature instead of just pissing it off.

After satisfying herself that the shelter would be sufficient, Lane constructed a small, almost smokeless fire and warmed some hash for lunch. While the fat boiled at the top of the can, she took the opportunity for some target practice, sending all the remaining arrows into flight. The dramatic improvement in her targeting in the fifty-foot range pleased her, and her shoulders grew more accustomed to the work.

After her high-fat, high-protein meal, she sent another volley off, strengthening her shoulders and arms a little at a time but stopping before the soreness caused any real pain.

With little else to do, she picked one of the tributaries and followed it north, taking with her only a few necessities: the bow, one quiver of arrows, the radio for hearing pursuers, and the binoculars for seeing them.

The walk not only kept her leg moving, giving her the physical therapy she had been avoiding, but it also cleared her mind, which suited her much better than some stupid shrink asking stupid questions about her stupid feelings. Best of all, it prevented anyone from getting a bead on her. It didn't take a genius to figure that out. Everyone knew that a running rabbit was harder to catch than one flaked out in the sun.

She didn't return to her small camp until late in the afternoon, when the shadows growing across the ground foretold the yielding of sun to moon but still left her with plenty of time to heat another can of hash. It had been a long time since Lane had been able to eat what she wanted, when she wanted, without counting calories or dissecting nutrition labels. She took her time, relishing every high calorie bite and licking every last bit of grease from the spoon.

As the sun dripped down under the horizon, the shadows that had toyed along the ground took complete possession of the landscape. Lane snuffed out the tiny fire she had built, extinguishing the flames long before the glow could blaze forth like a lighthouse on the shoreline, thereby drawing every human caught in the unforgiving darkness. Keeping a fire lit now was a rookie mistake, and Lane was not new to this particular game. Were she freezing to death, she would opt for a heat source, but right now she was evading human beings with eyes, brains, and cognitive reasoning.

One final trip to the streams before it got too dark allowed her to sink the hash cans, preventing the smell from adding to the savory aromas that might draw wild animals. It also gave her one last chance to refill her canteen for the night. Unfortunately, she still had no idea if the filter was doing its job trapping bacteria and bugs; she had no symptoms of any disease, but a parasitic infestation would likely take a week to manifest. She shrugged; for all she knew, the entire situation could blow over in that time, and she'd be either dead or back home in the cabin.

She crawled in through the open end of the boulder alcove and draped the sleeping bag along the wood plug before settling into the cushiony material. The bow stood at the ready, just a foot away from her left hand, with the quivers by the entrance on her right side.

She practiced the scenario, shrugging out of the bedding and simultaneously grabbing the bow in one hand and a broadhead in the other, arming herself quickly. It took another few seconds to nock the arrow and draw the bow.

Those few seconds could be enough to kill her, so to trim away any wasted time, she drew a razorback from the quiver, nocking it to the bow and setting the assembled weapon on the ground in front of her where she could react, retrieve it, and respond to any threat as quickly as humanly possible.

To make it just a little more difficult for whatever might try to eat her in the night, she pulled several stout logs into the hole, wedging them between the two boulders like a door.

Richard's jacket hung off her, the largest single piece of clothing she had worn since those days she had spent homeless, living on the streets and in the forest, scrounging for food, stealing it mostly, and making do with what she had. She pulled the edges together and zipped it up, glad for the Mandarin collar that snugged up tight around her ears. "Geez, he's got a big neck," she chuckled into the leather.

The coat would keep her warm for quite a while, but the temperature in the forest was still dropping; she wrapped the sleeping bag around herself and drifted off to sleep.

Chapter 60 – Fishing

Morning came without any more serious an incident than Morgan's ghost hovering among the trees. He disappeared slowly, fading away as sunlight poked tendrils into the forest and through his body. With her bow clenched tightly in one hand, Lane flipped the bird to the phantom with her free hand.

A quick tour of the area revealed no footprints, no scratch marks, and no scat that would signify that a wild animal had found her and lingered about, puzzling out how to get to her. And that was a good thing…with less to worry about, she could concentrate on catching some breakfast.

Lane pulled the two fish arrows from the quiver. They were easy to find with their smaller fletching. The hole drilled just behind the feathers helped, too. Unfortunately for her, she'd neglected to grab the line and reel when she was rummaging around the cabin, which made bow fishing difficult but not necessarily impossible. She hiked back to the water.

The creeks pooled into a small pond which dispersed water down the mountain through a single outlet on the south side of the basin. Lane slipped off her shoes and socks and rolled up her pant legs to the knee.

Cold water rippled up to mid-calf, stopping Lane before she got too wet. The jeans would dry fairly quickly, but she could see no reason to get soaking wet. If she caught a fish, great. If she didn't, no big deal. She still had Pop-Tarts and hash.

Her mind rolled through bow fishing. The light refracting off the water made the fish difficult to spot, and the distortion of the water impaired targeting. The barbs on the arrow would secure the fish, preventing the arrow from sliding out should she actually hit the target, but the lack of a reel and line meant he'd wriggle away. And if he wriggled too far, she'd have no choice but to go in after him, something she wasn't sure she wanted to do today.

"So why did I roll up my pants?" She considered what she was up against here...the catch twenty-two. She decided she really didn't want fish for breakfast, anyway. She could try again at lunch, or dinner, even. Besides, hanging out on the shore waiting for an easy target to swim by probably wasn't the smartest thing to do while armed killers were looking for her.

She reminded herself that if the assassins really planned to kill her while the Keates men watched, she was probably okay for now. If they were around, they would try to capture her, not kill her.

The realization hit her, peaking her eyebrows, and she hurried back to her camp and the quivers full of arrows she'd left behind. Not that a fish arrow wouldn't kill a man. But she only had two of them, and she sure in hell wasn't waiting for anyone to get close enough for an accurate delivery. With the rest of the arrows at her disposal, she would be able to present the appearance of a threat, letting arrows hail down on them. Maybe they wouldn't be smart enough to figure out she couldn't aim for crap.

Back at camp, Lane stoked a small fire, certain that a well-constructed heat source wouldn't attract much attention during the day, and that any smoke it created would trail and dissipate quickly.

The fire crackled its way to independence and readily accepted another can of hash as its new best bud. Lane settled back against the boulder, bow across her lap, listening to the tiny flames lick the label from the can.

Despite the danger, her mind settled into nearly complete peace. As near as could be when her family was in jeopardy, but peaceful none the less. There were no voices, no yelling, no stares, whether they be condemning or pitying. No second guessing everything she said or did, wondering if she'd made the right move or said the right thing. No worrying over every little detail of every little encounter.

And accepting nothing. Fighting with Richard over everything. What would it harm to just listen to him? She could clean the damn room, if she wanted to. She could do the damn therapy…if she wanted to. Making the bed, however, was a lesson in futility. "Not like it won't get messed up the minute I get back into it." And the well-rounded meal…

She chuckled aloud at the can of hash sitting on a rock in the fire. Doc Williams had warned them her weight would stay down for quite some time while her body recovered from starvation mode. He had said her temptation would be to gorge on high fat foods, that she'd be drawn to them, craving them. There could be no doubt about that, considering her propensity to eat hash, pastas, and snack food.

Doc had suggested using the fatty foods as side dishes or the occasional treat, limiting their intake while acknowledging and satisfying the cravings. But he said the best bet would be to stuff Lane full of fruits and vegetables, with large portions of protein. "Fill her up," he had said. "So she doesn't go looking for crap."

It didn't really work. Perhaps it was a subliminal desire to run her own life and maintain her independence. Or perhaps it was more conscious than that. Perhaps Lane just didn't want to do what anyone else told her to do. Of course, that meant doing everything that everyone told her not to. Her independence had been the only thing that kept her alive after the attack. Giving it away now just didn't feel right.

And how exactly will I tell Richard that? Butt out, old man, because I don't really need you? But she did need him, and she couldn't deny it. "So why do I fight him at every turn, for every little thing, all day every day?"

It was almost as if she was thirteen and testing her will against her parents, a child flexing her newfound adulthood, thinking herself bigger than those around her whose job it was to guide, teach, and protect.

She'd had Ray's guidance for years, but he rarely gave her an order. Richard, however, micromanaged every detail of her day to day life. Or at least, that was how it seemed to Lane.

Richard. There were times when he looked at her that it seemed he wanted to cry. And yet, for the most part, he maintained a professional attitude toward her. Somewhat distant, a tad aloof, firm, and struggling to be calm most of the time, though she knew of several occasions when she had sorely tested that patience. He had a way of gripping things like chair backs or counter edges, or leaning against the table top, pressed forward on flexed hands. Those were the times she knew he was just about ready to come unglued.

Though he hadn't actually. Yet. "So why am I pushing him so hard to crack? To prove he doesn't really care about me? To prove he doesn't really want me around? To prove that the only reason he pretends to be concerned is because it's the "right" thing to do. The "responsible" thing to do. Because the Sheriff, the pillar of the freakin' community, will do anything to maintain pretenses?"

Her head shook side to side. She knew that wasn't true. She was just transposing Morgan's behavior onto Richard, and the two men could not have been more different. That was evident in everything about them. In their simple versus ostentatious homes. In their humble versus haughty mannerisms. In their immediate versus non-existent acceptance of Lane.

Then what is it? she asked herself, puzzling through it like the shrink had tried to do with her. So he wants the house clean. Why does it bother me?

"Why indeed?" She used two forked branches to remove the hash from the fire. She would have preferred it fried in patties, with just a little crispiness to it. But hash was hash. Another of God's perfect foods, right behind Pop-Tarts.

Maybe she was just trying to punish Richard for the first eighteen years of her life. He was, after all, responsible for her even being alive. Without him, then Lane would have been Morgan's daughter...probably. With Jenna sleeping with everything that still had breath in its body, Lane could have been the bastard child of just about any man in the state.

But Morgan was known for his brutality. If she had to be like somebody, she'd rather it not be him. "So why won't I let Richard help?"

Entertaining the notion that perhaps fear was the culprit in her dilemma, she clamped her lips around a spoonful of hash and dragged the spoon back out from between clenched lips, leaving it looking fresh-from-the-box clean. Even just thinking about fear left her disturbed.

Goose bumps popped up along her arms, and her shoulders shrugged up tight to her ears as an unnerving sense of dread settled into her mood. Her eyes flitted along the tree line, and she half-expected that Morgan's ghost might suddenly reappear. But Morgan's ghost only came out to play after a long sleep.

She tried to shake the feeling off like a passing chill. "I'm not afraid of Richard." Sure, he yelled on occasion, and sometimes his knuckles turned white when Lane frustrated him into strangling a chair rail. But he had neither said nor done anything, since finding out he had a daughter, to indicate resentment or hostility about being saddled with an eighteen-year-old convict. She dismissed the idea that fear of her father kept her at arm's length from him.

But the sense of dread persisted, as if she had just stumbled into a little secret that only she could ultimately reveal. "I'm afraid...he'll leave...me?" If he did, she'd be alone again. But if she didn't want him to walk away, maybe she shouldn't be pushing him—with both hands and a sledgehammer—to hit the road and not look back.

Even if Richard did turn his back on her, she still had Ray. And Ray would never abandon her; he had said that he and Lane were all the two of them had ever really had. He'd also said Richard would try to earn my trust.

Her eyebrows peaked as she swallowed down another greasy bite of hash. "No, actually, that's wrong. Ray said I had to let him try."

And that left her. Fear of herself. Of making a commitment. And of failing it. Of hurting someone else the way she had been hurt. Of ending up completely alone because of something she had done.

A gentle wind blew through her campsite. Even though she tried to immerse herself in it, tried to find the laughter and playfulness she had always known in the wind, it eluded her. Still, it provided a good diversion, and she watched it dance through her campsite, rippling the leaves and branches, fluttering the edges of her clothes. She was glad for the reprieve...she didn't like going to the shrink and talking about the things that had happened to her, but she didn't like trying to figure them out herself, either.

She took a deep breath of fresh, clean air, let it fill her lungs until she could hold no more, and then exhaled slowly. "I'm gonna have to deal with this, Lord." And her eyes took a quick turn toward the sky. The breeze tousled her hair and sent a shiver through her body, and Ray's voice popped into her head, unbidden but welcome. "It'll take time."

Alone here in this place, surrounded by the wind and forest…this was easy. No pressures other than those of basic survival, and that was something she was fairly well-skilled in. On the flip side, dealing with people twenty-four seven in close, tight quarters was worse than eating live toads.

Perhaps, she decided, I'm not so much an angst-ridden thirteen-year-old. Perhaps she was more like a five-year-old struggling to make friends and fit in on her first day at school, unsocialized and unsophisticated despite living with the two most social and sophisticated people in town. Lane decided they'd done that on purpose.

A black-capped bird called his merriest chick-a-dee-dee-dee. It hopped between branches to investigate her, then flew off. It was a learned response for the bird, investigate and fly away. And it was true of Lane, as well. Only she hadn't learned to embrace the investigation, just the flying away. If she made a concerted effort to investigate and embrace the human condition, then maybe she could break free of the fortress she'd built around herself and let her father in. Because God knew that all Richard's trying wouldn't amount to an earthworm on a three-inch tuna hook if she wasn't willing to meet him halfway.

She decided to spend the day in the woods, thinking and planning. There was an apology to be made. "Probably more than one." She would take the day to hoist her britches up and make herself ready for the rest of her life. Tomorrow, she would venture into town, make those apologies, and get on with that whole letting Richard into her life thing. And spilling the beans on the little adventure at the cabin would probably push any hints of familial anger clean out of sight.

In the meantime, there was certainly ample time for a nap…and a haircut. She dug the scissors out of her pack.

Chapter 61 – The Capture

Noon brought increasing temperatures, and a sunbeam poked into the sleeping nook, spotlighting Lane's leg until she could take the blotch of heat no longer. She stared bleary-eyed at the radiating, vicious swatch of light, shifting her leg an inch or two to get it out of the sun.

Outside the alcove, something scurried about in the underbrush, scratching and rooting around in the leaf littler. She pegged it as a mouse, or maybe a shrew.

It could have been any of a half-dozen or so varieties, all of which were small, and all of which were insectivores. No eating of people. "Or at least, no reported incidents of eating people." She stood the bow and broadheads in the corner so she could squeeze out of her hiding place without slicing off her fingers.

Lane crawled out, hands and knee; the right leg took a free ride while the left did the bulk of the work. The scratching in the brush changed, stopped, and then the creature scurried quickly away. "Sorry," Lane said to the rustling tunnel of leaves.

"No problem." A low, deep rumble growled at her.

Lane backed into the cave, but a meaty hand grabbed her by the hair, what she had left of it, and stopped her in her tracks. Another hand reached in. "Come on out here," he said, dragging her up and pushing her against one of the boulders.

The skinny, short guy gave her a look that made her skin feel as if it might shake loose from her body and crawl away by itself. He loomed close. "It's about time. I still say we should've rushed her this morning at the pond."

"Yeah, but this way we didn't have to worry about getting shot." The hefty one gave her a thorough pat down, his hands running over her body and causing her no end of discomfort. Angelo fought to keep her still. "Let me get this done, or I'll just keep at it."

Teeth clenched together, Lane endured the humiliation.

"Huh. House full of guns but you ain't got a one."

"I'm on probation, you freak!" Lane slapped at the hand clamped onto her shoulder and tried to dislodge herself from Angelo's grip.

Jack's hands jabbed at Angelo. "We could've grabbed her hours ago."

"Yeah, and she would have still skewered one of us with that damn bow." Angelo kept one hand on her coat and steered her away, pushing her faster than her leg could carry. "So what's wrong with the leg?" She ignored him as she climbed back to her feet; he spun her around, giving her a rough shake. "This'll go so much easier for you if you just answer my questions."

Her brain screamed both fear and defiance. She wouldn't deny being genuinely afraid, but fear she had known before. She would bide her time, and then she'd run or fight if given half the chance. "Took a bullet."

Angelo checked out the leg. "When?"

"What freakin' difference?" Logically, she had no reason not to answer his questions. It wasn't like he was asking her where her father was. Oddly, she didn't think he needed to know that—she was his ticket to get Richard and Ray out of hiding. But Angelo's glowering eyes forced her to reconsider. "Six months ago."

"Huh." He steered her away again, only not quite so fast.

Chapter 62 – Lane Meets Barnett

The mansion hadn't changed. Not much, anyway. Jenna wasn't there, which Lane supposed was a turn for the better. But the reason these two guys were hiding out on the Harris estate baffled Lane. She wondered if Camilla and Anton had been dismissed, maybe to save money or to make sure no one witnessed anything illegal. Like kidnapping and murder.

As Angelo ushered Lane into the office, her legs seized up, her body went rigid, and she immediately back-pedaled, pushing against the hand wrapped around the base of her neck. Someone, the spitting image of Morgan only topped with brown hair, sat at Morgan's chair, puffing on one of Morgan's cigars, with his feet propped up on Morgan's desk.

"Hello, step-niece."

Lane had heard Morgan speak of Barnett, and to him, but she'd never actually met the man.

"What did you do with the priest?" he asked the big man behind her.

Angelo's voice growled in her ear, his hot breath raking across her face. "Got him locked up in his own cabin."

Panic rushed up from Lane's gut and out through her open mouth. She pulled away from Angelo, but his thick arms wrapped around her, crushed her back into his chest, and held her still.

"Yes, we have Uncle Ray." His eyes snapped toward Angelo. "I expected you earlier."

Angelo shrugged. "She's good at hiding, and dangerous enough with sharp, pointed things for me to wait for a clean catch."

"Apparently." Barnett flicked his cigar hand in the direction of an empty chair, and Angelo pushed Lane into it. "I decided to have them bring you here first so we could chat." He studied her, the crazy style of her hair, the mix of fear and hatred in her eyes. "Morgan really disliked you."

Lane remained silent; she couldn't refute the absolute truth.

"But you killed him." He stared at her, sucking on the cigar, pulling a deep draw which made the orange tip glow brightly for a few seconds. He waited.

Lane reviewed her options. It wasn't like Barnett didn't already know his brother was dead, or that he had met his end at Lane's hand. And she had just enough spunk left to defy Barnett, too. "I should have done it years ago."

Angelo snickered, but Barnett didn't share his amusement. "He was still my brother."

"And he still deserved it," she said, almost calmly, her voice only slightly betraying her fear. "You may want me dead, but everybody wanted Morgan dead. I just had the privilege of doing it."

Barnett smiled, like he knew he was being baited. "My dear girl. I don't want you dead. I want Morgan's money. To get it, I need your mother's cooperation. To get that, I need her out of jail. And to get that," the cigar tipped away from his body as did his head, a half-hearted shrug at best. "We need all the witnesses to disappear. You see, it's not so much that I want you dead…rather, I need you dead."

Lane imitated his shrug, a casual rise of her shoulders, her right hand flipping out from her side just a little. "Don't expect it to be easy. You might get us, but some of you are going down, too."

Barnett kicked his feet off the desk and leaned forward, trying to intimidate her much the way Morgan used to. Lane refused to turn away from his stare, meeting his eyes without so much as a flinch. Heat rose up her face, making itself known to her as well as her adversary. But that kind of flush could say embarrassment, fear, defiance, or butt-ugly anger. She went with it.

He rose from the chair in a smooth, calm movement, his body reminding her of Morgan's in so many ways. He moved around behind her, his hands brushing her upper arms, caressing up to her shoulders. "I am really not interested in you the way Morgan was," he said, enjoying the shudder that went through her body. "But it certainly worked to make you rather compliant."

Lane bolted to her feet, suddenly desperate to put distance between herself and her tormentor. Barnett grabbed her, slapped her across the face with enough force to flush tears from Lane's eyes, and threw her against the desk.

Jack grinned, ear to ear, as Barnett leaned over her and pressed her against the desk with his body. But Angelo, the guy who looked to be the most capable of violence, displayed a different emotion, something more akin to dismay.

Barnett grabbed her wrists, forced her hands wide apart, and pressed against her back. Leaning close to her ear, he whispered, "Of course, I could be persuaded to let you live, if I didn't need Jenna. But that means you'd have to provide the information she has, namely, Morgan's offshore accounts."

Lane's body shook violently. This is about the damned money! she thought. "I know where he hid it!" she blurted, hoping to stall both Barnett's current and future plans.

He nuzzled into her neck. "Tell me before I have to hurt you."

"No!" she barked, her voice cracking in fear. Her tactics didn't serve the purpose she had intended. Barnett didn't let up on her. He reached around her waist, one hand fumbling with the button on her jeans. Lane struggled against him, her newly-freed hand grabbing for objects with which to fight back.

Barnett laughed. "You're running out of time."

"You hurt me and I swear, I won't tell you a thing. I won't even give you the combination to the safe."

"Fine. I'll have to deal with your mother, then." His hands coursed up her sides, pushing her shirt toward her head.

Another shudder swept Lane's body, this time accompanied by goose-pimples that spread from each inch of skin Barnett touched. Lane croaked out a nervous laugh. "You're crazy if you think she's gonna give you all the money. She'll dupe you, just like she's duped everybody else she's ever known. Oh, sure, she'll give you some token, like you're the chauffeur. But the rest of it? A hundred mil? She ain't parting with that. Mostly because she don't even know where it is."

Barnett spun her around, his fingers crushing into her upper arms. "What do you mean?"

Lane suddenly had the upper hand, and she played the trump card as if Morgan had personally taught her all his deepest, darkest trade secrets. He hadn't exactly taken her under his wing, but he sure as hell didn't know about the peep holes in the attic floor, through which Lane had learned a multitude of valuable lessons. "Gimme a break. You didn't think he'd tell her where it all was, did you? She whored her way up the ladder until she found Morgan. He had contingency plans for when she decided to work her way up higher."

Barnett's eyes registered it, and the information spun around a while as his brain digested it.

Lane pushed on. "One seven five three seven two seven seven."

"What?" The numbers brought Barnett quickly back from his silent reverie.

"The code to the wall safe."

Barnett released her and swung the hideous picture away from the wall. "Once again, slowly."

Lane complied, waiting for Barnett to punch in each number on the keypad before giving him another. The safe popped open, but Barnett's disappointment sang out in his voice. "It's empty."

"Of course it is. I stole it all. I know all his secrets. And I know the codes for the two safes in the master suite."

"There's only one safe in there," Barnett corrected, turning his back on her and utterly dismissing her argument.

Lane had to get his attention back. Quickly. "Yeah, you wish." She whipped a pen off the desktop and wrote the combinations on the newspaper folded up on the blotter. "I even know where the phone numbers are for all the women he was banging in Olympia."

Pausing briefly, Lane studied Barnett's face, waiting for the precise moment before driving headlong and impaling him with his own greed. "I can give you the money. I can give you the account numbers and the pass codes, and you'll be richer than God in half an hour. But you're going to have to take me to my uncle first. And you're gonna have to let us go free."

She threw the newspaper across the room, nailing Barnett in the chest with it. "First code is the wall safe, which you obviously know about. Second one's hiding behind the vanity mirror, if you're interested. That's where they hid the sex tapes."

Barnett caught it before it fluttered open and considered her proposition. He dismissed his three guests with a wave of his hand. "Well, you heard her. Take her to her uncle."

Chapter 63 – Jack Gets Too Close

The feel of Jack's clammy hand on her skin was bad enough, but the way he looked at her made Lane's stomach inch closer to her throat. She slapped at his head and struggled against him as he escorted her into the cabin, forcing Angelo to get involved. The bigger man's steely hand clamped onto her arm, and he dragged her inside.

She didn't see Ray. "Where is he?"

"You didn't really think we'd leave him out here where just anybody walking by could see him, did you?" Angelo steered her into the living room and down onto the sofa, raising a single finger along with his eyebrows, and commanding she remain there without ever speaking the words.

While Jack secured the first floor, locking doors and windows and closing curtains and drapes, Angelo made himself at home in the kitchen, checking out the fridge and cabinets and pulling out all the makings for a meal. "You want eggs?" he hollered to no one in particular.

Only Jack answered. "Over easy." He coursed the floor, familiarizing himself with the layout, and then sat in an easy chair opposite Lane, one leg draped over the arm.

Angelo stood by the dining room table, eyeing Jack for a moment before his gaze shifted to Lane. "Kid. Eggs?" Lane looked at him, her body still quivering, but she managed to push out an obvious head shake.

"No reason not to eat. Might as well get something in your stomach." But her head shook again, just a little bit more than the rest of her body. "Suit yourself." Angelo returned to the kitchen.

"I want to see my uncle." Lane focused her attention on the coffee table, but the muscles in her neck cramped up with tension and fear.

"Yeah, later," Jack laughed. In the kitchen, eggs cracked, butter sizzled, and utensils clanked and shuffled around. Jack moved closer. "Maybe we should get better acquainted. That's Angelo. My name's Jack." He slid onto the couch next to her. His hand started on her knee and moved slowly up her thigh.

Memories she didn't want ever to remember came flooding back. Morgan grunting away as he took her innocence, the homeless boy on the street dying to protect a few dollars and change. Running for her life. Screaming herself awake in the middle of the night.

She slapped furiously at Jack. He laughed, grabbing her hands and dragging her out of the chair and across the room to the study, where he threw her on the bed.

A squeal of fear crawled out of Lane's throat. "Please don't." Her petition only made Jack laugh all the harder as he unbuttoned his shirt.

Angelo stood in the bedroom door, watching, waiting, studying. "Cool it," he said to Jack, his voice low, deep, and surprisingly calm. And filled with an authority that said he believed Jack would do exactly what he was told.

Jack pursued his own plans for the evening. "You don't always get to choose. I get to choose, too. And I want this one."

Angelo moved further into the room, approaching the bed as Lane scooched as far away from Jack as she could. "Let it go." He stared at Jack.

But the skinny geek defied the big man. "No." He stripped off the shirt. "You can have a taste or not. I'll keep her alive for as long as Barnett says, but she's going to die in the end, anyway, so what difference what I do to her in the meantime?"

He crawled across the bed at the same time Lane crawled off, positioning herself behind Angelo. "Please," she whispered, leaning in close to the giant's body and trying to hide behind him.

Angelo stared down at her, and Lane watched a subtle change flash in his eyes, as if he had shifted off the fence he'd been riding and landed clearly on her side. He pushed Jack away as the shorter man approached.

The confrontation grew more heated. A push led to a shove, and that led to a series of punches. Lane lurched her way to the bathroom, slamming the door and locking it behind her. She didn't expect it would keep either man out for long, but she hoped it would hold long enough for Angelo to win.

Their voices rose, escalating in intensity and volume, and the noise seeped into the bathroom. Assuming Jack didn't have the strength required to send Angelo across the room, the scraping of the bed on the floor meant the smaller man had landed on the platform with enough force to move it. "Can't you control yourself?" Angelo growled.

"What the hell is the matter with you?" Jack spat back. "Why is this one so special? It's not like she's not going to end up in the ocean."

"Barnett's after the money. If you do this and she clams up, maybe we don't get paid."

"Then we'll make her talk. And he'll pay, or he'll end up in the ocean, too. I don't get it. Suddenly you're a freakin' saint."

"I've told you before. I like to put them in their place."

"They all belong in the same place. On their backs."

A dull thud suggested someone had just taken another hit. "I said no. You know my game. I wipe the smug look off their faces. This one ain't got a smug look. And I ain't gonna tell you again to leave her alone. You've been a good partner, Jack. Don't make me kill you. You need something to help you sleep, have a couple beers. Or drive yourself into Shelton and pick up

215

something with fight in her veins. But stop thinking about that girl." Seconds later Angelo banged on the bathroom door. "Kid. Come on out."

But Jack continued to press him. "You mark my words. Sooner or later, me and that little girl are gonna dance."

Angelo's annoyance sang out in his voice when he had to repeat himself. "Come on. He ain't gonna hurt you."

Lane didn't know why her petition had worked, only that it had. For some reason, Angelo had no interest in her physically, and she had managed to instigate a dispute between the two men. She decided that capitalizing on it might prove beneficial.

It wouldn't require much effort for Angelo to smash the door in; Lane hopped in the tub. Pulling her knees to her chest, she crushed herself into a tiny, tight ball.

Chapter 64 – Angelo and Ray

Angelo wolfed down a plate of scrambled eggs while guarding Ray, who sat at the opposite side of the table, hands tied behind his back.

"Let me make sure she's okay." Ray said, his voice barely a whisper.

Angelo snorted through the eggs. "You ain't exactly in wonderful shape yourself. Not like it matters, though. It's likely you'll both be dead soon."

"Please."

Angelo shook his head. "Not happening, Padre. I got nothing against you or God. But this is business. A deal's a deal." He dropped the plate into the sink, then grabbed the phone and dialed. It took just two rings for the receiver to answer.

"Yeah, let me talk to Sheriff Keates." He waited a moment, scowling at whatever the person on the other end of the line was saying. "Tell him it's about his kid and his brother. I'm sure he'll change his mind."

He hadn't long to wait. "There you are. So right about now you're figuring out that I have them both. If you want to see them alive again, you'll come out to your cabin. Alone, of course, because if I hear, see, or smell more than one package of bacon, I start slicing." He hung up the phone and turned on Ray. "Very soon, in fact."

Chapter 65 – The Sheriff Arrives

Richard parked a mile from the cabin and hoofed it, careful to avoid areas which could easily be watched from the house and sticking to those which provided ample cover.

The thickets made it more difficult to travel, but he would be able to get quite close to the cabin before having to come out of hiding. He crept into the tributary side of the lake, putting him on the land Lane had inherited from her maternal grandparents, and hunkered down among the reeds. The lights in the cabin shone out the windows of the front door, but from this distance he couldn't make out anything more definite than that.

The road would be the most likely place for attack or arrivals, and Richard hoped the hired guns expected that. He slid out from cover, skirting the brush and picking his way through the marshland as he headed for the hillside.

Excessive caution cost him only a few extra minutes, and he slipped down to the kitchen door, pulling himself onto the back porch without using the creaky stairs that would give away his position. He reached for the door knob.

The unmistakable sound of a cocking shotgun froze him in his tracks. Richard slowly raised his hands and turned toward the sound. Angelo stared back.

"This isn't exactly how I pictured this," Richard said, avoiding the look or sound of a frightened man.

"I'll just bet," Angelo smiled his twisted, evil grin, urging Richard into the cabin with a flick of the shotgun.

Chapter 66 – The Beating of His Life

The battle raged. The two adversaries punched and jabbed at each other like prize fighters in the ring. But Angelo's last punch sent Richard careening backward, and he fell over the coffee table and wound up wedged between it and the sofa.

Richard waited, hoping that his opponent would make the mistake of reaching into the tight space. If Angelo did, Richard would have the opportunity to kick the big man right in the chops. When Angelo motioned him out, Richard gave up the ploy and pulled himself up using the furniture at hand.

Gobs of blood, some of it already clotting, flowed from Richard's nose and mouth, leaving red streaks down his shirt and trousers and spots on the furniture. He wiped his face with his sleeve, taking a few seconds to regain his breath. Despite getting several good punches in at his antagonist, Richard was dismayed by the lack of damage he had inflicted—a mere trickle of blood coursed a route down Angelo's chin before dripping onto his shirt.

The big Italian smiled, clearly enjoying himself, and just as clearly enjoying the conflict. Richard knew in that moment that the man opposing him was more than capable of beating him to death.

The skirmish paused long enough for Jack to drag Ray into the room and tie him into a dining room chair. "You're not going to want to miss this," he said to Ray, then took a chair for himself. "Don't mind us, fellas," he said, waving a dismissive hand at Angelo and Richard. "Carry on."

Richard watched as Ray struggled to lift his head. The priest had taken a serious beating, and exhaustion and pain left him just this side of consciousness. Probably if Jack hadn't dragged him in from the den, he'd be asleep right now. "Sorry, Rich." It was little more than a whisper.

Angelo charged, and he and Richard exchanged furious blows, a flurry of fists and elbows designed to incapacitate, but it was Richard who ended up on the floor again. He lay there, staring up at the ceiling, arms and legs flared apart, wondering how long he could just rest there before Angelo kicked him in the ribs.

But the giant made no move toward him, preferring to allow the beleaguered Sheriff the opportunity to regain his footing before the fight continued. Eventually Richard struggled back to his feet, and Angelo cast him a respectful nod.

Jack piped up from the sidelines. "Too bad she wants to be here for the end. We could just get this done with and be gone."

"Now you're seeing my point? Hopefully she'll be here tomorrow. In the meantime, he said we could amuse ourselves, right?"

Richard wiped the blood from his mouth again. "Jenna?"

Angelo's laughter was almost a growl. "That'd be her."

"You can't trust her." Richard's head waggled back and forth. "She'll betray you at the drop of a hat."

"I ain't working for her. She's just where the money's coming from."

"Morgan's brother? You can't trust him, either."

"Oh, I think he knows what'll happen if he double-crosses us. You really don't have any cards to play here."

Richard smiled, the weak twist of his lips making him look sad at best. "Forgive me for trying to keep us alive as long as possible."

"Absolutely. But your only hope of surviving is that kid telling us where Harris' dead brother hid the account numbers."

Richard tried not to act surprised. "She's a pretty smart kid."

Angelo nodded his agreement. "Yeah, she is. But everybody's got a weak spot for something." He turned on Ray.

Richard lunged across the room in a last ditch effort to defeat Angelo, but he was already too drained to accomplish much of anything. Angelo deflected the blow and clocked him a stiff right that spun Richard around and dropped his legs out from under him. He had enough time to watch the floor rush up to meet him before joining Ray in dreamland.

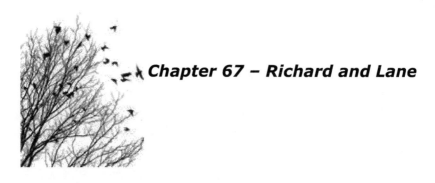 **Chapter 67 – Richard and Lane**

Richard awoke to Lane mopping blood from his face and applying Band-Aids to his eyebrow in a poor imitation of butterfly strips. The edges of his uniform shirt flapped open, and his tee was balled up high on his chest. The shredded remnants of a bath towel bound his midsection and stabilized his bruised ribs. He ran a hand down the length of his torso, probing, pushing...testing the extent of the damage.

"I don't know if they're broken," Lane said.

"I don't think they are. But that guy sure has a soft spot for ribs, doesn't he?" He winced as Lane pressed a little too hard on the slice across his cheek bone. He circled her wrists and eased her hands away. "Thanks."

"It won't stop bleeding."

Richard nodded his understanding, but he had other concerns. "Do you really have the accounts?" A silent nod answered him. "If you give them the numbers, they'll kill us all. And they've got plenty of ammo to use against you to get you to talk." He hoped that Lane recognized all the dangers facing them, that the two assassins would use father and daughter as tools against each other, and that the girl would bear the worse portion.

"I know," Lane whispered.

"I'm trying to figure out a way to get you out of here."

"Can't we just wait for your guys to storm the place?"

Richard shook his head. "Not sure when that'll be. Everybody's at the station, waiting for me to call...or not. Staties are probably there by now, too. But that won't save us if Angelo and his psycho friend decide not to wait for Jenna to show up. Depending on the timing, she may not be coming at all."

Lane's head twisted and her eyes flickered up to meet his; he didn't make her ask the question. "Because sooner or later, my guys will throw up roadblocks. They'll nab her the minute she turns onto the road."

"But…what if she walks in?"

Richard snorted. "You mean, like, through the woods, and the muck, and the dirt, and like, the bugs…I don't think we have to worry about that. But it figures that these guys would lock us in the only room in the house that has no window." He tried to muster an evil eye for his disobedient offspring, but her twisted smirk kept him from even pretending to be mad at her.

"Sorry," Lane said, failing to disguise a snicker.

"Don't be. Looks like you were right. Too bad you couldn't have stayed out of their hands a little longer. But I really gotta tell you that just once before I die, I'd like you to do what I tell you to do."

"I guess once wouldn't be so bad. I don't suppose you'd consider giving me a painkiller?"

"Top of the closet, behind the toilet paper." Lane struggled to get them, eventually using the handle of the toilet bowl plunger to pry them forward and bring them down. "Knew you couldn't reach them there. Just don't go back to eating them like M&Ms. I know exactly how many are in there."

He patted the floor with his hand, silently requesting that his daughter join him. While she washed a pill down with tap water cupped in her hand and pocketed the medicine bottle, he fished all the green from his wallet and offered it to Lane when she sat down next to him. "Put that in your pocket," he said, his voice soft and casual, as if the order wasn't an order at all. "If an opportunity presents itself, you split. It's not much, but it'll get you out of harm's way." To his complete amazement, she

223

complied without even an eyeball roll. He wished he had known earlier that dealing with her could be just that easy.

"Don't tell me where you'll go, just in case that ape out there tries to beat it out of me. But you could catch a bus out of Shelton or Bremerton. Or the ferry out of Port Angeles. Just pick a direction."

"Why can't I just go get Pete?"

"Because the minute these two know you're gone, one of them will try to get you back. In town, he'll have the advantage. Angelo's a puncher…I don't think he can run. Your experiences will outweigh his two good legs as long as you stay in the mountains. Once you are sure nobody is on your tail, go ahead and find a police station. But if you're being chased, don't risk letting him catch up to you. And be careful out there. I don't think these two are part of the first team that tried to take us out."

"But how will I know when to come back?" she asked.

"Watch the news," he said, glad that she didn't press him further, glad that he didn't have to explain that she should be watching for the untimely death of a Washington State Sheriff.

Richard wanted to wrap his arm around Lane's shoulders, but he couldn't raise his arm high enough because of the pain in his side. He settled for sliding his arm around her waist and pulling her against his chest, and they shared a quiet, tender moment.

"Lane…chances are that they'll end up getting physical with you. Please, as hard as it's going to be, just live through it. Whatever happens, we'll deal with it. I really want this to be the time you listen to me…if this goes down badly, all you have to do is survive. I know I'm asking a lot, but you have to submit. Don't worry about what they do to me or your uncle. Just live through it."

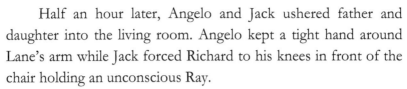

Half an hour later, Angelo and Jack ushered father and daughter into the living room. Angelo kept a tight hand around Lane's arm while Jack forced Richard to his knees in front of the chair holding an unconscious Ray.

"He's getting worse by the hour," Jack said as he zip-tied Richard's hands to one leg of the chair. He withdrew his hunting knife, displaying its business side for Richard to see, then slicing a button off the front of Richard's shirt without damaging the fabric beneath. "Doesn't get any sharper than that." Jack took up a position behind the Sheriff, his knife sliding along Richard's neck.

"Last chance," Angelo said. Lane burst forward, but Angelo held her tight. "Give me the account numbers."

With his hands secured, there was little Richard could do to draw his daughter's attention but speak. "It's okay. All I want is that you live. I love you." Panic screamed out from her eyes, but he continued to assure her. "Don't tell them. It's okay."

Jack pressed the knife to Richard's throat and Lane tugged, trying to free herself from Angelo. The big Italian wrapped a hand around her throat and pulled her back.

"It's okay," Richard repeated, a loving smile softening his eyes and the corners of his mouth. Jack dug the knife into the Sheriff's flesh, just under his left ear, angling the knife so Lane could get a good look at what was about to happen.

"Look at me. Lane, look at me. It's all right." But Richard's reassurance didn't prevent the knife from slicing through his skin. He ground his teeth and accepted his fate.

"No!" Lane yelled as hard as she could.

Jack's knife stopped, not quite an inch into its intended journey, a flow of rich, red blood marking a trail along Richard's neck.

"Where?" Angelo urged. When the answer wasn't immediately forthcoming, he whirled the girl around and gave her a resounding smack across the face, holding her erect when her bum leg gave out. Richard struggled against his bonds, but it earned him a crack in the skull from Jack's knuckles, which were firmly wrapped around the hilt of the knife.

Defiance surged up from Lane's toes and settled in her eyes. "Let them go and I'll tell you."

Bargaining was a skill Angelo had never acquired. "Do I look stupid?" Lane stared at him with the most lifeless, dead eyes and wondered if the question was rhetorical or if Angelo expected an answer. He must have been reading her mind, for his hand rose, ready to strike again. "Careful."

Lane flinched, but stood her ground. "I've already got the contents of the safe, remember?"

"Which means pretty much nothing from where I stand."

"It means you kill me, or either of them, and you don't get squat."

"Nothing now, nothing later. It's still nothing." Angelo slammed Lane against the wall and leaned in close, pressing against her. "You know what comes next, right?" he growled, one of his hands latching onto her face.

Lane's body shuddered, and the switch that controlled her memories tripped back and forth—Morgan grunting over her in the dirt, Angelo pressing her into the wall, Simon copping a feel at the group home. Her brain switched off.

"NO!" Richard yelled across the room. "Lane! Look at me! Look at me!"

The pleading, concerned voice drilled into the edges of her consciousness, demanding her attention, requiring she wake from the trance. She blinked back to reality and found Richard yelling at her from across the room. Then Jack started hollering, but Lane's hearing and conscious thought hadn't quite caught up with her vision. Angelo blurred, surprising Lane with how quickly he could move. He threw an arm across her throat, then relieved her of the trophy she had appropriated from a nearby table.

"You thought you could bash my head in?" Angelo wrapped both hands in Lane's shirt and tossed her across the room like an angry bull hurling a matador. "We'll see how feisty you are when I'm done with you." He pursued her across the floor, lifted her with one hand, and chucked her toward the den.

Richard yelled after them. "Lane! Just survive!"

Jack delivered a vicious kick to Richard's face. The Sheriff crashed to the floor, jarring Ray but not waking him.

Lane scuttled away from Angelo, but her eyes locked on Jack, kneeling on Richard's pelvis.

"Consider her lucky," Jack said. "Under normal circumstances, I'd climb on and then slide this little beauty right in here."

Lane watched the blade skim across Richard's stomach, settling in just under his rib cage. Jack pressed in just a little; Richard clamped his teeth against the steel bite. "Her lung fills up with blood, and she starts suffocating beneath me and squirming against me trying to get away. And I get to feel the life drain out of her body."

Angelo dragged Lane up by her hair and dropped her on the bed, slapping her soundly when she tried to rise and sending her sprawling across the bed. She lay still for a moment, stunned, then cupped the stinging flesh and blinked back tears.

The assassin stripped off his shirt, balled it up, and tossed it away, and Lane tried again to get away from the man whose intentions for her were all too clear. She pulled her legs to the other side of the bed and launched herself off the edge, getting just a few feet away before Jack entered from the living room. She veered away, but Angelo caught her and spun her around, his massive right fist smashing into her eye, glancing off her nose, and pushing her right to the brink of unconsciousness.

He dragged her back to the bed, tossing her on it like a limp pillow. His hand wrapped around her throat and squeezed; when her body registered the lack of air, she resurfaced from oblivion and fought off his attack, slapping without effect on his face and arms.

"That's better," he growled. "Fight."

And she did, stretching across the bed and snatching the lamp off the bedside table. She whirled, smashing the fixture into Angelo's head and knocking him back. She hobbled toward the door, but Jack had already moved to intercept. His punch knocked her head back and into the door frame, rendering her unconscious before her mind registered the pain.

Jack stood over her, watching blood pour from the split in her lower lip that wrapped from the skin side clean around to the tooth line.

Angelo glowered down at his partner. "Moron."

Bloody hand towels filled the sink. Richard wedged another towel against his neck, using his shoulder to keep it in place while he prepared a gauze and tape bandage to cover the bleeding gash.

A wave of dizziness washed over him, forcing him onto the toilet seat cover. He was sure he hadn't lost enough blood to worry about, but he kept pressure on the wound just in case.

His free hand inspected the damage to his face. The left eye had swollen shut, and the gash across the eyebrow held hints of purple and black bruising that would probably spread, but fresh Band-Aids kept the laceration closed. The other eye had avoided serious damage, but a thin, blackish stripe spread underneath the lower lid, looking like the shoe-black that football players used on game day.

The slice along his cheekbone had finally clotted and crusted over, but the split in his lip was red and angry-looking, and would no doubt continue to open every time he spoke, drank, or ate. Only stitches could help his lip, but the cheekbone could stand a bandage or two. He smeared a large swab of ointment on another square pad.

The assorted pains in the rest of his body screamed for attention, too. Abdominal muscles rippled against bruised ribs, knuckles raw from slamming against Angelo refused to flex, and the entire left side of his face throbbed from the blunt force trauma of the big Italian's vicious right hook. The best bet, he decided, was not to move at all, at least not from the waist up.

On the sink next to him, the gauze bandage lay open, ointment melting into the pad and adhesive strips dangling open like octopus tentacles. He positioned it against his face and smoothed the tape against his skin.

And he smiled. Angelo, for some reason, had sequestered Lane in the den, which, unlike the bathroom, had windows. One of those apertures would soon become his daughter's ticket to freedom and life. Her disappearance would save him and Ray for a little while, probably not very long, but that didn't matter. His daughter would live, provided she was smart enough to seize the opportunity. Since this wouldn't be the first time she'd escaped from someone via window, Richard felt confident she'd be gone soon, and that come dawn he would be in for another serious hide-tanning.

But that didn't matter. Not anymore. All he had to do now was give her time to carry out her escape. He would do the one thing every real father knew they had to do in a pinch, no matter what...he would give his life for his child. His shoulders squared, and he stuffed three bars of soap into a dirty sock pulled from the laundry hamper.

Lane woke with a gasp, bolting to a sitting position and scraping her right wrist along the handcuff chaining her to the bedpost. The moonlight streaming in the windows spotlighted Ray just a few feet away from her. No other people lingered in the dark room, and Morgan's ghost dissipated by the time her uncle spoke.

"You were dreaming," Ray whispered. "I'm sorry...I couldn't get to you."

Lane eased to the edge of the bed. Her face throbbed and she probed the wounds, deciding she looked much like her father and uncle at this point. She had more pressing issues to handle. Stretching to a nearby bookshelf, she pulled The Old Man and the Sea from its assigned spot and caught half a bobby pin that fell from it as the pages splayed open.

Already formed into a miniature golf club, the bobby-pin had been concealed shortly after Lane's arrival at the Keates' homestead. It was a skill she had acquired while living on the streets of Seattle, and she had been unwilling to give it up just because she happened to be living in a house now.

"How many of those do you have hidden in here?" Ray asked.

"You gonna tell Sheriff Stick-Up-His-Butt?"

"Probably."

Lane shrugged. "In that case, the one you see is the one I have."

Ray's chuckle at the carefully structured wording cut off with a sudden wheeze of pain. Seconds later, after freeing herself from her chains, she untied Ray from the chair and helped him lie down on the floor.

A roll of paper towels sat on her desk, looking like part of the clutter. No one had to know why she needed them or any of the other items she had sequestered in her room.

Tucking the roll under her arm, she hobbled back to the bookcase. From the second shelf, behind four books that sat further out than the rest, Lane withdrew a sixteen-ounce bottle of water. She snagged a pillow from the bed and returned to Ray's side, now armed with the tools of combat first-aid.

While she cleaned some of the dried blood off her uncle's face, Ray took her free hand in his. "You were unconscious when they brought me in here. Are you all right?"

Lane nodded, but kept working. When Ray took her hand, his grip felt like the clutch of a feeble old man, and his skin was cold and clammy. Lane was fairly sure that her uncle was going into shock. That could only mean that his injuries had to be severe, probably broken ribs to start with, but that could mean sliced organs and internal bleeding.

"Then you need to go. The window near the desk puts you into the forest faster," he said.

"I can't leave you here."

"I'm telling you to go." He pushed her hands away.

"Ray…you're pretty beat up…you could die…"

"Go!" His whisper didn't travel far, but Lane reacted as if he had slapped her in the face. Tears welled up, but she scrubbed them away with the back of her hand. She capped the water bottle and set it between his hand and his body, then raised his head high enough to slide the pillow beneath. Awkwardly leaning close, like a twelve-year-old sneaking a kiss from her first crush, she kissed his cheek and hobbled away.

Ray lay on the floor, aching from the waist up. Any movement caused intense pain in his sides, and he felt sure one of his broken ribs had sliced into his pancreas, his lung, or maybe his liver. Maybe all three. He'd been feeling weak and lightheaded, general symptoms of shock. He expected internal bleeding was causing it, and he expected to be dead long before this situation played itself out.

He listened carefully, unable to see what Lane was doing. He could tell she was fishing around in the closet for something. When she returned, he tracked her to the window, watching as she skillfully raised it without making any noise at all.

Tears stained his face and he choked down sobs as Lane whispered to him. "Goodbye, Uncle Ray." She peered out into the night, checking both ways as if stepping out into traffic. The window closed just as silently as it had opened, leaving him alone in the darkness.

A sob broke free, gnawing its way out of his throat. His hand slid toward his face, and he gently touched the spot where his niece had planted that goodbye kiss. It was the one and only kiss she had ever given him in her whole life, and it told him that she, too, knew he was dying.

Chapter 68 – Hitting the Trail

Lane snuck out onto the wraparound porch, clinging tightly to the sack she had pulled from the closet. Breathing calmly and listening intently, she studied her surroundings carefully before deciding on a plan of action.

She guessed that somewhere off towards the road the deputies and troopers might be amassing and planning their strategy, and she wondered if any of them could see her right now. Peeking into the darkness gave her no clues. They probably had night-vision goggles and could see her as clearly as a zit on the end of a nose.

If she struck out due east and swung south, she would probably run into them. That might be the safest course of action; on the other hand, running into a bunch of steroid-laden, buzz cut, testosterone junkies might not be a good idea in the dark. Downing one of them with a crotch-buster or a sternum-blow would only get her a serious walloping. Of course, if they weren't watching from the street, she was wasting time, giving Angelo a chance to recapture her.

Lane tiptoed to the front of the house, peering around to make sure neither of the assassins was outside. She did the same at the back of the cabin, confirming to herself that, for the moment at least, she was alone. Carefully avoiding all the creaking planks, she maneuvered down the stairs and into the forest, dropping to the ground several feet into the tree line.

She studied the house, watching, waiting, but all remained quiet, and the forest beckoned.

Chapter 69 – Danny Grows a Backbone

Now it was Danny's turn to pace the squad room like a trapped animal. He'd never been in charge like this before, and he doubted he was ready for this kind of responsibility. This wasn't like answering the phones or sending an ambulance. These were people's lives in the hands of a rookie who had been duped or subdued by an eighteen-year-old girl on more than one occasion.

Danny didn't want to place blame, but dammit! "If he had just listened to me. I told him not to go alone." And now Richard wasn't back, and he wasn't answering his radio or his cell phone. That left only one reasonable possibility: the Sheriff had been captured. Or maybe a second possibility…killed.

"Pete, you've got the station." Danny tossed him the keys. "Call the Troopers again, see what's taking them so long. And then protect that woman like she's your mother. Same orders: Anybody gets through, splatter the walls."

Richard's actions replayed in Danny's brain, so he took the opportunity to hand Pete a fresh radio. "Rotate off with what's-his-face when you need a spell."

Pete nodded, but an odd smirk carved its way across his face. It took Danny a minute to figure out why. "Uh, sorry, Pete. Of course, you should be in charge, you…"

Pete's head inched side to side, the barest move but enough to quiet Danny. "You got it. And I got this." He relieved Danny of the shotgun. "You know where I'll be if you need me." And without another word, the senior officer snagged a bulletproof vest for himself and prepared to play guard to the station's last remaining VIP guest.

Danny turned his attention to the others. He wanted the best with him, but he also needed serious manpower here at the station, protecting the two people who would be hiding in the basement. He split the difference. "Eckert, Bailey…you're here. You keep my partner and my boss's mother safe. But you," he pointed at Bailey. "You're rotating with Pete. That's your job. He needs a break, you're his relief." He got no response, so he jabbed his finger in their direction. "Got it?"

Only after they affirmed it did he move on, pointing to Nyugen and Santos. "You two are with me. We're taking three cars. You'll block the access road in case they make a break for it while I go in."

Arrogance lined Bailey's face and spoke out as clearly as if he'd said the words, "I ain't taking your orders." He searched the faces of his fellow officers, finding in them nothing but the resolute faith of men on the lower end of the chain of command. Bailey turned toward Pete. "He's the rookie."

Pete nodded. "Yep. But he's my rookie. And right now, he's giving the orders, so you best hop to. If anything else happens 'cause of you, I'm gonna drive my boot so far up your ass, you'll be using my shoelaces as dental floss."

Danny wormed his way through the forest, following the tracks Richard left behind. When he reached the edge of the marsh, he peered through the reeds with his binoculars, trying to get a feel for what was going on in the cabin.

Chapter 70 – The Getaway

Lane's eyes adjusted to the darkness, and she had no trouble avoiding the obstacles the forest spread out in her path. During the day, with a great deal more light, Lane might well have gone over the blockages, but at night those encumbrances could quickly turn from minor inconvenience to major booby trap. The last thing she wanted to hear was Angelo's laughter when he found her with a foot wedged between rocks.

She was sorely tempted to retrieve Grandpa Rainier's ride, making her escape both easier and faster. She could have been in that car and out of town, heading north and escaping into Canada before Angelo or Jack even figured out she was gone.

Too bad the Jeep sat alone on a hunting road just a mile away from Harris Lane, left behind at Richard's suggestion. Going back for it would put her much too close to Barnett.

Unfortunately, that left her with two incredibly crappy options. She could either steal a car, screw up her probation, and end up in prison—a particularly unpleasant thought, seeing as she would have to face her family. Or she could just hoof her way to Canada...as far as Port Angeles Harbor, anyway, where she would hop a ferry and sail on over to British Columbia.

The leg didn't hurt too much—just an occasional twinge of pain that stabbed throughout the knee and musculature—but Lane decided that even having her limbs ripped from her body one at a time by an angry grizzly had to be better than facing Richard's disappointment. She would do nothing to screw up, nothing that could land her in jail, and nothing further to upset her father...unless she had no other choice.

She paused often, listening in the night for sounds of pursuit. Hearing anything abnormal would give her a chance to hide from Angelo and Jack, and since the darkness of the forest made them equal competitors, they would have no better luck finding her at night than she would have of eluding them.

A sound carried on the wind and she dropped to her knee, pushing the bad leg out to the side and ducking behind a tree. At first it sounded like nothing more than branches in the wind, except there was no perceptible breeze. The brushing sound lengthened, as if an elk or deer was pushing through a long stand of trees. She stared into the darkness, sure that she should be able to see an animal that size strolling around.

Nothing stepped into view on any side of her. A new sound—a pounding, then an occasional grunt. Lane hunkered closer to the tree, fairly certain now that the sound emanated from the south. She eased around to block herself from view and leaned out to catch a glimpse.

The tan hide of an elk caught moonlight, but most of its body remained dark among the trees. It looked in her direction and gave a determined stomp, signaling its displeasure at her presence.

From this distance and in the dark, Lane couldn't judge the animal's full size. Considering the time of the year, the odds were high that if it were male, he would have already shed his rack. The fact wouldn't save her life; it just meant she wouldn't get gored. If the animal decided to kill her, it was thoroughly capable of doing so with its hooves and strong forelegs. But when its bugle split the still night air, Lane had no doubt that she sat less than fifty feet from an adult bull.

Fifty feet. The distance at which she could conceivably protect herself and win. Regrettably, the bow rested inside a makeshift shelter at Tippett Point—she couldn't hope to evade the bull long enough to get there. But elude him was exactly what she had to do, since she had chosen tonight to stroll through the forest without so much as a flyswatter or a rolled-up newspaper.

Lane waited, keeping watch on the animal. She had to get away from the cabin, had to get further into the forest, and had to keep trees between herself and this large, ornery creature.

But the beast was neither predator nor human. Elk didn't kill to eat, nor did they kill without cause. And since rutting season wouldn't start again until the fall, it might just be possible for Lane to alleviate any threat she presented to the brute.

Crouching low to the ground and keeping the tree in her line of sight, she backed away from the massive animal and headed for the top of Jensen Ridge.

Chapter 71 – Angelo Is Bent

Angelo threw open the bathroom door just after five a.m., his bark drowning out the crack of the door slamming against the wall. "Where is she?"

Richard's one good eye peeled open. "Get away, did she? Not at all surprising. It's kind of her M.O. You probably shouldn't have locked her in a room with a window."

"Your smart mouth could get you killed before the lady shows up."

Richard's hand closed on the knotted end of the sock wedged behind his back. "Well, if you plan on taking something else out of my hide, you best come help me up."

Angelo charged; Richard swung his soap-laden sock with all the strength he could muster.

The battle didn't last long. Richard delivered three furious blows with the makeshift bludgeon, nailing Angelo about the head and shoulders. But in his deliberate attempt to protect his bruised ribs with his left arm, he exposed his face to the giant's devastating right hook.

"Now what?" Jack asked, as Angelo dragged the beaten Sheriff from the bathroom.

"Now I'm going to have to go find that little bitch. But dragging that leg around behind her…there's gotta be a trail."

Chapter 72 – The Journey Begins

Once she'd cleared Jensen Ridge and left the bull elk on the south side, the trek had grown easier. Lane had worked her way to the path that led to her makeshift shelter, steadily putting more pressure on the artificial knee as she descended the hill, and growing pleased that the reconstructed joint wasn't hollering too much about it. Ray would be happy; Richard would probably just say, "I told you so."

After a quick stop at Tippett Point to pick up her survival gear, Lane struck out through the forest. Taking a northerly heading, she planned to avoid all the well-traveled byways, which would limit potential human encounters.

Her chuckle broke the silence. "Because God knows that elk aren't dangerous enough." Lane knew that by remaining free, her father and uncle would stay alive. And though forestry roads, ATV tracks, and hiking paths would make her trip faster, a chance encounter with anyone could jeopardize not only her future, but the lives of her family, as well.

She chose a route up into the mountains, only going high enough to break a sweat and make the climb difficult for anyone following her. Unfortunately, it all depended upon her knee, how much abuse it would take, and how long the painkillers would last.

"Kid!" Lane whirled toward the sound. Angelo, waving casually, emerged from the tree line in the valley she had just crossed. "I'm coming, kid!"

Chapter 73 – Reporting In

Danny stood beside the three cruisers, two of which were blocking the road and checking all vehicles going into or out of the area. "The Sheriff, Ray, and at least one other man are still in the cabin. I didn't see Lane, but there's some scuffing leading into the woods. My guess is that she got away, but it also looks like she's being followed."

He sized up the two officers, deciding who needed more attention. He hadn't had any sleep, either, but he wasn't going anywhere. "Nyugen. Go back to the station. Fill Pete in and then grab a few hours' shuteye."

Nyugen had other ideas. "You don't want to go in while there's fewer people inside? We could rush them."

"That house is full of guns. And I've got no idea how many killers we're dealing with. I need to have a better idea of what in the hell is going on. Like where Lane's off to and who's chasing her. And how long they'll be gone. In the meantime, tell Pete to call in a helicopter."

Chapter 74 – Grisdale Hill

In a fair race, Lane couldn't possibly beat a man with two good legs, but nothing said Lane had to be fair. Punishing this particular man with the terrain would still allow her to win, delaying him, keeping him out in the forest, and thereby keeping her father and uncle alive. Provided Ray hadn't already died. Soon Pete or the State Troopers would have figured something out. They would rescue Richard, get Ray to the hospital, and they could all live happily ever after.

"Yeah. What might that actually look like?" She paused for a breath, peering over the ledge and tracking Angelo's progress; he was keeping up, but the terrain prevented him from getting any closer to his quarry.

She couldn't fault him for being able to follow her—she left what amounted to a tornado track in her wake. In fact, his progress was admirable for a city boy; no doubt it was fed by his murderous rage. When he lost his footing and slid back down the rocks on his belly, losing several hard-gained feet, Lane settled on a rock and massaged her throbbing knee. She considered laughing over the cliff at him, but that would be incredibly foolish, especially since she hadn't exactly lost the city slicker in the forest yet. She would be laughing out the other side of her face if he caught up with her.

Down below, Angelo clambered back to his feet; Lane rose and ambled away, taking the most difficult route to make sure her pursuer had the toughest time possible. She needed to lose the big-fisted Italian before catching the ferry to Victoria, British Columbia, otherwise he would just follow her into Canada.

She veered northeast, steering a trajectory that would take her first to Grisdale Hill and then on to Dennie Ahl Hill. The course would require her to cross the valley and lowlands, which would give Angelo a chance to catch up, but if she reached Dennie, the climb would be more difficult, and the higher altitude would slow him again. She could continue to play games with him, leading him further north and onto even higher peaks.

If she really wanted to test the limits of Angelo's endurance, she could head northwest from Dennie, heading onto Prospect Ridge with its three thousand foot peaks. But that would also tax Lane. The easier route for her would be continuing northeast, skirting the southern shores of Lake Cushman and taking her to Dow Mountain. Its two thousand foot peaks wouldn't task her as much, making it easier to reach Port Angeles.

But Lane had time to decide where to go after Dennie Ahl. She smiled back down the hill and whispered, "Come on, buddy…keep up. I've got a surprise for you."

The whirring of a helicopter echoed in the mountains. Lane studied the firmament and located the mechanical bird southeast of her position. She made the assumption that they were looking for her, but God only knew why they were that far away. Apparently they expected her to follow the highway north. Below her on the slope, Angelo copied her movements, watching her and the copter. Lane's brows furrowed, studying the man who was learning from her.

She pushed on, reaching the top of Grisdale Hill just before nightfall. The cleared summit left her visible and vulnerable. Picking a quick route to the treeline on the north side of the slope, she hurried for the cover of the forest.

The decision had to be made: stopping for some sleep without knowing what Angelo was doing, or hiking through the night. One choice would let Angelo overtake her while the other left her at the mercy of the mountain. But if she holed up and

Angelo kept searching, then any cougars or grizzlies in the area would be drawn to him. And that wasn't a half-bad scenario. She could wake in the morning to find bits of his flesh strewn about the landscape, an intestine here, a limb there.

The trees caught her attention as she re-entered the forest. She should have been scouring the landscape for a likely resting spot, but instead her eyes sought the canopy. The wind danced in the branches, and the scratchy chatter of bough against bough sang a soothing lullaby.

And Lane heard it, sliding in through her ears and settling in her bones. She smiled, drawing in a deep, crisp breath through her nose. This felt good...this was something she could do...this was like coming home.

The moon rose, casting fingers of light among the standing timbers. Up ahead, a patch of ground contrasted starkly with the trees beyond it. Lane headed for the clearing and stepped out onto the dirt bed of a Forest Service road. It would make her easier to spot, but it would also help her move just a little faster and more easily. She followed it north, and it led her to a small river.

Nighttime would not normally be the time of day for a swim. Her watery forays usually occurred during the day so she had time to walk off the cold and wet and prevent hypothermia from setting in. Lane headed back into the forest and found a suitable tree in which to spend the night. She sized it up from all angles, circling the trunk and gazing up into its stout limbs. She placed a hand on the rough bark, as if appreciating a fine antique or comforting an old friend.

Her pack, bow, and quivers all hit the ground, nestling into forest debris which absorbed the sounds of her work. She dug a rope from the sack she'd taken before abandoning Ray to his fate and, after three tries, managed to toss one end over a branch several feet above the ground. While it dangled there waiting for something to hold, Lane quickly tied all her possessions on the other end and hauled it hand-over-hand into the branches. After securing the rope around the trunk, she climbed up after her gear.

The backpack held food and water, so she found it a resting place reasonably nearby, squishing it into a nook created by two convergent branches. The extra quivers of arrows would probably not be necessary...if she couldn't stop whatever was after her with the first two dozen projectiles, there was no reason to believe she could stop them with the remaining three dozen. Two quivers hung off the peg-like protrusions of broken branches some twenty feet off the ground.

The third quiver and the bow had to be close at hand, ready to protect her at a moment's notice if Angelo, or a cougar, jumped out of the night. She found a secure cranny to leave them in another ten feet up. One last job remained—retrieving the rope so she could use it in the morning, and so it wouldn't give her pursuer any clue as to her whereabouts.

Chapter 75 – Not Again

Bird song echoed in the forest, one very nearby waking Lane with its continual, and annoying, chirping. Sunlight filtered through the canopy, and squirrels scurried through trees in search of a quick and easy meal.

Lane stretched the kinks from her neck and back and carefully untied the rope that kept her from falling out of the tree. Maneuvering one appendage at a time, she withdrew herself from the sleeping bag, rolled it into a ball, and tossed it clear of the tree. It unfolded itself all the way down, but it did eventually make it to the forest floor.

Clinging tight to the rope so it wouldn't get away, she lowered herself the ten feet to the rest of her gear, tied them all back on the rope, and lowered them to the ground. When they settled into the pine bed, she released the rope and watched it snake between the branches, coiling itself in large swirls on the ground. Lane climbed down and packed up for another day's journey.

She didn't hear Angelo until it was too late. He grabbed her, spun her around, and slammed his massive hand into her face, knocking her back into the tree.

Lane's body collapsed, folding onto itself much the way the rope had during its descent from the tree. She sprawled in the dirt, pain zipping along the skin as it split wide open on her cheek bone. Fear seized her lungs, forcing them empty, and adrenaline surged through her blood. She scuttled away, kicking with her good leg in an effort to put some distance between herself and the big man.

Angelo fell atop her, his leg crashing into her artificial knee. The pain reeled her up from the ground, but he descended, knocking her flat, his rough hands wrapping around her throat and squeezing.

Lane pried at his arms and quickly shifted to punching him in the side of the head. It annoyed him just enough to release one hand from her throat; he used it in an attempt to backhand her into submission. The first strike pissed her off and she flailed at him. The second impact infuriated her and she rose up valiantly, swinging with both hands. The third blow finally defeated her and she fell onto the ground, completely spent.

"Damn, you're a pain in the ass." Angelo rose to a kneeling position, then stood. "Let's go. I wanna be back at the cabin by nightfall." He offered Lane a hand in getting up, but she declined, preferring to grovel in the dirt rather than accept his help. She tugged her possessions closer, the backpack, the bow—Angelo kicked it away and out of her reach—and the sleeping bag, which she started rolling up.

"Leave it. You're not going to need it again." Lane sat still for a minute, then pushed the sleeping bag off her lap and into the dirt. The rough fletching of an arrow brushed along her finger.

"Hurry up," Angelo barked. "And don't even think about running away from me."

That little piece of Lane that had remained hidden through the last twelve years of torment and neglect poked its little head out of the closet and reared up in defiance. "What?" Logic told her that Angelo could have no idea how his words would affect her, no idea what they had meant, or how those same words had been used against her so many times. How Morgan had used them to control her with fear. Nor could he have any real idea of the aftermath, the rape, the living on the streets, the destitution. The nightmares.

247

A jumble of memories rushed her brain, the torrents ripping in from so many directions and occasions that it would have been impossible to tell where the floodwaters began. Only a few lingered long enough for the memory to bring a tangible emotion—the darkness in the attic enveloping her, the sting of Jenna's slap, the intense pain of the rape. But as they all ran together, that little piece of Lane that survived grew angry, hostile, and went looking for someone to punish for it.

She launched herself at Angelo, knowing she couldn't possibly win, but too angry to care. And maybe, if she was lucky, he'd just kill her and get it over with.

The attack took him by surprise, but not for very long. And while Lane pummeled away at Angelo's head and chest, he landed a solid backhand that sent her sprawling in the dirt. As her head bounced off the ground, another memory surfaced—looking up at the sky and listening to the driveway gate clang shut after Morgan had thrown her into the street. The anger intensified. She rolled to her feet, climbed up and threw herself at Angelo again.

Chapter 76 – Lane Wins, More or Less

Lane spent most of the battle catching Angelo's hands across her face and looking up from the dirt. And every time she went down, the anger surged and forced her back to her feet.

One of the punches, Angelo's signature rib-buster, caught Lane just beneath her breast, knocking the wind from her lungs. Pain ripped along the ribs when she inhaled, which turned breathing into a focused attempt not to expand her lungs too much. She struggled to rise, clutching her side, and bowing forward so that the muscles wouldn't move across the rib cage.

The last hit knocked her senses and memories from her, and she stared up through the tree canopy, marveling at their beauty and wondering why she had decided to sleep outside, on the ground, in the forest, nothing more than a tasty snack for any predator in the area. She watched as the upper branches of the trees swayed in the gentle breeze, and puzzled over the identity of the man standing above her.

"Find some fight, did you?" Angelo descended toward her, his hands winding into her shirt and lifting her from the ground.

Pain seeped in at the edges of Lane's fuzzy consciousness, deepening with each slap of Angelo's big hand across her face.

He gave her a shake. "Are we done yet? I don't want to spend the night out here."

With a few more shakes, Lane returned to the realm of the cognitively aware, and she pushed against Angelo's arms. "Let me go."

Angelo drew her closer, glaring down at her, both amused and impressed by the girl's determination to hold her ground, and then he simply released her. "Head south."

"No." Lane took a step away.

"You haven't had enough? You want maybe I should beat you unconscious and then just carry you back?"

"That'll certainly make the trip longer."

Angelo laughed. "Yeah, but it won't make any difference in the end."

"Maybe not. But I'm not helping you destroy my family. And that means no matter what you want, you're not getting me back to Mills Valley before dark. Not if I'm walking, and not if you're carrying. So we need all my stuff, because we are spending another night right out here." Lane took a tentative step toward her sleeping bag, then turned her back on the big man, gathering up her possessions.

Once again, Angelo's speed surprised her, snatching the pack and tossing it away. "I'm gettin' damn sick of you."

Lane tracked the flight path of the bag, but the instant she turned to retrieve it again, Angelo grabbed her and threw her to the ground. He followed her down, grabbing her throat with one hand, and staring down at her with his death-filled eyes. "You're going to do what I say or, as God is my witness, I'll rip you from stem to stern and leave your body here for the animals." His empty hand jabbed into her pelvis and dragged up the centerline to her sternum as if he were gutting a fish.

Someone Lane hadn't known in a long time took control of her tongue. She couldn't hide the dismissive tone, even though the words slurred between her swollen and busted lips. "What? It makes a difference where I die?" Her hands thrashed against the ground, pushing against the pine debris on one side and the sleeping bag on the other. The arrow brushed along her finger.

Her brain leapt for joy, and her fingers clawed in the dirt, seducing the only available weapon into the palm of her hand.

"Careful...there's a little bit of your mother coming out there. You should trust me when I tell you that a bullet to the head is a whole lot quicker than getting splayed wide open. It won't take too long to bleed to death, but you're gonna feel every second of it. And it'll sure attract something, if only crows to pick at your intestines and drag them around the countryside. And because your mother wants your father to see you die, I'll capture it on my iPhone so I can show your old man before I put a bullet in his brain."

Lane's teeth clenched tight and her hands balled up into fists. A scream rose up in her brain, pounding at her eardrums from the inside out, and beating against her eyelids with flashes of squiggles and patterns.

It took longer than normal to funnel that command through the channel now serving as her voice box; the shriek clawed its way out of Lane's body like caged tiger. "I am nothing..." she whispered, clamping onto the graphite shaft, drawing it out from under the sleeping bag and rising into a sitting position at the same time. Her words amplified, grinding into a growl. "...like my mother!"

When Angelo latched onto her face in an attempt to subdue her, Lane experienced no black out or glimpses of past events. No memories surfaced to cloud her judgment. And she slammed the arrow deep into Angelo's back.

The giant roared, swung, and connected with her jaw.

Lane woke, her goose-bumped flesh pressed against the cold ground. Pain coursed up her leg, and a dull throbbing spread out from her face, but her mind was oddly silent. No thoughts jumbled about trying to get her attention, no worries snuck in to plague her.

The wind danced in the tree branches, tousling them gently and drawing Lane's eyes to those boughs as they embraced and released each other in a simple yet carefully choreographed ballet.

A tickle at the side of her face drew her attention, and she wiped at it, surprised to see a stripe of crimson on her hand. The vague throbbing turned to pain, spreading like fire along the skin, hugging the corners of her mouth, up along her cheeks, and around her eyes.

Her fingers toured the damage zone, finding splits on her lips, along one cheekbone, and above one eye. Inside her mouth, her tongue investigated the salty ooze pooling between lips and gums, then gingerly probed the three teeth wiggling loosely in their sockets. The only thing that came to her mind was *what in the hell did I do?*

As the clouds lifted in her brain, bits and pieces of the beating filtered in. The slaps had done damage on their own, but that last punch…that jaw-knocker…had brought a fog that settled into her brain like a shroud, and it left her wondering if a concussion lurked in that mist somewhere.

Lane didn't feel queasy at all or lightheaded, but she couldn't deny that, upon waking, it had taken several moments to figure out where she was and how she got there.

She wiped the blood from her fingers against the palm of her other hand, only then realizing that her injuries weren't limited to her face. Dried blood had caked in creases and tiny slices—one on her pinky and two on the side of the palm, all of which stung like killer paper cuts. When she closed her hand into a fist, the marks lined up as the tail-end of the razorback she had jammed into Angelo's back.

Angelo. He'd vowed to gut her like a fish. Lane's hands flew to her torso, probing the centerline, and she tried to rise up to get

252

a good look at her belly. Pain high in her rib cage made the move impossible, and Lane was forced to rely on her hands to probe her midsection. Relief flooded out of her, relief that her hands didn't slide inside her body, and that her intestines were not strung out along the forest floor. She laughed and cried and sucked air like she had been completely drained of breath for hours.

Focusing on the bruised ribs and breast, Lane rolled onto her side, tucking her left arm against her flank in order to cradle the damage, supporting the injuries as she fought her way to a sitting position.

Glad to be alive and in one piece, she sought out her tormentor. The quick snaps of her head back and forth brought a wave of that lightheadedness she had worried about. The fog slammed back down, and Lane braced herself with her hands until the haziness passed.

A pool of blood muddied the dirt nearby; a thin trail led to Angelo laid out several feet away. From the look of him, he had been twisting himself about trying to get the arrow out of his back and tripped himself up. Or maybe he had run headlong into a tree. Lane had no intention of getting any closer to figure it out; from this distance, she simply could not tell if he was dead or just unconscious—not that she cared. Dead was good, but alive wouldn't do much for him out here alone. He would be dead soon enough. As the mechanisms of survival kicked in, she packed up her gear and headed north.

With her head pounding a steady beat, Lane stopped often to drink and refill her canteen, utilizing every fresh water source between Grisdale and Dennie Ahl Hills. The ten plus mile drive would take about forty minutes by vehicle; walking, she expected it would take six hours, maybe longer, and that meant pretty much the rest of the day.

Breaking her own rule in order to move faster, she settled into a stilted hike along the Forest Service roads, listening for the sounds of motors and engines that would alert her to oncoming dangers.

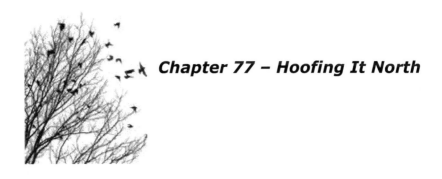

Chapter 77 – Hoofing It North

An assortment of pains vied for attention. The rib and breast ached, but Lane minimized the impact by bracing her arm against her side. The knee, however, worked harder to cripple its owner; agony stabbed along the tendons with each step she took.

Lane sat on a rock, digging through her backpack for the painkillers. Frustration built as she searched, until finally she dumped the contents on the ground, shaking everything loose until the pills popped out.

She popped one and rested for twenty minutes, waiting for the pain to fade before continuing the trek north to Dennie Ahl Hill. With no one else in sight and momentarily in charge of her own destiny, she felt invincible. Almost.

Wild animals roamed these forests. So did dangerous men like Angelo, if he hadn't already bled to death. If one listened to novel writers and newsmen, killers thrived in the Pacific Northwest, which had been dubbed the serial killer capital of the world.

Lane knew the drill, drummed into her head by Uncle Ray, who brought up the subject every time a new murderer was caught or a new victim found. Sometimes, if Ray became particularly distressed by an incident, he would even request she avoid the woods for a while. Whether or not she obeyed depended upon how disturbed her uncle became. But at the moment, she seriously doubted that there could be anyone more dangerous than Angelo in these woods.

If Angelo hadn't bled out—which Lane thought a long shot at best—then the odds rested at fifty/fifty on whether he was dogging her or had crawled back to the cabin for aid and comfort. Following now would be slower for him, what with an arrow sticking out of his back and every hungry, blood-loving predator in the forest zoning in on the smell of fresh meat.

During this leg of her travels, she had been more careful about not leaving a trail for the assassin to follow, making sure he wouldn't know what direction she had taken or what her destination might be; it pushed the odds to sixty/forty in her favor.

The forced march proved uneventful, as nothing more dangerous than birds and chipmunks chose to cross Lane's path. A few hours before sundown, she climbed away from the gravel road and up into the forest, scouting out a decent place to spend the night. Had she been more familiar with this area, she would have known where to go, but her woodland expeditions usually centered around Mills Valley, not Dennie Ahl.

As with any trip into the forest or mountains, several things remained constant—predators, shelter, warmth, water, food. Three of those concerns were easily addressed; her full canteen would get her through until morning, her sleeping bag was adequate protection from the cold mountain nights, and Pop-Tarts were God's gift to humanity, the perfect food, a combination of carbs and fruit filling, loaded with simple sugars.

Shelter didn't really matter. One night at forty degrees in a sleeping bag rated for thirty-degrees-below-zero wouldn't kill her. That left predators.

Dangerous creatures in the wilds were more likely to be four-footed than two, and those were the ones Lane planned to stymie. Bobcat and coyote seldom attacked people; if they did, the odds were great they were rabid, and that presented problems aside from being eaten alive. Bear didn't usually use humans as a food source, but that didn't mean that getting attacked by one wouldn't hurt or lead to death.

Cougars. Those were the scary ones. The big cats didn't see anything as off the menu; the size of the prey merely dictated whether it was an appetizer, an entrée, or the dessert. Lane didn't care whether the problem was a decline in their natural food source, or simply a decline in predator management programs that produced an abundance of cougar and thereby caused a shortage of food. Cougars were big, scary, dangerous, and always looking for a free and easy meal. Lane didn't plan to become an hors d'oeuvre.

With ample sunlight left to do the job, she scoped out the local trees. Many of the sturdier specimens lacked low-lying branches; there was no way to climb them without spikes or hoists. She settled for a stand of young trees, all roughly the diameter of her arm, in which to construct a nest.

She started with two specimens growing very close together. Alone, they probably wouldn't support her weight...together, they'd begin to do the job. Using the scarred ridges where older branches had already broken off, Lane looped a section of rope around the two trees and made a foothold.

Lane's intention had been to climb into the tree—the pain in her ribs made it more difficult than she expected. After taking a quick break for another painkiller, she fought through the misery, gritting her teeth and relying on her right leg to do the pushing while her right hand did the pulling.

The effort got her three feet off the ground but left her panting from the exertion. When she could breathe again, she made another loop around the two trees, this one about a foot above the first. Another loop, and another, and twenty minutes later—just about the time the painkiller kicked in—Lane stood fifteen feet in the air.

Perched above the ground, Lane leaned out and looped the rope around another young tree, drew it closer, and tied it off to her ladder-trees. After three more trees met similar fates, she climbed into the nest of ropes and tested it for strength.

The opposing force of trees trying to get to their original upright positions held the ropes taut, supporting Lane's meager weight without question. Once the sleeping bag was rolled out and positioned, it would be almost comfortable. With her pack and canteen hanging from nearby branch stubs, she would be able to reach whatever she needed, be that the simple joy of a Pop-Tart or a long, leisurely drink of pure, filtered river water.

As always, the day replayed itself in living color, perhaps a bit exaggerated due to her jaded perspective, but true for the most part. She had taken a serious beating at Angelo's hands, and it reminded her of Morgan's brutality. Those memories flooded back, reminding her of her vulnerability and mortality. Of how close someone had come to killing her, and how easy it had been for them to do it.

But that hidden part of Lane's old psyche, the fragment that screamed in Angelo's face and hinted that being murdered wasn't any big deal, that tiny allotment of spunk hadn't gone back into exile when the emergency was over. That little piece of the old Lane had steered her northward, eyes seeking a suitable route, legs overcoming obstacles like she had been born a three-legged mountain goat. That little piece of the old Lane didn't want to go back into hiding, and grew exponentially bolder.

Lane sank into the rope webbing and wrapped her sleeping bag around her, pondering the events, the meanings, and the outcomes, staring up at the stars hovering calmly in the sky, little pinpoints of light billions of miles away. Tiny auras glowed down from heaven, miniature versions of the big one surrounding the moon. Tons of them together, but all alone in a sea of ink. Separate. Islands of isolation.

Lane wanted to be one of those stars, cooling slowly but burning brightly. Strong. Independent. Unaffected by the actions of man. At one time, she thought she had been nearly unaffected…avoiding Morgan, staying just outside the reach of his anger and animosity. She had been able to endure the isolation and loneliness, relying on Ray as her sole companion. But she hadn't been able to avoid the rape, and that one incident now defined everything she was, everything she did, and everything she thought.

Her body was sore from courting Angelo's wrath, but the rest of her—her spirit—felt good. Alive. Powerful. Unbridled and unbroken. Determined to go on living because that one event would not have a lasting impact nor alter the natural course of her existence.

"Why should it?" she asked the sky. She believed God was up there, watching, listening, and helping. She didn't expect an answer, but she did figure she would get something close enough—insight, guidance, or understanding.

It was easier to talk to God about it than to anyone else. She hadn't even told Ray, the one human being she had always been able to talk to about anything. She had found that she just couldn't say the words, "Morgan raped me." Ray knew it. In fact, everyone in Mills Valley knew it. It was in their eyes every time they looked at her. Just like Jason had said. Everybody knows.

"Of course they freakin' know." God was so much easier to talk to. He had no face, no eyes to show condemnation, regret, or pity. No eyes at all. No frown, either. He didn't say much, certainly didn't pry, and if he wanted something, he always made it a point to make it sound like some random thought popping into her head. God also made no comments about her colorful language or the condition of her bedroom.

"It really is there every time they look at me."

One of those random thoughts popped in. Maybe it's the presentation.

Her face screwed up as she delved into a conversation with herself. "I was raped. He crushed my larynx and ripped me open. I ain't exactly spilling my guts about it."

But am I subconsciously saying it every time I walk into a room?

"No, no, no, no, no…am I?"

Of course I am.

"Yeah, right. I need a pill." But while she dug through her pack for another painkiller, the little voice prodded, suggesting that if she didn't walk into a room looking like a pitiable waif, maybe people wouldn't treat her like one. The voice merged into her conscious thought.

"Like Richard. Yeah, just like Richard. I am not pitiable. I'm afraid. I'll give you that. But I'm not pitiable. I don't want to remember it, I don't want to think about it, and I sure in hell don't want to talk about it." She focused on the tiny, cool pinpoints of light in the sky. "Not with the shrink, that's for sure."

And Richard?

Her head wagged back and forth. "I dunno. I know he'd listen. I know he's trying to help."

He needs me.

"Then why in the hell am I running away? Again."

To be safe?

"To keep them safe. This is like, the last-ditch attempt to keep all of us alive. Man, this is too confusing." She closed her eyes and studied the inside of her eyelids while waiting for sleep.

Dawn didn't come quickly enough. Sleep eluded her, coming in spats but not staying long. When asleep, she dreamt of her father and uncle, needless fights, and missed opportunities.

260

When awake, she scanned the countryside for predators, at one point staring down at a passing coyote that had found her hiding place but quickly realized he couldn't get to her. All the while, she raged against the one-sided conversation in her head.

It made her want to scream until the sound echoed back from the mountaintops. Jumbled thoughts merged with rape statistics, and mental images whizzed through her head...the shrink, her family, even Morgan taking his pleasure and then dropping dead at her feet with ten bullets in his body. She couldn't turn it off.

Any other day, even if her family and doctors were trying to get her to "open up" about the incident, she would be able to shut them out, push them aside, and drown the noise into silence. But last night she couldn't pull it off.

Three times more likely to be depressed. Four times more likely to consider suicide. Twenty times more likely to abuse drugs.

She could have laughed out loud, remembering the aftermath of her overdose, but managed to stifle that, at least. As desperately as she wanted to be quiet, she also needed someone to talk to. "Not like we don't know why Richard hid the pills," she whispered into the dark, hearing the sound of her own voice and letting it provide some small measure of comfort. "I really was popping them like candy. But I ain't killing myself. No way. I'm surviving this. Millions of women get raped. They don't all kill themselves. I'm gonna survive this." Determination drove into her gut. "I am going to survive."

A gentle breeze wafted down from the mountains, a slow current carrying the crispness of late spring snows. It danced among the branches and tousled the hair of a human it hadn't seen in quite a while. It coursed through the trees and Lane turned her face to meet it, letting it slide along both cheeks and feather her hair away from her face. Head tipping back, she

261

listened, and she heard it sing, heard the chatter of rustling limbs and felt the loving hand of God.

A deep breath brought the smell of lush greenery, mountain streams, and coyote scat to her nostrils. She filled her lungs and held the scent until she thought her lungs might burst.

She had thought them gone, the wind, the trees, the life she'd had. But they were all still there, right where she had left them.

Right where I left them. "It's me. And it always has been." Tears stung her eyes as they crawled their way to the surface. Ray had come close to sacrificing the priesthood for her, and he had done it willingly. Richard had stepped outside his comfort zone of solitude to be her father. Willingly. No one had to fight with him. No one had to say anything to him…as far as Lane knew. No shame, no admonishment, no threat. Perhaps it had started out as a responsibility he had to perform, but he never treated her like it bothered him. He hadn't punished her for it. He simply accepted it.

Sure, there were times when it was more than obvious that he hadn't a clue what to say or do. But isn't that the case with most fathers? They don't all know what to say and do, do they? They screw up, right? Right?

A tear brimmed and fell, coursing down her face in slow motion. It had been a long time between cries; she had almost thought her tear ducts had dried up and withered to dust. Another tear slipped the dam, this one traveling faster on the moist slide left behind by the first one.

"Not like I made it easy for him. Not like I wasn't trying to see if he'd screw up." She stared off into the sky, the stars now fading with the morning sun. "But he said he loved me."

The dam broke. Flood waters trapped by months of repression surged out, set free by the simplest of revelations. She cried until no more tears would come.

Lane wiped away the remnants of sorrow with her shirt, catching a whiff of Richard from his jacket. She pulled the leather closer to her face and sank her nose in it, breathing deeply, knowing she would never forgive herself, wondering if he could. And why he would even bother.

She surveyed the area carefully, peering high and low for animals, the kind that kill either out of intention, fear, or just plain orneriness. A bull moose, generally an uncommon sight on this side of the state, drank from the stream several hundred yards away, but he could cover that distance quickly if he wanted to. Safety said wait him out, and ten minutes later he wandered away, heading back into the forest.

With nothing in sight besides a barking squirrel who apparently hadn't heard her wailing, Lane dropped her pack and canteen to the ground. She glared up at the furry beast, all of seven inches tall, his tail flicking about as he scurried down the trunk, then back up, then around the side. "You even try to beat me to that pack, and I'll have you for breakfast."

He screamed an alert, no doubt to warn any other squirrels in the area about the surly human invading their trees, and scurried away as Lane pulled herself out of her bed. She dropped the sleeping bag to the ground, then eased the trees loose of their bindings, setting them free to once again be trees and not bed framing.

Packed and ready to go, with the area as pristine as it had been when she arrived and perhaps a little more fertile for her salty tears, she continued her trek north along the Forest Service road.

An hour passed slowly. With each step, Lane felt like she was wading through waist deep mud. It was all she could do to move forward, because her mind kept looking back, dwelling on all the yesterdays that had gotten her into this position, on the family she had left behind on her run to safety, on the mother

263

who so desperately wanted her daughter and the name Keates wiped from the Earth.

Lane's ankle twisted and she stumbled, catching herself just before she slammed face first into the ground. Behind her, a rock sat on the edge of the road, all of six inches across and maybe three high, and certainly not invisible. "You gotta be freakin' kiddin' me."

She climbed up, dusted herself off, and continued on her way. Four steps later, she stopped, staring up the road ahead of her, then turning and staring down the road behind. Another step, and another, and she stopped again, turning sideways. Richard popped into her head, then Nana, and finally Ray. Another step, dragging her right leg behind her.

Her breath caught in her throat, her skin flushed, and numbness tingled in her arms and legs. Beads of sweat popped out on her forehead, and the muscles in her chest felt as if they were crushing her lungs flat.

The ground came up quickly as Lane crashed to her knees. Seconds later, a new thought pushed all the others clean out of view, but this time it came with Richard's voice. These guys are professionals. Sooner or later, they'll just kill whoever they find wherever they find 'em.

Lane braced her hands against the ground to keep herself from falling prone, and she stared into the gravel, trying to rein in her breathing and calm her shaking limbs. She was about to lose her family, the family it took so very long to get and which had come at so high a cost to all of them. Jenna would see Richard and Ray dead, even if she couldn't get Lane at the same time. "Oh, dear God...what have I done?"

Chapter 78 – Jenna Arrives

After a quick stop in Mills Valley to advise the Sheriff's Office—where all the deputies behaved rather poorly—of Jenna's status, Barnett pulled the car through the gate at the Harris Mansion and parked at the main door. Jenna took the opportunity to survey her estate, admiring her home, the grounds...her empire.

Barnett ushered the woman inside. "There have been some changes since you were last here, Jenna. First, I'm in the master suite."

A barefoot young woman dressed in skin-fitting blue jeans and a cropped tee shirt which revealed her belly button ring and tramp-stamp tattoo bounced in from the kitchen. A smile full of teeth graced her face when she saw Barnett, and she set a bottle of beer and a plate of fruit down so she could wrap both arms around her current client.

Barnett's hand squished down into the rear pocket of her jeans. "Lindsey...have you found the pool?"

Her eyes flashed, and her smile grew just a little wicked as one eyebrow peaked. "I was hoping we could explore that."

"Every nook and cranny. But let's start upstairs first. I'll be up in a few minutes." He silenced Jenna's argument until Lindsey was safely out of earshot, watching her sashay up the staircase and out of view.

He turned to Jenna. "And you are free to take any other room you'd like. Maybe Lane's room. Or maybe that first room. I've seen a number of recordings that suggest you know exactly what to do in there. Wonderful acting. I must say, I never would have looked for a second safe in the master suite, especially one so cleverly hidden, if your daughter hadn't been so gracious as to point it out."

He didn't retaliate to the slap that crossed his face, knocking his head to the side. Not that he was above physical confrontation, but at the moment he was far too amused by Jenna's reaction.

"You throw me out of my room and take a whore to my bed?"

Barnett shrugged. "Why not? It's fairly obvious that Morgan took a whore to that bed every night." His finger rose in warning as Jenna's hand cocked back for another blow. "Don't. I gave you the first one."

Barnett sauntered through the great room as if he had lived there his whole life. At the bar, he poured himself a drink and showed enough courtesy to offer Jenna one.

She declined. "No." Her mouth had pinched tightly shut, and her eyes shifted between Barnett and the staircase, giving Barnett the feeling that Jenna was still watching Lindsey skank her way up to the third floor.

"Envy is unbecoming, my dear. Don't hate her because she's beautiful. Or even because she makes no bones about being a whore. She's here to make my stay tolerable. Of course, there was a time when I might have considered taking you to my bed, but really, Jenna. Look at yourself."

Chapter 79 – Off and Running

Skirting the forest road under full pack and five dozen arrows, with a bow in one hand and a sleeping bag bouncing off her butt, topped the list as the granddaddy stupidest thing Lane had done this week. She smiled, thinking that Richard would probably challenge her decision on granddaddy stupid things. No doubt he would point out a dozen or so other dumb things she had done that could rank up there on top of the list, too.

To move faster, she had only to drop the excess baggage, tuck it under a bush somewhere, and leave it. If she really wanted it, she could come back for it after the emergency was over...provided Richard didn't lock her away for the rest of her life.

But to move safely, she needed all the gear she had. If she didn't make it back to the cabin today, she would need to be warm tonight, so the sleeping bag had to stay with her. And if an overnight stay was called for, she would need to eat. Canned food maybe hadn't been a wise choice, but it was all she had.

She also needed to stay hydrated, and she stopped at every stream and river she passed, filling her canteen once to drain it immediately, and then filling it again for the road.

That left arrows and odds and ends. The arrows didn't have to speak on their own behalf, being both offensive and defensive in nature. But the odds and ends were hidden in the backpack; digging them out would waste time and probably wouldn't save her more than a pound or two. She mused over it. "How much does a pair of socks weigh, anyhow?"

But pushing harder and walking faster strained the knee, and it wasn't long before the leg throbbed like it had during that last session of PT with Erika. The longer she coerced it to obey, the more the knee hurt. No doubt if she mentioned that to anyone, she would get a lecture about her reluctance to participate in her own recovery. She regretted being such a baby, balking, complaining, and squirming instead of doing her physical therapy. She had no one to blame at the moment except herself. More and more it looked like her father and uncle were right more often than not. And that just sort of pissed her off.

When the joint refused to support her weight any longer, she settled onto a fallen tree, hoping to entice the leg back into service with a little massage. The rest of her body ached, too. Muscles that hadn't been used in a long time resented having to work now. Bruises, cuts, and scrapes wanted her to move slower. But at least the rest of her body obeyed her commands. The reconstructed knee, however, declined, screaming its displeasure along the nerve endings and into Lane's brain each time she even attempted to extend the leg.

With time on her hands that she didn't necessarily want, multi-tasking seemed a good way to make it seem less wasted. Another Pop-Tart bit the dust, chased down by half a canteen of water. But that killed all of three minutes, and the leg wasn't any more ready to do its job than it had been before the Pop-Tart left the security of its foil wrapper.

She could certainly force it to move, though odds were that she would be moving even more slowly. What she really needed was a way to pick up the pace. "If I had just done the damn therapy, maybe I could run…"

The words hung in the air with the steam from her breath and were promptly joined by one of the more pertinent statistics she had tormented herself with the night before. Twenty times more likely to abuse drugs.

Chapter 80 – Jenna Goes to Richard

Barnett, water dripping off his swim trunks and spattering the floor, set a pair of hiking boots on the settee next to Jenna. "You should be going over to the cabin now. Looks like you'll have to settle for two out of three."

"Who's missing?" Jenna demanded. The sneer she gave her brother-in-law held almost as much contempt as the glare she cast at the footwear.

"The girl. She apparently slipped out a window. Angelo is chasing her, but it's only a matter of time before the Deputies call in the State Police. Your window of opportunity is closing. I suggest you settle for what you can get."

Jenna rose from the chair, a fluid motion of sophistication and elegance, and glanced down her nose at large-breasted but poorly styled Lindsay, whose bathing suit revealed far too much skin for Jenna's taste. "Fine." She drew her long, trim leg onto the cushion. "But since you didn't deliver on our deal, don't expect full payment. Help me remove this." Hiking up the leg of her slacks, she revealed the ankle bracelet that the police were using to monitor her.

"I'm afraid you'll have to take that with you, my dear. I do not want the police showing up here. Even if Lindsey and I are "busy", I certainly don't want to be implicated in your apparent escape."

"I'm not escaping."

"Of course you are. Removing the tether is the same as escaping from jail."

"Well, I can't take it with me! What if I'm at Richard's when they try to call me?"

"The instant you cut that strap, it will transmit a distress call to the authorities. No amount of money can stop it. I can, however, control a computer generated phone call to record your whereabouts, so you needn't worry about that." He checked his watch—rather, his dead brother's watch, a Tour de I'lle manufactured by Vacheron Constantin and cast in 18k rose gold with a sapphire crystal. Barnett flashed it for Jenna. "Nice, isn't it? That dear, sweet child gave up the combination so very easily."

Jenna's mouth dropped open into a gaping cavern inviting enough for house wrens to take up residence.

"Problem?" Mock innocence dripped from his tongue. "Not like anyone else is using it. You've got just under four hours. That should be plenty of time for you to get your gloat on, see them dead, and be back here. And just to be gracious, I agree that you shouldn't have to pay full price when I wasn't able to complete all the requirements of our arrangement. Let's call it seven point five, shall we? And I'll just keep the watch."

"And what about Lane? She's what? Running around the countryside somewhere?"

"What difference? Very soon now, both the men in her life will be dead. Not something I think she'll be getting over very quickly. Isn't that enough?"

Jenna fumed. "I guess it'll have to be. I'll need the car."

His head waggled back and forth. "The road is blocked by police officers. I'll take you as far as I can, but then you'll have to hike through the woods."

"You're joking."

Barnett ignored her. "And while you're gone, I think Lindsay and I will watch some more of your videos...for inspiration."

270

Jenna's Manolo Blahnik pumps bounced off Barnett's leg as she kicked them off her feet.

The princess from the Peninsula tromped around the edge of Jensen Pond but could find no way to cross the tributary without walking in muck. The ooze sucked her foot in, slipped over the top of the boot, and wicked down along the sock. By the time she pulled that foot free, the other was stuck. So it went for the thirty feet of marshland she had to navigate before standing on the cabin side of the lake, but by that time her feet were wet, and everything below the knee was muddy. She stamped up the stairs at the front of the cabin.

The door flew open and Jack stared down the barrel of a shotgun at her. He quickly lowered it. "Sorry, ma'am."

Jenna left a track of brown goo footprints as she entered the cabin, demoting Jack to her personal servant and leaving him to close the door. Ropes bound the unconscious priest to a chair, but his breathing definitely sounded like something inside was broken. Seriously broken. "He's half dead. He won't even know what hit him. I doubt he'll even figure out that I'm here."

But she didn't wait for a response. Instead she toured the house, fingering things, finding Lane's bedroom, heading upstairs to tour the rest of the house. The corner of her lip peaked up and her chin tucked in tight to her neck as she inspected the bedrooms. The larger room served as the master suite, but only its size made it any different from any other room. It had no his-and-hers armoires, no matching side tables, not even its own lavatory. It was nothing more than an oversized bedroom.

When she returned to the first floor, she planted herself in front of Richard, who sat on a throw rug with his hands tied behind his back.

He looked up at her, then down at her boots. "Track enough mud through my house, did you? What? Couldn't find the stepping stones?"

She raised her foot, planted it on his shoulder and dragged it down his body, wiping off some of the mud and aggravating his damaged ribs. "What? No maid? It won't matter soon." She draped herself on the couch, removed her filthy shoes, and dropped them on the coffee table. "You haven't found Lane yet? Is it that difficult to subdue one cripple?" she asked Jack, eyeing the mud on her fingers and wiping it off in stripes on the arm of the sofa.

"You have no idea." Jack's flat tone drew a chuckle from Richard and a glare from Jenna. "Don't worry. Angelo'll get her. She says she has all of your dead husband's bank account numbers."

"Fools. She's playing you. I have them all."

"She says Morgan didn't tell you about all of them because he didn't trust you."

"Really? Well, indulge yourself. When you figure out you've been duped, do be sure to make her pay you for that, too. In the meantime, I'm going to take a shower. Richard, be a love and help me?" Jack didn't approve, but Jenna laughed at him. "What's he going to do? If he tries anything, you kill his brother. In the meantime, we'll have one last chance to reconcile our differences."

Richard followed Jenna to the upstairs lavatory, producing items as she requested them: towels, shampoo, soap, a robe, fresh clothing. While he didn't have much to offer in the way of women's clothing, he managed to find some jeans his mother stored at the cabin. He returned to the bathroom to find Jenna butt-naked, waiting for him.

She drew his body against hers, the body he had enjoyed so many times. Gently pushing her away, he declined her obvious offer.

Her behavior turned homicidal, her eyes wide and her features stern. "I'll have Ray killed."

"You'll have him killed anyway. I'd rather you just did it than teased me with a lie." And he headed back down to the living room. Her scream chased him, reaching him before he hit the bottom stair.

Jack motioned the sheriff back to his spot on the floor, and Richard knelt down, interlocking his fingers behind his head as well as he could with the pain in his side. "What happened?"

"I guess I'm not the man I used to be."

Chapter 81 – Back to the Rock Shelter

Fifteen miles alternating between a swift walk and a light jog on uneven terrain took the better part of seven hours. Lane thumped onto Tippett Point feeling good enough to bounce another fifteen if she had to. Fortunately, she didn't. The cabin sat just over a mile away, and with good luck, the good Lord, and a good wind, she would be there in half an hour, tops.

Now it was possible, feasible even, to shed some extra weight and shave some time off her anticipated ETA. After knocking back another hydrocodone to keep the knee responsive, she tossed all the extraneous gear into her boulder-bound sleeping nook, keeping only the bow and its arrows at hand.

But five dozen was no longer an acceptable number of projectiles. She wouldn't have time to draw that many, not with Jack firing a handgun or a shotgun at her. Or any of the rifles Richard and Ray kept at the cabin. Five razorbacks remained; they would have to be enough. Strapping on a quiver and sliding four arrows in for safe carrying, Lane nocked the final arrow to the string before heading down to the cabin at double time.

Double time for her, anyway. In the old days—she smiled as Ray's favorite saying sprang to mind—in the old days, back when she had two good legs, back when she was a cross country runner with scholarship options and promises of a bright future, back six months ago, she could have covered that mile in five minutes.

But that was ancient history. Her knee had been torn asunder by the Sheriff's bullet, a move designed to keep her from escaping half-dressed and freezing to death in the mountains.

Lane knew he'd had no choice, and she never held it against him. There had been an occasion or two when she thought maybe he wanted to talk about it. She knew he felt bad…she saw it on his face every time she struggled to get the leg to take orders. It behaved pretty much like she did every time Richard tried to get her to take direction. Isn't that odd? she thought.

A new idea gnawed at the back of her brain. A sudden teasing suggested that maybe the mile between her and the cabin could still be crossed in five minutes flat. While she contemplated the bedeviling notion, the logical half of her brain reminded her that forcing a true run right now could result in her never walking again.

It didn't take long to make a decision. In the grand scheme of things, walking just didn't seem that important when compared to the very real possibility that if she didn't run, she might never see her family again.

She popped another pain killer for good measure.

Chapter 82 – Danny Gets Nailed

Still in the position of not knowing where Lane was, who was following her, or how many armed combatants he could expect to encounter, Danny decided to take a chance trying to free Richard. He followed the sheriff's path, swinging around the pond and approaching from Jensen Ridge.

As he neared the cabin door, he expected to hear something going on inside the house, but at the moment, all remained quiet. He brought his rifle to bear, wedging it against his shoulder as he eased the back door open.

The shotgun blast nailed him in the chest, striking with such force that it knocked him clean off the porch and into the dirt. Unconsciousness claimed him the instant his head slammed into the ground.

Chapter 83 – Lane Arrives

The shotgun blast echoed through the forest. Had it been a gun battle, Lane would have expected more shots to follow. When none came, her mind jumped immediately to another scenario: execution.

A shotgun was acceptable as a short range weapon in an execution…it would certainly kill whoever it was pointed at. Its one big flaw was the spray of body goo that would cover everything in sight, including the shooter.

Lane calmed herself with a simple reminder: Jenna was involved in this. Jenna. Mother, wife, heart-breaker, whore. Jenna. Little Miss I've-Got-A-Vendetta. That screamed handgun to the frontal lobe so she could watch her victims' eyes as they died.

Lane ran faster, scrambling through the woods over Jensen Ridge. The foolishness of overdosing on pain killers had gotten her to the cabin faster, but the leg hurt anyway. Seriously hurt. Split the knee open and slap her in the face with angry tendons hurt. And if that wasn't enough, her brain seemed to be in on the conspiracy, periodically washing confusion over her eyes.

How many pills did I take? It hardly mattered. They had gotten her where she needed to be, but the downside of such an overdose was most likely a sudden, serious crash. Before that happened, she had to get into the cabin, do what she had come to do, and free her family…whoever was still alive.

She shook off the fuzziness and coursed the top of the ridge, traveling the crest until she knew she could not be seen from any of the cabin's first floor windows. She forged a new trail down the slope, carefully picking her steps, avoiding sticks and leaves for their potential to make noise and stones for their propensity to trip her up and invite her to eat muck. From her vantage point, she saw Danny, laid out on the ground outside the back door, arms and legs splayed apart, completely motionless.

A quick detour took her to the deputy's side and she knelt in the dirt next to him. A small puddle of blood pooled under the deputy's head, and Lane eased his hair out of the way to see the split across the back of his skull, the blood just starting to clot. Setting down her bow, she stripped off Richard's jacket and one of her shirts, which she wrapped around the deputy's head and tied into place using the sleeves.

She shook him, whispering close to his head. "Danny, wake up. Danny, please." But Danny couldn't quite pull himself up from oblivion. The front of his shirt bore multiple holes through which she could clearly see his Kevlar, but a quick search revealed no bleeding from his torso, no bullets that had slipped around the sides of his vest and inflicted terminal damage.

Unable to remember if she should elevate the victim's feet or head, Lane folded up her father's leather jacket and made a quick battlefield decision. The deputy's feet weren't the issue…she tucked the coat under the deputy's head and left him where he lay.

A slight flicker of movement near the pond sent Lane scurrying for the safety of the forest. Not until she peered from behind a tree did she realize Santos was waving at her from his hiding place in the reeds, encouraging her to join him.

Lane hadn't come this far to leave her family's future in the hands of strangers. She ran for the house, pressing her back against the wall as she peeked in the windows and sidled to the door. She wasn't sure what she would do when she got inside the house; she only knew she had to get in, had to draw Jack's attention, and had to do something to save Richard and Ray.

An errant thought popped into her head and she dug in her pants for the whistle Richard had gotten for her. Her teeth clamped tightly on the red plastic, but her mouth remained open so that any uncontrolled breathing wouldn't send a sudden blast through the whistle and ruin her plans.

The door knob turned easily. Pulling the bowstring to full-draw, Lane ducked inside the kitchen, aiming the arrow directly ahead of herself. She ignored the open door behind her; she needed to get in quickly and get established before Jack figured out she was here.

She tiptoed to the front of the house, rolling onto the sides of her feet to reduce noise and pulling the bowstring to her face. It kissed her cheek and she felt its tension, the flutter in her shaky arms, and the ache in her shoulders.

Ray sat in one of the dining room chairs, his arms strapped to it, dried blood crusted on his face. Both his eyes had swollen nearly shut, and his breath rattled in his chest.

Richard knelt on the floor with his back to the front windows, making him clearly visible from outside of the cabin. His fingers interlocked behind his head, but his left arm wasn't as high as the right, tucking in closer to his body, pulling him into a lean, and suggesting a great deal of pain in his side.

Jack stood nearby, but had obscured himself from outside viewing by hiding behind the window drapes. He was prepared for a frontal assault, ready to take on Richard or the front door, whichever proved to be the first threat. At the moment, the shotgun pointed at Richard's head easily kept the Sheriff compliant, since a shot at this distance, even with birdshot, would likely cleave his noggin from his neck.

Richard's eyes flicked up when Lane entered the room. A storm of emotions raged there—joy, pride, sorrow, pain, despair. Hope.

279

Lane didn't waste time trying to analyze her father's state of mind. She squeezed her lips around her teeth, sealing off the air chamber, and blew down the center for all her worth. The whistle came out strong and piercing. Jack whirled on her, his gun coming to bear.

The arrow sang its way across the living room, covering the distance in a split second and knocking him off balance and closer to the front door.

If Lane had taken more time to practice, she would have been able to nock another spike faster. In the time it took her to clear a second arrow from the quiver, Jack had recovered from the initial shock.

The skinny assassin's sole experience with this type of weaponry apparently lay in movies he had seen. He expected to snap the arrow off, but Hollywood producers seldom used aluminum shafts. Jack screamed in pain when the shaft wouldn't break, and he changed his tactics, trying to pull the barbed steel back out of his shoulder. The foolishness of the endeavor rang forth in his agony. He gave up and brought his shotgun to bear. "I should have killed you when I had the chance!"

"You're probably right," Lane said without emotion.

Richard launched himself toward the gun cabinet, where his own handgun waited to be utilized. The move drew Jack's aim away from Lane, buying her some time.

Jack fired, the bullet tearing into the oak chest and sending Richard rolling in the opposite direction.

A second arrow whooshed away, its dull thud audible as it entered Jack's body. It pierced his neck and impaled itself in the front door. Jack grabbed at it, a weak gesture at best.

"Dance for me," Lane spat. He did, a little, his body spasming, nerves twitching. Jack died upright, the arrow holding him in place.

A gun butt to the back of her head dropped Lane to the floor, but she didn't stay there long. A thick, meaty hand wrapped around her throat and dragged her back to her feet. "Forget about me?" Angelo smiled at Richard. "Told you everybody's got a weak spot. Looks like hers is both of you."

Richard grabbed his gun, rolled onto his knee, and aimed.

"Drop the gun," Angelo said.

Richard declined. "The only thing keeping you from killing her right now is the knowledge that when you lose her as your shield, I'll put a slug in your head."

"So you'd let me kill her?"

"Let isn't exactly the word I'd use. I think we both know you have no intention of leaving any of us alive."

Angelo laughed, but his hold on Lane's neck eased as his arm slid down around her shoulders, pulling her into his chest and peering around her right ear. "Well, aren't you the smart one."

Jenna strolled out of the den, retrieved the shotgun from the floor in front of the body pinned to the door, and swapped weapons with Angelo. She had no need of the pistol, so she tucked it in Angelo's waistband. "But according to his orders, she goes first, then you two. So he shoots her, uses her to block your bullets, then nails you. The priest isn't really an issue anymore, is he?" She whirled on her daughter. "Of course, that depends on you, doesn't it, Lane? I've considered that Morgan might not have given me access to all his accounts. So tell me what you know, and I'll let you all live."

"No, you won't," Lane said. She knew the only way for the Keates clan to walk away from this alive was to take out Angelo first. Unfortunately, as Angelo's shield, she had no idea what Richard was thinking. From this distance, any move she made in anticipation could get her killed, not that they weren't all facing their mortality at the moment, anyway. She searched his eyes, and he stared back.

This time Lane had no trouble sorting through the emotion in Richard's eyes…pride. His shoulders squared back, even though his hands and arms were holding a perfect shooter's stance. His nostrils flared as he inhaled, his head tipping back ever so slightly in acknowledgement of his daughter's spunk.

Lane met her father's gaze, but she could think of only one way to walk away from this knee-deep vat of hooey. She firmed up her position, bringing her feet closer together, pasting her hands to her outer thighs like a soldier in formation. "Richard," she said quietly. Her head nodded before she got the rest of the words out. "I do trust you."

The Sheriff took the shot.

Heat seared along Lane's shoulder as the bullet tore through her clothing and singed a streak across her skin. She tried not to pull back, her body freezing in place.

In that same instant, the bullet slammed into Angelo's shoulder, splattering his blood all over Lane and knocking him away from her. Lane hit the floor, but she didn't know if that was an instinctive removal of herself from the line of fire or the aftereffects of the bullet.

Angelo let loose on the shotgun, spraying the room with birdshot even as Richard dove out of the way. At this distance, the shot would still be in a tight pattern, but he didn't completely get out of ground zero.

Lane saw the effects; the pellets slammed into Richard's leg, shredding cloth and skin, and generating crimson blossoms that spread along her father's pants. His gun went flying and Angelo trained his weapon on the defenseless Sheriff.

Lane staggered away from Angelo; the gloat on his face not only said that he had won, but that he wanted Richard to acknowledge it before dying. All Lane could do now was delay the inevitable. Sputtering, straining to see the wound high on her shoulder, she turned toward her father. "You shot me?" She wiped some blood off her face and neck. "Again?"

"I don't think that's your blood," Richard answered, but his eyes never wavered from Angelo.

The big Italian laughed in agreement. "I think that's mine." With his gun trained on the family Keates, his smile shifted just slightly toward pre-meditated murder. "You done toying with 'em, or you still think you can get the money out of her?"

Jenna sidled in beside Angelo, casting a smug look at Lane, then Richard. "I think we're done. I don't think there are any other accounts. I think she's just been playing us all for fools."

Angelo raised the gun and Lane struggled forward, standing before Jenna. "You want me dead? Do it yourself."

Jenna scoffed. "Please. I pay people to do my bidding."

Lane shook her head, laughing at Angelo. "How's it feel to be her butt-monkey? Tell me something, Mother. Did you ever love me? Or have I just been a tool all these years?"

Chapter 84 – Jenna Freaks

Lane's earliest memories consisted of nothing more than bits and pieces of daily life when she was four or five years old. A room here, an incident there. That fuzzy, spotted stuffed cat she clung to at night. An occasional glimpse of one of a multitude of nannies who breezed in for a month or two and then left before Lane ever really got to know them. None of them ever stayed long.

It could have been by design, to prevent Lane from ever getting attached to anyone, but it could just as easily have been the nannies' inability to deal with their employers. Either way, Lane spent a lot of her formative years alone.

Now, all these years later, with few ties to humanity, Lane watched as her words created a fury in her mother that Lane had seldom seen. Veins popped out on Jenna's forehead, and her tiny, delicate hands balled up into fists. "He raped me because of you!"

Things that had happened when Lane was a child had seldom made sense to her. In the years that ensued, maturity and time lent themselves to understanding, and she'd come to realize so many things about her mother. And about Morgan, as well.

Jenna, as if anyone in the state didn't know, inclined toward romantic interludes with men other than her husband. She never used the master bedroom for her entanglements; instead, she would stock one of the spare third-floor bedrooms with an assortment of skimpy negligees, lotions, and oils whenever she planned a tryst. She simply led her current interest there and tempted him with her pleasures.

Lane probably would never have known had it not been for Jenna's single-mindedness and predictability. Lane discovered the pattern one night by looking through the attic light fixtures. Jenna carted her collection of lotions to the first bedroom near the stairs using a box, then arranged them all like they'd been in the room the whole time. And then Morgan followed her in, carrying three or four negligees he thought were appropriately enticing.

Lane expected to see them strip off their clothes, but neither did. Instead, both of them went to the room next door. Lane followed in the attic, peeking through the light fixtures to find her parents playing with a computer, checking the angles, and making sure the video feed would be captured on the hard drive. Morgan, as it turned out would blackmail people after they'd slept with his wife—that Morgan planned the event eluded most of his victims.

Lane stayed home sick from school the next day, and every other day Jenna planned her little adventures. She watched through the light fixtures, learning about love-making when she was far too young to understand it. When Morgan got home, he and Jenna would watch the tape from the comfort of the second bedroom, and then Morgan would impose himself on his wife. Lane always got the sense that unions between her parents were more about Morgan possessing Jenna rather than loving her.

Jenna waited, but Lane said nothing. "You and that stupid drawing." Contempt lined her face.

Lane took a deep breath. "You slept with everything in the state. You would think that you wouldn't have minded sleeping with your husband. And that's why he raped me."

"That is not true."

"Oh, I think it is. He wanted you to sleep with all those guys. And you did. But he didn't want you to enjoy it so much."

"That is not true!" Jenna's eyes grew like saucers, giving her the wide-eyed look of someone who wasn't comfortable with their contact lenses.

"Of course it is. Even I could tell when you were faking it. And you only faked it for Morgan. That's why he has all those secret accounts. 'Cause he knew what you are. Whore."

Jenna's rage grew and she stalked across the room. Her arm drew back and for the second time in her life, she prepared to strike her daughter.

But that girl had other ideas, and Lane let loose a punch that landed dead in Jenna's kisser, sending her backward against Angelo. He laughed out loud, a roar that came from his belly. Jenna wasn't so amused, but Angelo didn't mind letting her in on his pleasure. "She is one feisty little bugger."

Richard chuckled, and Lane couldn't believe, under the circumstances, that both father and potential killer were laughing. At her.

Danny woke to find himself staring at the sky, the echo of a shotgun blast ringing in his ears. His sidearm sat properly snapped in its holster, but his rifle lay several feet away, tossed into the air when he flew off the porch.

The thing that struck him odd was the motion of the trees overhead, moving away from him. Next to him, a pair of jackboots scuffled in the dirt and someone else's arm, hooked under Danny's armpit, dragged him backward across the ground.

Pete looked down at his partner. "You're okay, Dan. Just getting you out of the line of fire."

Reasoned thought hadn't yet returned to the young deputy. He couldn't know that Santos had radioed for backup when the shotgun blast rang out, nor that Pete, Bailey and four Troopers had answered the call, joining Nyugen and Santos on site. All he knew for sure was that his boss, the girl he wanted to be as smitten with him as he was with her, and at least one other innocent were trapped in that cabin while he was out here in the forest taking a nap.

Danny pulled free of Pete's grasp, scrambled to his feet and raced through the open back door of the house, drawing his pistol as he ran. Assessing the situation as best he could with one eye shut and a headache splitting out his skull, Danny fired a single shot before collapsing onto the kitchen floor.

Angelo ducked, the deputy's bullet having gone wide. But in relinquishing his advantage, he had given Richard time to retrieve his weapon. Angelo grabbed Jenna and raced toward freedom, firing a barrage of lead into the trees and using Jenna as a shield to prevent return fire as deputies emerged from the forest.

Richard lurched forward, desperate to reach Lane. When his leg gave out beneath him, he slammed into her, and both father and daughter crashed to their knees. The only thing that kept them from kissing the floor was their arms wrapping around the other and grappling for a hold, with Richard's stronger arms crushing the girl into his body. He would have been content to hold onto the girl for hours.

"You shot me. Again," Lane whispered.

"It really isn't your blood." He lifted the material from her skin, pinching the frayed edges of the bullet hole between his fingers. In one quick tug, he peeled the sleeve off the shirt, verifying that the wound was not severe, and using the severed sleeve to mop the red streaks from his daughter's face.

After that he checked her arms, shoulders, hands, and legs, patting her down like he would search a suspect for contraband.

His hands lingered on the swollen tissues around her fake right knee. "Are you okay?"

She seemed to be thinking about his question; then she graced him with full eye contact and held it. "Yeah." Her head bobbed up and down. "I think I am."

Relief flooded his body. "Tell me right now. Is there ever going to come a time in your life that I'm going to tell you to do something, and you're just going to do it?"

"Not if you keep shooting me." Her body went limp and she fell forward.

His arms wrapped around her as she sagged to the floor. He looked down into her pinpoint pupils just before her eyelids slammed shut. "How many did you take?"

Her eyebrows rose high, even though her eyelids refused to reopen. Her lips pinched together and pulled to one side of her mouth, and she produced the hydrocodone bottle from her pocket. "You tell me."

Richard stuffed the bottle in his pocket and leaned Lane against his chest, tucking her head against his neck and struggling to lift her. That his daughter barely weighed a hundred pounds meant his inability to get the girl off the ground was more likely due to his own deteriorating condition.

Pete looked on from a few feet away, close enough to be of service if Richard needed him, but discretely waiting for an actual invitation. As Sheriff, Richard appreciated his senior deputy for so many things—his professionalism, his strengths, his understanding. Even the occasional intrusion.

Pete stepped up and inserted himself between Richard and Officer Insensitivity. "Think twice before touching his kid," Pete said, trying to keep his voice soft enough so that only Bailey could hear him, but not quite succeeding.

Bailey didn't take the hint until the smoldering eyes of the Sheriff ripped him to his core.

Chapter 85 – Richard and Danny

With the slam of the ambulance door, Richard consigned his brother and daughter to the capable hands of the EMTs. It also served to cut off Lane's complaining, though Richard heard enough to know what her problem was.

"I'm sleeping here!" she grumbled. That the EMT had deliberately roused her, and would continue to do so because of the amount of hydrocodone in her system, was apparently lost on Lane.

Pete laughed out loud, though Richard couldn't tell if his senior deputy's amusement was based on the girl in the ambulance or the look her antics produced on her father's face.

"She's never gonna stop fighting, is she?"

"Don't look like it, but I'll be happy enough if she just stops fighting with me." And now that the girl had put love, or at least concern, for her family above her own personal safety, Richard felt a twinge of hope that she might actually be coming around.

The Sheriff had already decided he wasn't waiting for the ambulance to come back, and he headed to the cruiser parked in the driveway, flicking his fingers at Pete and thoroughly expecting to receive the keys.

Pete finagled Danny into the backseat. "I got it."

Richard thought otherwise. "I'll drive."

Pete closed the door on his rookie. "I may have taken orders from Junior today, but I ain't taken any orders from you. Not if they're all gonna be that stupid."

A staring match ensued, Richard determined to drive to the hospital to be with his family, and Pete absolutely determined that the injured man wouldn't see keys until timeshare rentals became the hottest properties in Hell.

"I'm fine to drive, Pete. Just give me the keys."

Pete's head tipped away. "I'm seeing a decidedly left-sided lean going on there. I think you're all banged up. I think steering's going to be a problem for you, and I think at high speed, you'll get us all killed." Pete slid into the driver's seat. "So unless you plan to stand there and bleed to death, I'd suggest just giving in for once in your life."

"Fine, but you better drive faster than you've ever driven in your life. I want to be there before the ambulance parks." Richard climbed into the passenger's side, resting his head against the seat, and he released a sigh that came from far down in his body, perhaps all the way from his toes.

He had no idea why Pete had taken direct orders from Danny, of all people, or why Danny was in the field rather than guarding Dottie. He could assume that Pete was pushing the junior officer toward independence, but Richard could just as easily make the argument that Creepy Danny's affection for one eighteen-year-old probationer might be coming out into the light of day.

Outside the car, the four temporary officers assembled with the Troopers. Richard's eyes locked on the insignia of the officer barking orders, a Captain who paused long enough to issue a respectful nod in Richard's direction. The gesture assured Richard that the hunt for Angelo and Jenna was far from over.

"Drive, Pete."

"More than happy to, but I think if I run down these Troopers, I'm going to be in a great deal more trouble than you can fix right now."

Richard wanted to crawl out of his skin, or maybe just out of the car, and he wondered if he would get to the clinic faster if he walked all the way. Logically he knew it was the situation, not

290

knowing how seriously injured Ray was, or if Lane had actually overdosed herself again. Logic, however, moved into second place and allowed emotion to rule the moment. "Give them the damn horn!"

"Absolutely," Pete said, though he didn't do it. Instead he snapped on the cruiser's lights. Seconds later the Troopers moved out of the way, and Pete swung out of the driveway and onto the street.

Even though he couldn't see the speedometer, Richard had a pretty good finger on the speed of the car, guessing they had reached sixty-five, maybe seventy—he still couldn't relax. He felt fairly sure that Lane wasn't in any serious danger. Doc would more than likely flush her system, pump her stomach, patch her up, and maybe hang onto her for a day to make sure she was all right. Ray. Richard's mind twisted around the possibility that he might lose his brother, that the rattling in Ray's chest signaled a serious injury.

"Drive faster, Pete."

"You got it, Sheriff."

Richard didn't feel the additional acceleration that would tell him that Pete had actually obeyed the order. He turned his frustration on Danny. "You need to stop letting that girl control your actions, Dan."

Like a screen door straining against its spring, Danny's head pulled forward. A slight pink hue rose up along his jaw line. "Sheriff, I—" Danny stammered.

Richard shut him down, unwilling to indulge in any foolishness right now. "I'm talking, Dan. You had better figure out if you want to be a deputy in my department or a schoolboy with a crush. And you had better figure it out pretty damned quick, Mister."

"Sheriff?" Pete said.

Richard ignored the senior deputy, choosing instead to continue venting his steam. "Any little bit of attention a man gives Lane right now could be misconstrued by her. Or misused by him. You know what I'm saying, right, Dan? You do know what I'll do to you, if you hurt her?"

Danny nodded. "Oh, yes, sir. I expect nobody would ever find the dismembered parts of my body."

Pete stifled a chuckle in the front seat. "Sheriff?"

The longer it took to get to the clinic, the more certain Richard became that Ray had already died. Nothing he said to himself alleviated the fear. Since he was already on the track, the train took over and dragged him down another unproductive line of reasoning.

Lane. Richard had no reason to believe she would be okay. She could be crashing right now, and here he was—stuck in a damn cruiser with a deputy who didn't know what the gas pedal was for.

He chose to ignore Pete. "That would be illegal, Dan. But I will make it virtually impossible for you to work for me, or pretty much anywhere else in this town or on the Peninsula in general."

"Sheriff!" Pete yelled. "Relax, will you? We're here." He slammed the car into park; across the lot the EMTs popped open the back doors of the ambulance.

"And one other thing," Richard said, pulling himself from the vehicle, but leaning back in so he could glare at Danny. "Understand it right now. If you can convince Lane that you're not as creepy as she thinks you are, you best get an apartment, because there is no way on God's green earth of goodness and light that I'm letting my daughter live in your parents' basement."

Chapter 86 —Barnett

Nursing a bourbon, Barnett watched from the doorway of the kitchen as Camilla packed and bandaged Angelo's wounds. Both looked rather nasty, but neither would prove fatal unless infection set in. The wound to his back wasn't even bleeding anymore, but the through-and-through bullet hole in his shoulder still oozed.

"Jack's dead. I want his half, too."

"Why should I pay you?" Barnett queried. "You didn't complete the job. In fact, you didn't manage to kill any of them." Without another word, Barnett tossed back the remains of his drink and left the room.

A low growl wound up from Angelo's belly, and he shrugged away from Camilla. He never even turned to face her as he headed after Barnett. "You should return to your quarters now. You should go there, and stay there, and not come out until the police come." Camilla didn't need to be told twice, and the kitchen door closed quietly behind her.

Angelo found Barnett in the great room, lounging on the white sofa and sipping a fresh drink. He eyed Jenna, slamming the front door in some big-breasted girl's face.

Jenna strode past Angelo and into the cavernous area, parking herself at Barnett's elbow. "I need to get out of here." Barnett's total lack of response forced Jenna to become more demanding. "Now!"

Angelo moved closer, placing himself in a position to watch both Harrises at the same time. "I want my money," he said. As if the tone of his voice wasn't sufficient, even his eyes screamed, "Don't play with me." Barnett's smile only infuriated him more.

But Barnett reconsidered. "Tell you what. I'll keep the original deal if you rid me of one nagging problem. We'll call it square. Instead of three, you do just one." And his eyes shifted to Jenna.

Her jaw went slack, and she took a single step away from the two men. Angelo pointed a single finger at her and whispered a soothing, "Shhh. I've got a better idea." He pulled his pistol from his waistband and shot Barnett square in the forehead.

Except for his head flying backward against the sofa, the spray of blood settling on the floor behind him, and the red lava cascading down the cushion, anyone entering the room might well have thought Barnett had fallen asleep there.

"You got a car?" Angelo asked, casting a glance back at Jenna.

Chapter 87 —Jenna Meets Her Demise

Angelo parked the Matador Red Lexus IS-C at the marina and hurried to the rental. He didn't wait for Jenna to catch up. At the moment, she was as eager to get away as he was. But his eyebrows furrowed deeper as she spoke, and his twisted grin grew.

Jenna tried to climb aboard, but she had trouble bridging the gap between dock and gunwale. "You could at least help me, you fool." Jenna dismissed the man as casually as she dismissed any other servant. Angelo latched onto her and gave her a yank. "How dare you?"

Silence was her only answer as Angelo untied the yacht and cast off. To get to the wheel, he had to walk through the cabin. It wasn't huge, but it was well appointed, complete with a bed and a small shower. Jenna followed him. "Make yourself comfortable," he growled over his shoulder.

"And you think this will do it?" She sneered at him, turning her head and nose up in disgust. "This is just a trailer on water. If I had wanted a camper, I'd have married the damned Sheriff."

He popped open a closet door on his way by. "Barnett sent over some things for you...before his demise."

He disappeared into the adjoining room, and Jenna examined the dresses in the closet, pleased with the selections. "Well, he wasn't all bad. Where are we going?" she called out.

"I'm headed to Canada."

"Fine."

The engine roared to life, and they soon sputtered out into Puget Sound. Jenna indulged in a short, not very luxurious shower, but the waterproof bandage kept the sutures on her abdomen dry. She fingered her way along the scar, wondering if a decent plastic surgeon would be able to remove the hideous deformity and return her body to its perfect, pre-prison appearance.

Hair wrapped up in a towel, she settled on the bed and soon drifted off to sleep.

Five hours later she woke, stretched widely and rose, discovering that her robe was just slightly askance and wondering who might have seen what. She tossed the towel to the floor and quickly fixed her hair in a tight bun. She hadn't put on any makeup at all in the last few months, but she hadn't forgotten how, and it took all of ten minutes to make herself presentable. She slipped into the black dress that Barnett had so thoughtfully provided.

Carrying the matching heels, she stepped out on the deck barefooted, all full of herself, looking down her nose at the dirty man at the stern. Angelo, she reminded herself.

The boat puttered softly, churning through the waves without its pilot. Jenna looked around, scanning the horizon. In five hours, they could have crossed the channel between Canada and the USA three times, but there was no land in sight. "Canada is due north. Did you miss it?"

The look on her face screamed her contempt for lesser mortals, and Angelo made no attempt to hide his disdain for her as he changed from barely controlled thug to an out-of-control monster waiting for the right moment to unleash his full potential.

"Head east for the Sound."

Angelo stepped forward. "I've got a better idea." He grabbed her and dragged her back to the bedroom. Her struggling did nothing to delay him, and when he slapped her, she went sprawling on the bed.

He stripped off his shirt and fell atop her, one hand twining itself in her hair, the other pressing into the bandage on her abdomen. Her cry of pain egged him on. "Shhh. Isn't this what you wanted for the kid?"

The CT scan showed several issues that needed tending. Ray's broken nose and arm lacked significance when compared to the rib that had snapped in two places and sliced into his liver and one lung. The other two broken ribs would heal by themselves in the next six weeks or so.

All told, Doc Williams had high hopes for a full recovery, but he launched into his standard cautionary tale of all those things that could go wrong whenever a surgeon performed his art, including but not limited to death.

Williams hurried off to the patient who needed him the most, leaving Danny, Lane, and Richard in the capable hands of a Nurse Practitioner. Nathan promptly took control of the three patients left in triage, ordering an assortment of X-rays and scans, urine and blood tests, and assessing the order in which each would receive treatment.

Danny became the only other patient admitted. The bruising under his Kevlar wasn't particularly serious, but the concussion caused Nathan no end of concern, especially when it took five minutes to rouse the sleeping deputy.

An orderly wheeled Danny out of triage, and Nathan pulled back the curtain on the Sheriff's gurney.

Richard's voice boomed along the ceramic tiles. "Take care of Lane first!" Not that anyone listened to him.

"Put the johnny on," Nathan ordered. "Or I'll have the orderlies strip you naked and slap you in four-point restraints."

"She's overdosed on hydrocodone!" Richard blurted, pushing past Nathan and making enough commotion to draw three male attendants. While the three orderlies tried to subdue their birdshot patient, Nathan filled a syringe from a vial of fluid.

"Indeed she did. Again. Which is why we're pumping her full of charcoal and fluids. But those pellets have to come out of your leg. So you get ready for that, and I'll go do the rest of my job, which just so happens to coincide with your little teenager who can't read dosing instructions." He jabbed Richard with the needle, quickly ending the battle over who would be treated first. Then Nathan turned to Lane.

The teenager, for all the wear and tear, needed the least treatment. Stitches closed the split lips and the gashes across her cheekbone and eyebrow, gauze and ointment soothed the bullet burn, and ice slowly worked away at the swelling of one seriously pissed off knee.

The process took less than an hour, some of which she was awake for and some of which she slept through, and included Nathan stabbing her with a tetanus shot. Unfortunately, it excluded anything remotely resembling an analgesic. "When I know you're clean, I'll give you a Tylenol. In the meantime, you can have all the ice you want." He didn't waste time on small talk, but returned to Richard, now silent on the gurney, and used a pair of shears to cut the Sheriff's pant leg wide open.

One of the orderlies previously assigned to watch over the Sheriff now shifted tasks and packed Lane up for transport. While the aide rearranged her IV tubes, Lane strained to see the extent of Richard's wounds, concerned by the ground-beef look of his leg. "Can I stay?" she squeaked at Nathan.

"No," he hollered back, waving the orderly off.

The escort deposited Lane, and several ice packs, in the surgical waiting room. The area had been designed to be an oasis of calm and peace during a time when people were far from either. Overstuffed armchairs and a couple of sofas provided ample seating as well as the opportunity to spread out and sleep.

A cabinet held blankets and pillows for the anticipated overnight stays and bins for the dirty linens. Vending machines offered hot broths as well as coffee, sandwiches, and snacks.

Lane selected the sofa that faced the television. Not that she actually watched the box. She certainly wouldn't be able to do a book report on it in the morning.

The pain in her side prevented spreading out and getting comfortable, so Lane propped herself up in the corner, planting an elbow on the arm of the couch and supporting her head with her hand. And waiting for word of Ray or Richard. Or Danny, not that she had the same concern for him as she did the first two, but simply the concern one human being showed for another. Not at all concerned the way he apparently was for her.

Three hours later, Richard joined her in the waiting room. She jumped a little when he tapped her on the shoulder; using his newly acquired cane, he limped to the cabinet for bedding before gimping his way back to the sofa. The back of his johnny flapped open as he walked, but thankfully the staff had given him pajama bottoms.

Richard wedged himself into the opposite corner of the couch, wrapping a blanket around his shoulders and stuffing a pillow behind his head. He tossed the remaining linens to Lane.

She eyed her father, deciding her next step. After a silent deliberation, she picked up the extra pillow and moved it to Richard's side of the couch, dropping it next to him, and easing in beside him carefully so that she didn't brush against his injured leg or ribs. He folded her into his arms and she allowed it. "Why didn't they admit you?" she asked him, her words slurring.

"Doc says he's filled his quota of Keateses for the day. You don't sound so good."

"Rough couple of days," she said, working hard to be understood. She leaned against his chest, finding just the right position for her shoulder so that her father's arm didn't rub against her bullet burn. Her eyes grew heavier by the second, and she fought the mini-blackouts signaling that full sleep would seize her if her eyes stayed shut just a millisecond too long. "You're pretty pissed, huh?" she asked.

Richard smiled. "That'd be an understatement."

"I'm grounded for life," she said. It was a statement of fact.

"Oh, yeah." His tone suggested that she shouldn't even have bothered to ask.

The smile moved to Lane's face. "I can live with that." The silence returned, briefer this time. "You're not done yet, are you?"

Richard's lips puckered, relaxed. "Get some sleep. We'll talk tomorrow."

"I can take it. It's okay if you want to get it off your chest."

"I'm thinking I'm the least of your worries right now. And we can both use some sleep. But I promise…you and I will have a serious talk. Okay?"

Lane nodded against his chest. "'K."

"And then when we're done, you're going to have to face your Nana. I'll tell her to go easy on you."

A few seconds of silence passed, but Lane no longer had an interest in the quiet. It was like she had just learned to talk and couldn't stop. She wondered if it was shame, embarrassment, trepidation about the future, or just making up for lost time. "This is kinda nice," she whispered.

"Yep."

Lane drew a slow, deep breath. "Hey…they let you take a shower?"

"There's that word "let" again," he said.

"You smell good."

301

Richard's silence made Lane twist around to see his reaction. "It's okay if your kid tells you you're hot."

"Um...thanks?"

"Marigold thinks so, too." She watched as a red ring edged up from the collar of Richard's gown and flicked her finger against her own neck for emphasis. "Got a little something on your neck there, Sheriff."

"Why is everybody so fixated on Marigold?" Richard asked.

"You don't know, do you?" His silence confirmed Lane's suspicions. "She dyes her hair for you. She's been trying to catch your eye since, hell, forever. You're, like, Marshall Dillon. You should make your move before she decides to color her hair again. Red is next in the cycle."

"You don't know that," Richard said.

"Uh, Sheriff's daughter. Sees all, knows all." She twisted back around and settled against him, pulling the blanket over herself.

"Yeah, right. Pete says she's bringing over some dinner. She'll breeze in and out of here with barely a word."

"That's because of you, Stone Face. But you try touching her hand, or saying something other than "I'll have the three ninety-nine special," and you see what happens." Richard's harrumph signaled the end of that discussion, but Lane had other things she wanted to discuss, anyway. "Tell me about Grandpa Rainier?"

"First thing. Nobody called him Rainier except Nana, and then only if she was mad at him. Rainy. I see him when I look at Ray. I expect Ray sees him when he looks at me. We both saw something different in the man, and we both tried to emulate it. Came out pretty different, didn't we?" Lane snorted; the puff of breath rippled across Richard's johnny. "I think if you could combine me and Ray into one person, we'd be Rainy."

"Ray says I've got his eyes." Lane turned her head, meeting Richard's gaze. She watched a smile tug its way across his face, lighting his eyes and softening the hardened, all-business features he had spent the last eighteen years perfecting.

"Yep, you do. Let's see…Oh, you know how you like to call me Sheriff Stick-Up-His-Butt? Well, for Rainy, that was more like a telephone pole."

Lane settled in, breathing easily, feeling more peaceful than she had felt in months. It wasn't until she heard Richard speak that she realized she had been slipping along the edges of the black hole of sleep.

"Just don't break my heart like your mother did," he whispered.

Lane's eyes flickered open, but Richard couldn't see it…nor could he see the silent deliberation she had undertaken. She wrapped her fingers around his hand and drew it closer, wondering if she should comment or just let it slide.

"Richard?"

"Mm-hmm."

"I have to ask you a question. Do you think maybe you can assume I have a reason…do you think you could try to answer it?"

"I promise to keep an open mind and try to answer all your questions," he said.

"Why do you care? I mean, it's not like we knew each other. We were complete strangers. Nobody would blame you. Is it just a responsibility thing?"

It took a minute for the response. Lane assumed it meant that Richard was deciding what to say. "I suppose any decent man steps up and fulfills his responsibilities, but that's not it. Not for me. You're my daughter. My daughter. And I'm your father. And that's the only explanation I can really give you." He squeezed her closer.

303

"I'm gonna call you Dad now."

"Are you sure you don't want to wait until you're actually awake?"

As her lips pulled up at the corners to laugh, they also pulled tight on the stitches holding the torn edges together. She winced, pressing her fingers against the sutures to keep them in place. "Don't. I'm serious."

"Sorry…I'm just afraid you'll forget all about it by the time you wake up."

She ignored him. "And when I do, when I call you Dad, there's no going back. Not for me. Not for you. I can't ever call you anything else. And you have to always be Dad, no matter what happens. No matter what I say, or what I do. Even when you're being the Sheriff, you have to be Sheriff Dad. Okay?"

"I can handle that."

"No matter what. If you're angry, or I screw up, or whatever. And I may forget sometimes. Like if I'm angry. Or not thinking. Or something."

"I'll remind you."

A minute later, Lane piped up again. "Dad?"

"Mm-hmm."

"I just wanted to hear how it sounded."

"Sounds good to me," he offered.

Her head nodded against his body. "And I want to change my name."

Richard's voice changed, just a little, and Lane imagined a wry smile tugging at his lips. "How does "Mouse" hit you?"

Again pain reminded her not to laugh. "Stop! I'm being serious."

"Shrew, then, though that's got some negative connotations, doesn't it? Pup?"

"That better be short for puppet."

"I was thinking young wolf, really. Sprout?"

"Stop! You know what I mean!"

"Yep, I do." He squeezed just a bit tighter. "Lane Keates. That sounds good, too." She scooched closer to his body, grimacing as her swollen knee dragged across the sofa.

"You ran, didn't you?" Richard quizzed her.

"Oh, yeah," Lane said, mimicking her father's earlier tone.

Crinkling paper bags yanked Richard from dreamland. He didn't move, afraid to rouse the girl sleeping against his body like he was a King Koil mattress. Marigold tiptoed to the end table, trying to set the bags down without waking anyone.

Richard reached out and touched her hand, softly, the barest whisper of a connection. But from her reaction, he would have guessed that electricity had just shot up through the floorboards and out through her head. She froze, staring at his hand, her mouth falling open but nothing coming out.

He seized the moment. "I like your hair," was the only thing he could think of to say. And it was true. This light brown color gave her features a softness he had forgotten all about, a tenderness he hadn't seen in years, and it was much more pleasing than the garishness of her usual colors: Vampira Black, Nearly White Bleach Blonde, Fire Engine Red, and God Awful Beet Maroon.

Richard had also never seen her stammer. Marigold's conversations always centered on the food, the specials, the coffees, and how much of what he wanted.

"I...you..." Her hand self-consciously withdrew from under Richard's and played with the tresses that had suddenly become the center of attention. "Really?"

The door was open. Richard could walk through it, or just let it slam back in the waitress's face. His fingers wrapped around her hand. "Thank you for dinner."

"Yeah. Absolutely. You bet…" Her tongue slapped around searching for intelligent things to say, but it was apparently tied directly to her hand. As Richard's fingers tightened around her digits, her tongue faltered, forgetting its part in the communication game. Redness spread on her face, starting on her cheeks and expanding like mushroom clouds.

An awkward moment passed before she came up with a topic of conversation. Marigold looked down at Lane and the fresh hair cut. "Couldn't get her to go to Dahlia?"

Richard's chin inched side to side. "I don't know why she does that to her hair."

"Because Morgan did it," Marigold said.

"All the more reason to change it."

"I don't think that's imitation. I think it's revenge. Like by looking scruffy, she's making him look bad, too. Probably the only way she could get even."

Marigold studied Richard's hand, still holding a tender grip on her digits. "I should go." She slipped free of his grasp. "I'll be around in the morning. To check. On you. All…all of you. I'll bring some, um, breakfast."

"You could stay…"

"No, this is family time. I'll be back in the morning." Her hand brushed along Richard's shoulders as she moved around behind him, and that electricity he had witnessed in the room earlier jumped between bodies and grounded out through him. A tingling seared along every inch of skin Marigold touched.

"Call…" Richard hesitated, reining in the order-barking Sheriff. "You should call first. I'm not exactly sure where we're going to be."

Marigold nodded. "No worries. I'll touch base with Pete."

Richard watched her move away. She threw a glance over her shoulder, almost bouncing from the room, changing from skilled restaurateur to giddy schoolgirl with a crush in less than five minutes. She tossed a wave in his direction, then turned down the aisle and vanished from view.

"Told you so," Lane whispered.

"You were awake this whole time?"

"Oh, yeah," Lane said, just a hint of amusement coloring her voice.

"Is she right? Is that why you chop your hair off like that?" Richard's tone dripped sorrow.

"Maybe she should be Sheriff."

Chapter 89 – A Second Step

Richard awoke to the sound of a cart passing the waiting room door. Apparently, it woke his daughter as well for she yawned and stretched as widely as her battered and beaten flesh would allow.

"You're still here."

"I'm not going to leave you. Ever," Richard said.

Lane smiled. "Have you been stuck like this the whole time?" He smiled down at her. "Sorry." Her apology was soft but it sounded sincere.

"Don't be. You were tired. But it's only been a couple hours. Not even dawn yet. How's the shoulder?"

"Stiff. I can't believe you shot me again."

"You're really not going to get over that, are you?"

"Um, no." Her attention shifted to her toes, and that seemed to make it easier for her to talk. "And I'm sorry for making you nuts. I'm not used to having to depend on someone. I've sort of had to figure a lot of stuff out for myself, and take care of myself, and do for myself." She pushed herself into a sitting position, carefully avoiding any spot on Richard that had endured damage.

Richard drew his arm from around his daughter's shoulders and braced it against her in case she needed support. To him at least, it seemed as though Lane had more to say, so he kept quiet. He also didn't stare at her, hoping not to make her any more uncomfortable than she already was. And one last touch, something else he had learned from Ray. He leaned forward—slowly to prevent straining his damaged ribs. His arms rested on his legs, and his hands clasped together, matching his daughter's contemplative posture.

"I've just never really had to worry about anybody else before...their needs, how they felt, how they fit in. Or appearances, or..." A heavy puff of air escaped her nose and her hand flipped in acquiescence. "Or keeping a ton of crap in order."

"Surely you had to keep the attic clean?" Richard had assumed Morgan was a vicious and cruel taskmaster in all things, including the state of the attic bedroom.

Lane's head sagged. "I didn't have any stuff. A few clothes, a few odds and ends. And half of it fit into that hole in the floor." A silent pause forced Richard to reach across the sofa and take her hand, and his reassurance spurred her on. "I've just never really had to worry about this stuff before, and it's tough. I don't think this'll be easy, but I promise to try."

A twinge tickled around Richard's nose, and he knew it was the sting of heartache. "That's as honest as you've been with me in six months." He hadn't meant it to sound like an admonishment and quickly covered, just in case she took it that way. "Thank you."

He swapped over to the coffee table and faced her, their knees nearly touching, their heads close. Mindful of the bruises marring Lane's knuckles, Richard took her hands in his, leaning forward and gently resting his forehead against hers. "And I know that was hard for you, so I think you deserve just as much honesty in return. I haven't had to put somebody else's needs before my own in eighteen plus years. Since your mother left me for Morgan."

The memories couldn't help but flood his mind, but perhaps Ray was right. Perhaps the secret lay in sharing those memories, acknowledging them, and setting them free. And it was, after all, what he expected Lane to do. Of course, he would never tell Ray any of that.

"I was hurt. And when you were born, it was a double blow. I assumed you were his, but I should have been smart enough to figure it out. And I should never have blamed you for it because whether you were his or mine didn't really matter. You weren't responsible."

He gave her hands a light squeeze. "If I had been smarter, or perhaps just more courageous, neither of us would be in this position. Maybe I'd have gotten to know you sooner, maybe we'd have developed the sort of bond that comes from infancy to adulthood. But maybe doesn't help us now, does it?"

She remained quiet. The only sign that she heard him at all were the tears puddling on the floor at her feet.

"I resigned myself to spending the rest of my life alone. And now I'm scared to death of it. Scared you'll leave. Scared I'll lose you. I don't expect this will be easy, either," he said, acknowledging her earlier words. "But I do expect it'll be worth it. And I do promise to try." Richard eased her face up, only realizing the mistake after he had a grip on Lane's chin. He braced himself, not quite sure what she would do but knowing that he had crossed the same line that Jason and Angelo had.

Richard didn't have long to wait. Lane flung herself into his arms. He stifled a grunt of pain, but it took a few seconds before he realized that she wasn't pummeling the crap out of him. Her arms wrapped around his body, squeezing, and pressing her body against him. Richard's arms encircled her, and he decided that the touch of his daughter was well worth any discomfort his ribs might feel.

Dottie barged into the waiting room, casting the evil eye at both her son and his daughter. Her finger jabbed at Richard first. "You and I are going to have a serious talk about how you treat your mother. You locked me in that cell."

Lane's eyebrows popped up and she cast her father a sidelong glance, her face screwing up in amusement as she released her grip on him.

"And you." The finger dipped toward Lane. "It isn't particularly funny. You take off without a single thought to the concern you cause others."

Her diatribe went on for another second or two, causing Lane to flinch and find her feet worthy conversationalists once again. But Richard had driven over the cliff of fatherhood…and he had other plans.

"Mother," he rose to his full height, sucking his stomach in and forcing his back ramrod straight.

"Don't you even try that on me, Mister."

Now Richard's eyebrows popped and he cast his daughter a squint, a "now you know where I get it" look. But his tone softened just a smidge. "Mother, I've got this."

Dottie's mouth fell open and the finger jutted more aggressively at him. Richard knew she had a ton more to say.

His peripheral vision caught Lane rising, dragging a sleeve across her face to dry her eyes. She eased in closer to him, just behind his shoulder. The flutter of cloth against his skin told him exactly where and how close she was, and his hand reached out, drew hers into his palm, and closed around it.

And Dottie's hand fell to her side. "All right, then. The doctor says Ray's going to be out of it for hours. You two should go get some real sleep. The Troopers are still at the cabin though, so go to my house."

Chapter 90 – Redemption

Richard and Lane swung by the station. He only planned to spend a minute updating the staff, but during the course of his conversation with Pete and the other officers, he caught a glimpse of Lane heading down to lockup. Casually repositioning himself so he could view the monitors, he watched her progress: down the stairs, across the length of the cellblock, and into the last cell on the women's side—her cell.

"Sheriff?" Pete asked, a smile tugging away at the corner of his mouth. His eyes danced between Richard and the monitor. "They kinda worm right into your heart, don't they? Worse than damn Cocker Spaniels."

One of Richard's eyebrows cocked up. He would have preferred not to let anyone catch him in a decidedly human moment, but if someone had to, Pete was the man. Professional, respectful, usually silent, and a proud member of the "I'm a father" club. "Sorry, Pete. Just a little distracted."

"Want I should wait 'til she's asleep?"

Richard's lips peeled apart, but he fought back the temptation to smile. "Don't give me any more grief."

"No, sir, wouldn't dream of it. Like I was saying, we found Barnett Harris dead in the mansion. The State Police are working with the Royal Canadians. They tracked Jenna's monitor to Sooke. Found it on an abandoned boat, along with the foot it had been strapped to. This Angelo character didn't even bother to clean the boat when he was done hacking her up. The Organized Crime Division thinks maybe it's a warning to you not to come looking."

"It could also be a message to me that I don't have to bother." His eyes never left the monitor, and when Lane slid down onto her bed, Richard decided to do something he should have done long ago. "Gimme a lift out to the cabin, will you, Pete?"

"Troopers got the investigation, Rick."

Richard turned, and Pete's adamant stare nailed him in the eye. "Relax, Pete. I'm just after clothes for me and the kid. And when we get back, you guys can all go home for some sleep." Richard turned as quickly as his battered body would allow. "Except you." He pointed at Officer Insensitivity. "You get to stick around for another shift. And God bless you if you let anyone else escape out the bathroom window."

The troopers greeted Richard and Pete, asking about the Sheriff's injuries and the prognosis for his brother and daughter. Even though he was all beat to hell, he appreciated the concern of the officers, opening up and sharing with them everything he knew to date. The camaraderie served more than a social purpose though; those personal tidbits gave the troopers a reason to share morsels about the investigation, the evidence they had amassed, and what kind of progress the Royal Canadians had made in their search.

The first glimmer of sunrise poked through the windows, reminding Richard that he had come here for a reason. "Kid's got some clean clothes in the den," he pointed Pete in the right direction. "Just check the mountain in the middle of the floor."

Richard headed upstairs, taking them slowly and amazed by the extent to which Jenna had tracked mud all over the house. He fished clean clothes out of his dresser and closet, dropping them in a simple duffle for easy carrying. Nestled beside his TV sat his

313

engagement picture. He and Jenna sat in their favorite booth at Marigold's Diner. Hugging. Smiling. In love. He picked it up, his thumb glancing across the glass. And he dropped her in the trash.

Because Dottie and Ray had spent the night at the clinic, one watching the other sleep, Richard found himself completely alone with his daughter. He wasn't alone with her often, but at the moment, mostly because of the progress they had made during this crisis, he relished it. No buffer between them, no referee, no parenting instructors. Just him. And his daughter.

He had tons of things he wanted to say to the girl, but he shoved the garbled mess out of his mind; at the moment he was content just to watch her sleep. She almost looked as if she had passed out and collapsed onto the bed. One leg hung off the edge, and the rest of her body trapped the blankets beneath her.

Richard pulled the blanket off Dottie's cot, laying it across the bulk of Lane's body and drawing it toward her chin. As gentle as he thought he had been, his actions roused Lane from her slumber. It could have been the weight of the blanket, but it could also have been her inability to tolerate closeness. He suspected that a butterfly flapping by the window would snap her out of REM sleep just as easily as a rhinoceros crashing through the wall.

She rolled over to face him—or tried to. She sucked in a sharp, quick breath through clamped teeth. Her eyes popped open wide, as if she had just remembered her injuries, and her left arm clamped down against her side.

"Sorry," he said. Lane met his gaze for at least two seconds, maybe three. "Ribs?"

Lane gave him a sort of sideways nod, not quite saying yes, not quite saying no; a bit of heat rose up from her neckline, and

Richard hoped she would soon be able to trust him with more than just his ability to shoot straight. "And the boob," she whispered.

Richard's head cocked to the side. "Nathan check it out?"

"Hell, no."

"Lane…" he started, but she cut him off.

"He sent another nurse in. Some woman. I sort of assumed if something was seriously wrong, they'd have done more than strap me up."

Richard accepted the explanation and pressed no further, assuming that was the end of it. But Lane did something completely unexpected…she lifted up her shirt, revealing an elasticized-bandage wrapped several times around her torso. The slightest hint of blue peeked out under the last strip of bandage. He found himself wanting to know how it happened, but not knowing exactly how to ask. "Hurt?" She nodded. "They give you anything for the pain?"

She smiled, and Richard got the feeling a whopper of a lie was about to come out. "Nathan said to treat it with ice. Or maybe it was heat. I forget. But I can take Yankee Doodles and M&Ms as needed for the pain."

"We'll have to stop and get some before we go to Nana's. Think you might want to head on over there?"

Her head shook again. "I'm kinda beat."

Richard nodded. "You and me both." He watched her carefully. "Think you can answer a question for me now?"

Her nod came easily. "Absolument."

"Where are those account numbers?" Keeping the shredded leg stiff, he eased down onto the bed.

"Rolodex."

"FBI has already been through it, top to bottom, in and out, every which way to Sunday. They even had their code guys take a crack at it. There's nothing there."

"It's there. Hidden among his assorted mistresses. Phone numbers, addresses, dates. Even shoe sizes."

"You'd have to show them."

Her face screwed up. "Will you be there?"

"Not about to turn Uncle Sam loose on my daughter, but I'll put them off until Ray's well enough to advise you." He looked around the small space. With Dottie at the clinic, the second cot would remain unused today. "Okay if I crash here with you a while?" It was really just a courtesy. As Sheriff, he could damn well sleep any damn place he wanted to. Lane studied him, albeit briefly, and nodded her head, giving him permission to take off his boots and get comfortable.

"We can talk for a while, if you want to." Richard didn't really expect her to just open up and gush forth information on her time in the woods, her encounters with Angelo, or how she had gotten that bruised breast. Nor was he sure he was really ready to discover she had been manhandled once again. What he did was more important than any of that; he waited. He waited for her to choose the time, for her to choose the what, and for her to start the conversation.

"He slapped me around but he didn't...you know...and then I stabbed him in the back." Her mouth clamped tight, and the muscles rippled along her jaw. It took a moment for her to get the words out. "I've killed two people now."

"You've been through a lot, Lane. You've had to protect yourself. It isn't an easy thing, but it is sometimes necessary. What do you..." He paused, searching for the appropriate wording. He didn't want to ask her about her "feelings", not after what happened last time he made that mistake. "Is it bothering you? What do you think about it?"

"I think I wish he weren't so big around so that I could have reached his freakin' spine."

Richard chuckled. "I think we need to maybe work on some self-defense techniques that don't result in permanent maiming or death. I'm thinking that's something Pete and I can fit into your PT. Just doing a little at a time, just as much as you can comfortably handle."

"No Creepy Danny?"

"I'm letting you win that one. But I think you put up a pretty good fight," Richard said, gesturing to her battered hands. "Looks like you hit him pretty good."

"Not so much hit as bounced off." Lane drew a deep breath, her eyes flitting up to meet her father's for a second. "Ri...Dad...There's this thing between us." Her eyes darted in, finding his, then flitting away, and she pushed herself into a sitting position, tucking her left arm tightly against her body.

Her other hand drifted back and forth in the air between them, and it took her several tries to actually maintain eye contact. "And I don't want it to be." Her mouth fell open, and then snapped shut again, repeating the process a few times as if practicing for the real deal.

When she finally spoke again, a breath of air split each word from the one that followed it. "Morgan...hurt...me." Her voice cracked, and the volume vacillated between normally soft and incredibly hard to hear. Her eyes dropped to the center of Richard's chest, and a silent moment passed, but getting those first three words out seemed to make it easier for her to continue. "A lot. And sometimes, it still does. Physically. Hurts physically. I can feel him...tearing me. Sometimes I can hear him..."

She fell into another silence, but the pauses continued to get shorter. "The nightmares are different. He's there every time I close my eyes. Either he's...on me...or I'm putting ten rounds in his face."

Her legs slid out from behind Richard, and she turned herself onto the edge of the bed. "If he wins, I wake up just

317

before he kills me. Otherwise, I kill him. Then I get to stare at his ghost when I wake up."

Richard had seen the pictures—the blood, the bruising, the tearing. He knew exactly what she'd endured. If he had known he was the girl's father sooner, maybe he could have spared her that and the aftermath—the turmoil, the emotional and physical disabilities, the nightmares. If he had known her sooner, maybe he could have helped her sooner. He reached over and wrapped his hands around hers. "Is he here now?"

She nodded, reciprocating his tenderness by holding on tight. "Behind you."

Instinct had always been a good friend to Richard, and instinctively he knew there was no ghost in the room. Superstition, on the other hand, convinced him to cast a glance over his shoulder just to be sure. That he didn't see a ghost meant Morgan's spirit was only visible to Lane. And that meant she could be hallucinating.

He reminded himself that her anti-depression meds could cause the illusions, as could the pain killers, and if that wasn't enough, the trauma itself could do it. The deck was seriously stacked against this kid.

Lane turned his hands over in hers, studied them, gently probing his calloused palms. "He doesn't win very often anymore. Once in a while. And I know he's not really here...he'll disappear soon...I just can't make him stay dead."

Short of ordering her to do the one thing she didn't want to, namely telling this to her shrink, Richard had to find a way to get her to do exactly that. "Why won't you tell your doctor, or Ray?"

"I wanted to tell you first, 'cause you're...my dad. And that was hard enough. Maybe I can tell Ray now. Maybe. But a stranger is..." The conversation died in midsentence.

Richard picked up no vibes from Lane, no attitude or indignation. Her clamming up signaled more of an inability to speak rather than a lack of desire. "What if I go with you? Into the room?" His thumb coursed a line up and down the back of her hand. "You can talk to me and just pretend she isn't there."

She nodded, now studying the back of his hand, running her fingers down the bruised and battered knuckles. He gave her hands a gentle tug in his direction. "Hey," he whispered, then again until she actually looked over. "I know that was tough for you."

Lane's features struggled. Her mouth opened and shut again as if she might want to go on, but then the muscles along her jaw rippled like she'd never open her mouth again. She withdrew one of her hands from Richard's and scrubbed the tears from her face with her arm. "I was raped." Her head rose, and she looked him straight in the eye. "And there's nothing you can do about it. I know you would if you could, but you can't. And I know you'll do anything in your power to keep it from happening again, you both will, and that's good enough. But there's simply no way you can change what was."

He searched her eyes for meaning, and his mouth opened before he had even thought of something to say.

"Please," she cut him off. "I have to do this before I lose the nerve. You have to stop looking at me like that."

Richard's confusion came out as a slight shake of his head. "Like what?"

"Like the only thing you see is a little raped girl. Sometimes you look at me like you want to cry. Every time I look at you I see either regret or pity. You have nothing to regret. You didn't know me. You didn't know who I was. You didn't get me attacked. You said you wanted me around, so I don't think you regret me…but you have to stop regretting the other stuff. So if it makes you feel better, just say you're sorry, and I'll forgive you, and then we never have to go there again."

Tears brimmed in Richard's eyes. He hadn't cried since…he couldn't remember. He hadn't wept when his father died, nor when Jenna left him for Morgan. It was fitting, he thought, that his tears be so well used, so skillfully released. He pulled Lane's hand to his chest and held it against his heart. "Lane, I am so sorry that I wasn't there for you."

Her smile couldn't have been more genuine. "Now you're forgiven. And we're free. Almost." His daughter may have inherited his determination, but she seemed to have Ray's propensity for wisdom. "The pity thing. Don't. I can't use it. I can't do anything with of it. Give me your strength, or your love, or your sense of humor. Just don't pity me. I'm doing my best to forget what happened, or at least…subdue it. I think that my killing Morgan in my dreams more than he kills me means I'm winning. You have to let me win, Dad."

He drew Lane closer, wrapping his arms around her. "I'm proud of you, for so many reasons. For surviving, for your spunk, even your stubbornness. You took a damn crappy situation and came out of it pretty damned good. But I haven't said it before, and I don't know why. And right now, I'm proud of you for taking these very difficult steps." He kissed the top of her head.

When he finally released her, they both mopped their faces with their sleeves and shared a chuckle over it. Richard's eyes beamed his joy. "If you're still sure you don't want to go to college yet, I'll be more than happy to break it to your uncle for you."

Lane's eyebrows burst up. "That would be great."

"Is telling Ray stuff that much harder than telling me?"

"Depends on what it is. I'm, like, walking proof that all of humanity isn't inherently good."

"He knows that, but his job sort of requires he act like everyone he comes across is salvageable. Only you and I seem to know the truth." Richard smiled, and his hand slid down her arm.

"Get some sleep. We'll go see how the old man's doing in a few hours."

He rose gingerly, putting more pressure on the right side of his body than the left, and hobbled over to the spare cot as Lane settled back into her own bed.

"Dad?"

"Mm-hmm."

"Just checking."

Chapter 91 – Morgan

Sleep played cat and mouse along the inside of Richard's eyelids. Every time the mouse dragged him closer to Never Land, the cat pounced on his brain and insisted he remain awake and vigilant, guarding the girl sleeping across the room.

Now he lay there staring at the ceiling, listening to the few sounds that were audible inside the cellblock: a cricket outside the window casing, boots walking the floor upstairs. A tense gasp from his daughter...

Richard fled his cot as if it had been sprayed with lighter fluid and set on fire. He rushed to Lane's side, praying for an idea that might prevent what he expected was about to become a nightmare—the nightmare—the ongoing battle between Lane and Morgan.

He eased onto her bed and risked touching her arm, thinking that it might wake her, and guessing that she wouldn't mind missing out on a single night of bad dreams.

She didn't wake. Instead, her breath became ragged, and her arm thrashed out. Her hand clenched around Richard's leg.

He slammed his teeth on the gasp of pain, sliding his hand onto hers, hoping it would be enough to loosen her grip and urge her thin fingers off the birdshot holes in his thigh. It didn't work. "Shhh. I'm right here. Everything's okay."

Richard's voice cooed over Lane's shoulder. "I'm right here."

His presence did nothing to stop Morgan's advance, but Lane thought it odd that Sheriff Stick-Up-His-Butt had ventured into her nightmares. Still, she felt more calm than in any other battle. If nothing else came of it, at least it was new, a little variety to an otherwise repetitive phantasm.

Morgan loomed closer with each step. Dried blood stained his shirt, but fresh blood dripped from the nine holes in his chest. The final shot, the one that had blown away part of Morgan's face and drilled into this brain, was now little more than a blemish on his skin.

On other nights, the damage to her leg prevented her from running away, but she would hobble as fast as she could. Eventually, she would freeze up in terror or stumble over a branch, just like the girl always did in a horror film…something that would allow Morgan to catch her. But so much of this dream was different already; Lane stepped closer to Richard.

Some of the dream hadn't changed at all. At fifteen feet away, Morgan's hands balled into fists. His stiff-armed strut put him within arm's reach in seconds. Perhaps the dream hadn't changed at all for him. Perhaps he couldn't see Richard, or the Sheriff's presence made no difference to him.

Lane moved closer still to Richard, waiting, hoping he'd draw his firearm and shoot Morgan in the face. Nine bullets to the chest hadn't been enough to keep him down, and the tenth had miraculously healed. Maybe an eleventh would do the trick.

But Richard didn't move on his weapon. Instead he unsnapped his handcuffs from their case and stepped efficiently into Morgan's path, twisting the dead man's arm behind his back and dropping him to the ground.

Once he had cuffed Morgan's hands, he turned to Lane. "I'm right here."

Lane's breath caught in her throat. Three quick inhalations followed, and Richard grimaced, bracing for her to dig her fingers even further into his leg. But her fingers loosened. A long, slow exhalation released all the air trapped in Lane's lungs, ruffling the hair on Richard's arm. Her features softened and her body relaxed. Lane snuggled down into her pillow, but her hand remained on Richard's leg.

Chapter 92 – Truces, Healings, & Family Ties

Ray waved his visitors in, assessing each in their turn. Mom looked mildly annoyed, a sure sign that Richard had done or said something to upset her just a little, something she would come to terms with relatively easily.

Lane's face bore the same injuries that Richard's did, and having pawed his own face, Ray knew he bore them, as well. Angelo had a routine, and he had used it to beat three of the Keates family into submission. Two Keates, he corrected. And one Harris. But Lane did look relieved.

And Richard looked downright paternal.

Lane dragged the guest chair closer to the bed and ushered her somewhat displeased grandmother into it. The other patient in the room snored softly, so Lane hobbled in and swiped his guest chair, much to the amusement of her uncle and displeasure of her father. She slid the chair next to Richard, her intention clear.

"No, I'm good," Richard said, but by then Lane had moved on, figuring out how to climb onto Ray's bed without injuring herself. "Or maybe I'll sit here in this chair you very thoughtfully stole for me."

Lane leaned over and took Ray's hand. "You okay?"

If it hadn't been for the stitches in his lips pulling tight at the first sign of tension, he would have been inclined to laugh. "I look like you and your father. Except for this."

He pulled his johnny up and the blanket down, revealing the sutured incision that attested to the now-repaired internal damage. "Hurts like hell. Feels like I've been kicked by a jackass."

He almost smiled again, stopping at the first twinge of pain in his lip. "I suppose, depending on your definition of jackass, the argument could be made that I have indeed been kicked by one. How 'bout you?"

Lane managed a smile, then eased up her shirt, just high enough for her uncle to see the bandage wrapped around her torso.

"You, too?" Ray leaned around to see Richard.

Richard ran a hand along his left side. "Angelo was nothing if not consistent."

Dottie snorted. "Maybe someone should have locked the three of you in a cell instead of wasting time with me."

Ray didn't respond to her, turning his attention to Richard instead. "You apologize?"

"Several times. Doesn't seem to work."

Ray shrugged as best he could. "It will. Time heals all wounds." The quiet truce growing in his midst—the ease with which Lane revealed her injury, the calm in Richard's voice—confirmed it. There was something else in the room, or perhaps it was the lack of it that caught his attention. Lane and Richard—together, close, congenial. Familial, with no barrier and no trepidation from either of them.

He decided against bringing it up and changed the subject completely. "Zavier was here. He'll be sticking around for a little while longer so I can recover. He'll be heading back to Seattle sometime in July."

He had already had the conversation with both Richard and Lane, so he knew their thoughts. But neither balked at the announcement, nor did they seem at all fazed by the fact that they would be alone in the cabin in just a couple months. Both his brother and his niece wore matching smiles, and Richard gave him a little nod, like he was finally ready to do the job.

Dottie was considerably more vocal. "Well, it's about damned freakin' time." Lane stifled a giggle.

"Your grandmother likes to swear, too, just to see if it'll get my dander up. You two have a lot in common." Ray squeezed Lane's hand. "I know you've got something to say."

Lane squeezed back. "I won't choose between you."

Ray did sort of expect a fight. "Lane," he said, but he didn't get to finish; she silenced him with the raised brow stare she had learned from her grandmother.

"I won't choose. It's all or nothing. Both or neither. A family. Or not."

Ray admitted, albeit silently, that those had to be the most mature words he had ever heard her speak. He exchanged a glance with his brother, who smiled a proud yet sheepish grin, his eyes laughing a "don't look at me" taunt.

"I can live with that," Ray said.

"Mm-hmm. Me too," Richard added.

Dottie snorted. "And that's about damned freakin' time, too."

The nurse popped in, all authority, and rounded up the visitors, assuring them all that they were welcome to come back in a few hours, after Ray endured a fresh battery of tests and exams.

"You're sure you're okay?"

"I've never been better than this," Ray whispered quietly. He doubted most of the folks in the room understood; if they did, they didn't let on. But Lane did—that knowing smile, that easy way she trusted him with her deepest feelings and harshest secrets. Except one. The big one, the important one. The one she kept trying to hide. But when he looked between his brother and his niece, he knew she had shared it with someone. "The real question is, are you okay?"

The tiniest smile tugged the corner of her mouth, just enough to say it was there without pulling against her stitches. And her head bobbed up and down, just a little. "Yeah. I'm good." Nana Dottie gathered her up and ushered her toward the door. "I'm thinking about horseback riding," Lane called over her shoulder. "There's a place in Shelton…Crossroads Equestrian? Oh, and camping. I want to go camping again. We could all go."

"Okay, whatever you want," Ray said. "Might be a few weeks, though."

Richard dallied at Ray's bedside. The nurse looked liked she wanted to kick his butt for him, but Richard was still Sheriff. "Official business," was all he said. When she was gone, Richard peered down at his brother. "You look like crap."

"You've seen yourself, right?"

"Actually, no. But my eyes just don't feel as swollen as yours look," Richard said.

"How's Danny doing?"

"He'll be fine. For now. But I think his attraction to that girl almost got him killed."

The damage to Ray's face made it impossible for him to conjure up a decent frown. "He's five years older than she is."

"So what?" Richard said, dismissing the issue. "She doesn't want anything to do with him, anyway. Listen, there was a heart-to-heart. Couple of 'em. I think we're gonna be okay. I think she's let me in."

Ray smiled as if some grand plan had just come to fruition. He and Richard were reunited, and Lane and Richard had found sufficient common ground to become united for the first time. And all it took were some sleepless nights and a few broken bones.

Going forward, theoretically, would be easier. Instead of forging ties that didn't exist, all he had to do was nurture new-born ties, feeding them the nutrients that would make them grow stronger: acceptance, a serving of humor, attention, and a double dose of love.

And there was plenty of time for that, since Lane apparently wasn't going to college in the fall. He wondered when someone would actually get around to telling him. Not that it really mattered. If she wasn't shopping or packing by August, it would be a dead giveaway.

All in all, a year or two off wouldn't hurt anything. It would give her plenty of time to come to terms with Morgan's attack, Jenna's homicidal tendencies, and her own emotional state. She would even have a chance to work off her community service. And as the all-knowing, wise old uncle, he felt sure he could talk her into taking some online courses or maybe a couple classes at Shelton Community College.

Ray's head eased back onto the pillow, and he looked up at Richard. "It's about damned freakin' time."

About the Author

Carolyn Gibbs began writing in the sixth grade and hasn't put the pen down since. Credits include an award winning debut novel, *Tuesday's Child*, articles and essays in newspapers, poems in insurance industry newsletters, and training manuals for a local insurance company. From 2001 through 2004, she edited and published a monthly community newsletter, *The Good News of St. Thomas Parish.* She balances her time furthering her education and volunteering at her church.

tuesday's child II: redemption

For more information regarding Carolyn Gibbs and her work, please visit www.TuesdaysChildNovel.com.

Additional copies of this book may be purchased online from www.Amazon.com, www.TuesdaysChildNovel.com, and other fine retailers.

All books sold from the author's website, www.TuesdaysChildNovel.com, will be autographed by the author prior to shipping.

You can also obtain a copy of the book by ordering it through your favorite bookstore.

Made in the USA
Charleston, SC
17 October 2011